Love and Loyalty

KD Call

ISBN 978-1-940429-24-3

Book Cover by KD Call through Canva

Map by KD Call

Edits by Jacob D Law

Proofread by Alicia Whitaker

1st edition 2025

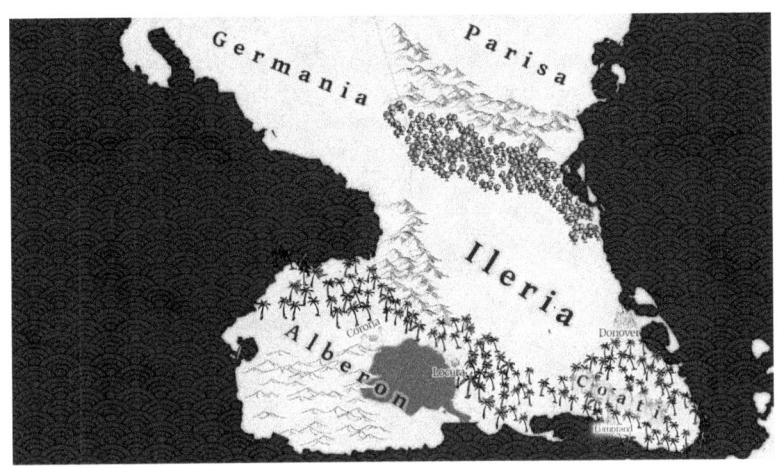

To my cheerleaders.
Thank you for believing in me
and encouraging me to chase my dreams.

Contents

Prologue

"Can you feel it, Aloura?" Mama's voice is weak, but I can hear it as clearly as her rattling breaths with my head resting against her chest. Her hand strokes my hair softly as we cuddle on her bed, a quilt she made before I was born pulled over us. It's too hot in the early summer air, but Mama is always cold now.

"Feel what?" A whisper. Papa is asleep in the chair by the bed. He has hardly left her side since the sickness hit. It started as a cough this winter, nothing serious, but it persisted until she couldn't breathe. It sapped her strength and energy, and now she is fading before our eyes.

"The magic of The Eternal." I glance up and her eyes are closed. Maybe if I close my eyes, I will be able to feel it too. I close them tight and try to recall the wonderful feelings that accompanied picnics in the forest or baking bread for our neighbor, but it's not there.

"The Eternal has abandoned us," I say, scowling at the unfairness of it all. At eleven years old, I was about to lose my mother.

"No...No," she says, grabbing my hand with her weak grip. "He is here. In this room. He is bringing me peace."

"I wish He would bring you healing," I say, sitting up so I can look at her. Her eyes are open, but she hardly looks like my mother anymore. The sickness has stolen her from me. She gives me a weak smile, but I can't give her one back.

"Sometimes miracles happen, and sometimes we have to accept that this is the course of our lives. He has offered me peace, and now my only wish is peace for you and your father," she says, reaching up and cupping my face. Her thumb wipes at the tears that have started to run down my face.

"Oh dear. Come here," she says weakly, pulling me towards her. I lie back down, trying to hold in my sobs. "Let's think happy thoughts," she says, trying to distract me. "Let's see... Did I ever tell you about how I found out I was pregnant with you?"

"Yes," I say reluctantly, smiling through my tears. "Only about a hundred times."

"Well, I'm going to tell you again because it is one of my favorite memories. It was eleven years ago, and your father was away. He had just finished with his apprenticeship, and we were newly married. We had some big choices to make about our lives. I was praying to The Eternal, attending temple, and lighting candles, but none of our options felt right. Finally, while praying, I heard a voice. It said, *I have a special gift for you.* I soon learned I was expecting a baby, and then everything fell into place," she says, her voice fading with her energy.

"I was your special gift," I say quietly, not wanting to wake her if she has fallen asleep.

"Yes, and you still are," she says. Her voice is only a whisper now. "This may not make sense now, but The Eternal has always been aware of you, even before you were born. You are my special girl, and I love you."

Her breathing evens out into sleep. I lie next to her until Papa wakes and carries me to my room. She is gone by morning, taking any magic I believed in with her.

Chapter 1

8 years later...

I bite my lip and stare hard at the little spot on the counter that refuses to be clean. A bit of ink covers it; it spilled when Papa carried the ink pot to talk with a customer at his drafting table. Sweeping, I missed it, and now the ink has soaked into the old wood. Papa promised to revarnish it months ago, but it still hasn't happened.

Giving up on the spot, I take up the broom and slowly brush it across the floor, not wanting to disturb Papa in his work. The task is methodical, leaving my mind to wander down the path I promised myself to stay away from. A promise I was failing. I pause and breathe in deeply, repeating the words that I need to hear to calm my growing agitation.

Aiden travels. I close my eyes to ground myself, breathing in and out with each sentence. *It's important to him, and he is good at his job. He was promoted to captain of his patrol. He knows what he's doing.* Another deep breath, and I continue sweeping. The strokes of the brushes against the floor mirror my mood.

"What did that broom do to you?" my father asks, and I jump, whipping my head around to look at him. I didn't even hear the customer leave. He gives me a knowing smile before beckoning me over.

"Come look at these before I roll them up," he says, as I wander over to his table to see the parchment he has been working on. Charcoal shavings cover the desk, and bits of discarded parchment litter the table in the dimming light, but my eyes are drawn to his new designs.

"Oh, Papa, these are stunning!" A picture of chairs covers the paper with notes written on the side. They will be a set with winged backs and intricate carvings.

"They will be made with oak. Roses, I'm thinking, and daisies. They will cover the back, and their leaves and vines will curl down the sides," he says with a thoughtful look, rubbing his hands absentmindedly. They will need salve on them tonight before bed, or they will ache worse tomorrow. He needs to take an apprentice.

"They will be lovely, Papa, just like all your creations," I respond, and he kisses me on the head before heading back out to the shop. Is he moving slower than before?

I wander behind the counter and look down at the books for the shop. Papa has been taking in fewer commissions, each one taking longer to complete. Every time I bring up an apprentice, he brushes me off, telling me that it is not time yet. I am not sure what he is waiting for.

I make a note on the account of the new client before I pick up a rag to continue my chores. The light is fading fast, and soon I will lock the door, completing another day. One day closer to Aiden being home.

"Sickness or accidents can take enough people, but did he have to choose a job where he deliberately puts himself in danger?" I say out loud. I knock the shavings from the table onto the floor before grabbing the broom again to sweep them into my pile and out the door.

"It's fine," I tell myself, trying to convince myself it's true. "It's fine, I'm fine, he's fine, and life is great." I sweep the dust out the door and place my hand on my hip, looking at the busy city street. It doesn't matter what time it is, there are always people out. I miss our little cottage outside the gates, where it was quiet and peaceful. There is nothing wrong with our shop and the little apartment above it, but it doesn't feel like home. Of course, nothing has felt like home since Mama died.

Shaking my head, I walk back inside, placing the broom away and tidying the desk. I glance at the clock. It is time to close for the night. Thinking about dinner, I reach for the handle just as it turns.

"Sorry, we are closed," I say, trying to grab the handle from the person before they can even come inside.

"Perfect, then no one will walk in while you give me my welcome-home kiss," a familiar, mischievous voice says. My hand slips off the handle as my eyes find his mesmerizing green ones. I fling myself into his arms. My Aiden is home.

He laughs as he moves us inside, locking the door for me, as I won't let go. He is here, and I plan on staying by his side as long as I can.

"Hello, my love," he says in his beautiful voice, rich with a hint of an accent thanks to his foreign heritage. I could listen to him talk all day, but I tilt my head up and accept his kiss. This is as close to home as I've felt in a while.

My hands tangle in his curly golden-brown hair as he pulls me close, making sure to communicate how much he has missed me through his kisses. "I missed you too." I smile as he pulls back, resting his head against mine.

"How was it this time?" he asks quietly. Sighing, I pull out of his arms, turning to fiddle with the papers on the desk.

"Not so bad," I say, making sure to keep my voice light. "But this was not a long trip, so I didn't have time to work myself up into a proper worry." I turn to smile at him, but his raised eyebrow tells me he sees right through my weak attempts at humor. I launch into questions before he can say anything. "How long are you home for? Are you well? Are you hungry?" The tension in my shoulders eases when he lets it drop.

"I am well; do I need an inspection?" he asks, grinning at me before taking a slow spin so I can see every angle. I laugh as my eyes scan over him. After a quick glance for obvious injuries and seeing none, I take my time taking him in.

He cuts a handsome figure in his guard uniform, a tan tunic covered by a leather vest, leather arm gauntlets, and his sword belted at his waist. Brown pants tucked into his leather boots keep mud and dirt out, and a red band encircles his arm, showing his rank as captain. With his tan skin, golden-brown hair, and glowing green eyes, he is the most handsome man I have ever seen.

"Do I meet your standards, my lady?" he asks with a teasing glint in his eye. I look down, but I can't keep the smile off my face. I've been caught admiring him. I glance back up, and his soft smile indicates he doesn't mind.

"Yes, I believe you are well, although the fact that you are still in armor makes me think that you snuck away again before check-in," I say, and he gives me a guilty grin before gathering me back in his arms.

"Gareth is handling it, and Rupert won't mind as long as all the paperwork is done. I did it before we entered the city because I knew I wouldn't be able to wait a moment to see you." He nuzzles my neck, drawing out another laugh before placing a kiss on my lips.

The kiss turns more serious, but before he can deepen it too much, I draw back. "You never did answer my question," I say, determined not to be distracted by his kisses again.

"Which one?" he mumbles against my jaw as he trails his lips to just beneath my ear. He is doing an excellent job of melting my thoughts.

"How long are you home?" I say, grabbing hold of the thought once more before it flutters away again along with the butterflies in my chest. I'm amazed my feet are still on the ground.

Sighing in defeat, he pulls back to look at my face, and I have a moment of disappointment that the kisses are done for now. His knowing smirk tells me he noticed. "I'm not sure, but most likely at least a week," he says, and I can't keep the frown off my face. A week is not a long time to be home.

"And dinner?" I ask, deciding not to dwell on that while he is here with me.

"I need to go check in and give my report. It was just another boring delivery, so it won't take long. As long as I'm not in too much trouble with Rupert, I would love to have dinner with you. Your cooking is fabulous." I give him a brilliant smile and a blush. I know I'm not an amazing cook, but I am pleased by the compliment anyway.

"Then later, I was going to head to The Goose for a drink with the squad. Would you like to come?" he asks, as though the answer is not a resounding yes. It has been a while since I have gone out at night, and it is silly that he would think I wouldn't want to spend every moment with him that I can. That hasn't changed since he saved me at eleven years old from being lost in a strange new city, and it isn't going to change now.

"The Goose sounds great. Who will be there?" I inquire. I already know to expect Aiden's patrol, but I am hoping that it will just be them.

"Probably the entire squad and whoever is in town," Aiden says casually, like it's no big deal, but by his tone, I can tell he is trying to hide something. He is talking too fast. "There will be fresh stories from our recent trip, and I think a ship has come in as well, so it will be a full house." He stops and looks down. Seeing my pinched face, he sighs and gives me a sympathetic look.

"I'm sorry," he says, immediately knowing that I am thinking about John. "He is part of the job, and honestly, if you get to know him, he is not so bad." He tries to explain, but he doesn't understand that it's not *my* dislike that is the problem. It's the fact that John doesn't like me.

"Aiden, you've heard his comments. They are subtle, but he is always saying mean things. It's like he thinks he is better than me," I say with a pout. I know it's childish, but I don't want to be around the man.

"He is part of the squad, and we can't exclude him." Aiden looks down at me with a shrug. "We won't sit by him. Maybe he won't talk to you tonight." I give him a skeptical look. It's not like I haven't tried that before, but if enduring the man means staying with Aiden, then I can put up with him for the night.

"It's okay," I sigh. "I still want to come. You just got back; I want to stay with you as much as I can." I snuggle up to him again, loving how perfectly I fit against his chest, my head just resting against the front of his shoulder.

"And I want to be with you," Aiden says, leaning down and nuzzling my ear, getting a giggle out of me.

"Well then, how about you help me finish closing up, and then I can get dinner started while you finish your check-in." I pull back to grab the rags.

It feels amazing working together, and I can't help but long for this feeling to last forever. One day, when we are married and have a home of our own.

Maybe someday, I tell myself as I watch Aiden finish wiping down the front window and checking the door.

Maybe someday soon.

Chapter 2

"How was your trip this time?" Papa asks between bites of food. Dinner is normally a quiet but comfortable affair, but it is nice having Aiden here tonight. Papa has always loved him like part of the family.

"Good, but cold. Luckily, even in the north, winter has been mild," he says, spearing a bit of potatoes. "It was just a small caravan, but it was my first trip as patrol captain, and I think it went well. Rupert was impressed, I think."

"He actually told you that?" I ask, my fork suspended between my mouth and my plate. Rupert, the head of security at Machiavelli's Merchant Guild, is not one for compliments.

"Well, he told me, 'I knew you could do it, lad,' but for him, you know that was a compliment," he says with a boyish grin, earning a beaming smile from me. I know he values Rupert's opinion.

"That is praise indeed," Papa adds. These are my favorite moments: when the two men I care about most in the world are together with me. It makes our little broken family not feel so small.

"He told me that we shall be in town for a few weeks. Our next shipment will be a big one, but he won't give me more information yet," he says, digging back into his food. He is excited about this next assignment, but my heart hurts at the thought of him leaving again. I just got him back.

"Lana wants to go dress shopping tomorrow," I say, trying to change the conversation as I play around with the food on my plate. "She says we need new dresses before the Founders' Festival, even though it's only a week away."

"Well, you could use a new dress," Papa says, not even looking at me. He's probably right, though. The shop makes enough to keep us comfortable, but we don't have much extra for frivolous things.

"What do you think, Aiden?" I ask, smoothing my hands down my green dress with little embroidered flowers around the collar. It's not fancy, but it's one of my favorites because it brings out a hint of green in my gray eyes.

"I think you look lovely no matter what you are wearing, but I do love you in green," he says, glancing down at my dress. He loves green because it reminds him of the jungles of his home country, Alberon, but I wonder if it is because I match his eyes.

"Well then, if I find a reasonably priced ready-made one in green, I will buy it," I say, making both men smile.

"I've heard prices will go down soon now that Alberon is opening its border again," my father says casually, but it causes both Aiden and me to freeze with forks raised.

"Where did you hear that?" Aiden asks while I chew my bite slowly, watching his reaction closely.

"The chairs that were commissioned earlier, the man mentioned fabric prices coming down because of trade reopening in Alberon." He says it like his news is trivial, but I know to Aiden, it is not. He has been waiting for news from family still on the other side of the border.

"That's great," I say, because it really is. Even though Alberon was the country wracked by a bloody civil war, it has affected the entire continent. It wasn't so bad at first; the war was small and the rebels ineffective, but the past several years have been tough on everyone.

Dinner finishes quickly after that, and cleans up even quicker with Aiden's help hauling the dishes down to the pump in the courtyard outside the shop to rinse them. Before I know it, we are on our way to The Goose.

The tavern is not far, and the streets are fairly well lit. The slight breeze from the ocean ruffles my coat, and I pull it closer as we walk. The winter chill has not yet lifted, but spring is right around the corner. Aiden is quiet, and I let him have his peace for the moment, content to be in his presence. By the time we get to the tavern, though, he is back to his cheerful self.

"Will you have any fun stories to share?" I ask as we near the noise from the tavern bleeding out into the night.

"You shall just have to wait and see" is all he will say, so I give him a playful scowl in return. Familiar faces from Machiavelli's employ fill the tavern tonight. The employee housing and warehouses are nearby, so it is a popular haunt for most of them.

Many shout a greeting as we enter, and I look around the familiar building, soaking up the atmosphere. The place feels friendly, the barkeeper is attentive, and the food is decent. Tables are scattered around the room, and a fire burns in the fireplace on the far wall.

I spot Gareth, Aiden's second-in-command, at a long table in the middle of the room, surrounded by the patrol. As we make our way over, we catch his eye, and he stands to greet us. "Hello, beautiful," he says, enveloping me in a friendly hug. "It's great to see your pretty face again after looking at this one for so long."

His booming voice vibrates through me, drawing a smile before he lets go to pull out a chair for me. I glance up at Aiden and catch his friendly glare. He knows there is no competition for my affection, but Gareth loves to tease. "When are you going to ditch this guy and finally go out with a real man?" he says, giving me a wink.

"A real man? Who are you thinking of because, obviously, you don't mean you?" I ask innocently before breaking out into a giggle at Gareth's surprised look. Aiden smirks and drapes his arm around my shoulders.

"She is much too smart for you, so don't even try."

"That's true," Garth says innocently before a mischievous glint enters his eyes. "It makes me wonder what she's still doing with you." I roll my eyes as their teasing fades into the background as I take in the rest of the room. Rupert sits at the bar nursing a drink, and he gives me a nod as our eyes connect. The man is tall and formidable-looking, with orange hair streaked with white and a strong Northern accent, but I know he is a big softy. I smile at him before my eyes continue traveling the room.

My eyes next connect with John, who is staring at our table. Low lights gleam off his balding head, and he has gathered the halo of long stringy hair he has left into a tail that falls down his back. He converses with Machiavelli's other guard instructor, but his eyes stay on us. I look away quickly but peek at him from the corner of my eye. His eyes drop down to his drink but quickly return to Aiden, like always. It's creepy and weird, but Aiden doesn't notice. They get along just fine. I make the mistake of making eye contact and catch the look of disgust that crosses his face before I turn back to the table with a shiver.

Aiden notices and pulls me closer to him with a smile. I remind myself that he is here, and nothing can hurt me. I sip my drink, a mild spiced cider. I close my eyes and soak in the warm atmosphere and think of my mother. A magic moment has found me.

"Well, Aiden." A thin voice intrudes on my warmth, and the magic flees. I frown as John sits in a chair across from us, a pleasant expression on his face. "How long do you think we will be home this time?"

"You probably know better than I. You're the one who works with Rupert and his schedules," he responds, before he gets a gleam in his eyes. He sits forward with his hands on the table as he lowers his voice. "Rupert hinted that he has a special project coming up. Do you happen to know anything about it?"

"I don't. Rupert has been in meetings with Machiavelli and some important guests recently, but he has not shared anything with me. You shall just have to be patient then and enjoy your time at home."

At this, he glances over at me, a smile on his face that feels patronizing. I look up at Aiden to see if he notices, but he just smiles, sitting back and looking down at me. He loops his arm back over my shoulders. "Of course, that is one of the best parts of being home. Although sleeping in a proper bed comes in as a close second."

"Of course," John says. "It is lucky Aloura has so much patience with you. It must be hard to always have him leave. It's a wonder you have stayed with him all these years," he says, addressing me.

"Of course, I would wait for him as long as I need to. I love him," I say, and am rewarded with a kiss, which is met with a few whistles and good-natured groans from the rest of the table.

"Yes, of course. Sadly, not all of us have that pleasure of someone so dedicated to us," he remarks in a flat voice, causing an awkward silence to settle over the table. Fortunately, Gareth has a knack for saying the most interesting things at probably the wrong time. In this case, I could kiss him for breaking the tension, and at John's expense as well.

"What? No girl for you, ol' Johnny boy?" he exclaims loudly, drawing some laughs. John scowls, though not amused. John is not what I would call a good-looking man. He isn't old, but he isn't young either, maybe late thirties. He is tall, but despite all his guard work, he is still lengthy. And with a long, pointy nose and small dark eyes, he looks decidedly ratlike. John turns red as all eyes turn toward us.

"Well, it's not like you have one either," he spits out, but Gareth doesn't even bat an eye.

"That is because I have many," he replies with a wink, causing another round of laughter and good-natured teasing around the table. John huffs and grumbles something under his breath in Alberonian before excusing himself back to the bar. My tense body finally relaxes, and I feel Aiden squeeze my side in reassurance before going back to the conversation with his other guards, mostly centered on what they enjoyed most about being back in the city.

My eyes flutter shut as the night grows later and the conversation dies down, turning to more serious topics. "We are going to see an increase in bandit gangs since the trade has opened back up from Alberon," one guard remarks, reminding me of the news my father shared earlier. "The first caravans arrived today, and it doesn't sound like they encountered any trouble."

"That's because they are the first. Mark my words: now that people know that it's open again, there will be an increase."

"But won't prices go down on luxury goods now that they are more accessible again?" a young guard asks.

"That's *why* the number of bandits will increase. Keep prices high by keeping stock limited and only accessible through certain buyers," one of the older guards explained. "We see it with the mines from Parisian. It's the purpose of the military bases in the mountains to discourage the bandits from taking the valuable metals."

"Do you think Machiavelli will send us into Alberon soon?" someone asks, and I open my eyes to see the question was directed to Rupert.

"I would not be surprised if Machiavelli tries to get a ship there before the summer storms, but if I were you, I would prepare to be sent into the jungle sometime soon," he remarks, and I can feel the excitement of the guards. I'm sure they are all anxious to be in that first caravan into Alberon.

"I can't wait to have coffee in the morning with a bit of sugar. The prices have been unaffordable for the past couple of years."

"I've heard the new king is working hard on getting his country back in working order. It's why borders were still closed for so long, even though the war was over. He has been working on rebuilding his country."

"I think that is very admirable," comments Aiden. I know he has been keeping close tabs on the news from Alberon. He and his mother fled the country right before the fighting got bad, but he left behind a brother. It's been hard for him not knowing what happened to him.

"The king has been implementing some major programs as well, trying to clean up the poor and reduce taxes and the like," John adds. He is also a refugee from Alberon. I think that is why Aiden sees past his flaws. He is a piece of home.

"He sounds too good to be true," I respond and then blush at the scowl Aiden sends my way. The comment was for John, not a sarcastic remark about the king. I feel bad anyway.

"If his programs work, then they would be worth looking into. Can you imagine a world where no one has to beg on the streets for food or worry about the king's creditors taking you away after a poor harvest?" he says. This is a topic close to his heart because he has always been the kid begging for food, whether in a rebel camp or on the streets of a foreign capital.

"I'm sorry," I whisper, leaning close so as not to be overheard. "You're right. There is much to admire in this new king's efforts."

"If anything, he is already doing better than our own king," John remarks a little too loudly, probably because of one too many drinks.

"Be careful," Rupert warns, a dark look in his eye as he stares at John. Everyone knows his loyalty to the king, having been on his guard for many years. Even after he left to marry his wife, his loyalty is still strong.

"What? There have been complaints lately, you know. Many of the lords on the council are upset that Prince Jude is not the heir," John says, looking around for support, and while no one agrees outright, he is telling the truth. There are quite a few who think having a crown princess makes us look weak.

"The Prince has made it clear he doesn't want the crown and supports his twin," Gareth replies. "I've heard he is working his way up through the royal guard and plans to become a military leader—a noble profession," he says, looking at John. "If he wanted to be king, I'm sure he would be fighting more for it instead of doing grunt work and earning his respect."

At this, many of the guards agree. In this crowd, that type of work certainly earns respect. Still, there are groups, especially among the nobles, who see the line of succession broken by placing the Princess on the throne, even though she is the oldest, and there is no law against it.

"Well, the Alberonians replaced their king. Maybe someone wants to replace ours with a new line," John quietly suggests, starting a few murmurs of protest from several surrounding tables.

"I think you have had enough to drink, friend," Aiden says, standing and placing his hand on John's shoulder. Rupert is standing as well, and they have a quiet conversation before John storms out, brushing them off.

As if his exit were a cue for everyone, the tavern starts to empty. "Come on, love. Let's get you home," Aiden says, coming back to my side. We say our goodbyes before making the walk home. On the way here, I let Aiden process his thoughts, but now I want to know what he is thinking.

"So," I say casually, not sure how to start the conversation. "Alberon." I leave it at that, hoping he will share his thoughts, but he only hums in response. It is up to me to pull more out of him.

"Do you think…" I start to ask, hesitant, but he cuts me off.

"He will contact me if he can, but I'm planning on going after him as soon as I am able."

I take this in, not really surprised that this is his response. He has been waiting for this for a while now. The borders to Alberon are open, and he is ready to find his brother, who was left behind when his mother fled to Ileria during the war.

"When will we leave?" I ask, looking up at him, but he stops and looks down at me, his eyebrows furrowed. "I'm coming with you, of course," I say confidently, like there is no question that we would do this together.

"Aloura, this is something that I need to do by myself," he says, reaching out to me, but now I am the one with my brow furrowed.

"I'm going with you. You might need me. We have no idea where your brother is, and what if he didn't make it?" I hate to bring it up, but it has been years with no word from him. Even though they are half brothers and he was quite a few years older, Aiden has always loved his brother and talks about him like he could do no wrong. "I want to be there for you, whether good or bad," I say quietly, looking up into his face.

He looks down at me before softly kissing my head, and I know he is going to say no. "I need to do this alone," he says, his eyes begging me to understand, but I don't. Why would you want to be alone when you could have someone you love there to support you?

"No, you don't have to," I start, but he interrupts me again.

"Your father would never allow it, and it would be unseemly for us to travel alone," he says, but it's a simple solution, really.

"Then marry me, and we can travel together. It can be like a honeymoon."

"To a war-torn country?" he asks skeptically.

"To the country where you were born. Please?" I say, begging, but I know that I have not won him over. If I had my way, we would have been married when I turned sixteen, but here I am at twenty, still waiting.

"No," he says. "Aloura, this won't be a trip for fun. There won't be enough money to stay at inns and have enjoyable meals. I don't even know how long I will be gone. I will be sleeping on the ground and traveling in a country that is still recovering from war, asking questions about a rebel fighter. It is not a place I want to take you or a position I would put you in."

I look away, knowing he makes sense. I'm not incapable, but I've also never lived on the road, and as much as I want to marry him, I don't want it to be like this.

Taking my face in his hands, he meets my eyes. "You know I've had a restless spirit; I haven't been ready to settle down, and now I can finally find answers to some questions that I've been dealing with. I have to take this chance." I look into his eyes, and I know I have to let him go, just as he knows that I will be here waiting for him.

He pulls me into a hug, my head snuggled under his chin. "I'll come back for you, and when I do, I'll be ready," he promises, and I can only trust that it is true. It will break my heart if it isn't.

Chapter 3

The conversation with Aiden still hangs over me like the ocean fog hangs over the city. The gloomy skies match my mood as I wait outside the dress shop for my cousin Lana. The shopping district is close to the docks, so I close my eyes and listen to the gulls' calls and the low crash of waves under the regular bustle of the city. The ocean is probably my favorite thing about living in the city. It always helps calm me.

"Hello, darling," Lana says. Her hips sway as she glides up to me, giving air kisses like the nobility. As the daughter of a wealthy business owner, she is always trying to imitate them. "Don't you look dreary?" she says, taking in my expression. "Is Aiden still out of town?" She slips her arm around mine, linking elbows, before walking into the dress shop. The little bell above us chimes, but no one rushes to assist us, instead leaving us to wander to the premade dresses that line one wall of the shop.

"No, he arrived home yesterday, but we also learned that Alberon has officially opened its borders again," I say, detangling myself from my cousin and picking up the first green dress I see.

"Not that one, darling; it washes you out," she says, switching it with a darker-colored green. This is why I take her shopping with me. "So," she says, turning to look at some dresses for herself, "I take it he wants to go find his brother now, and he said you can't come with him."

My head whips over to look at her. "How did you know?"

"Please, if you could be attached to that man's side every second of the day, you would. I'm surprised you're here with me right now," she says casually, holding up a pink dress that complements her complexion nicely, but she shakes her head and places it back.

"He's in meetings with Rupert today," I say, shaking my head at a blue dress she holds my way. It's pretty, but I'm looking for green.

"Why does the festival have to be held at the beginning of spring when it is still cold and miserable?" She pouts, holding up a lovely short-sleeved dress with ruffles down the front. "Summer styles look much better on me. These winter styles will be covered by my coat anyway," she says, putting it back and lifting the sleeve of a maroon dress.

"It's supposed to represent a time of new beginnings; plus, it gives us something to look forward to when the weather is still cold and miserable," I say as I pull the perfect dress from the wall. It is a darker green that will go nicely with my brown hair, and it won't require too much altering. I'm worried about the price, though, and look around for a store assistant to ask.

"Yes, that's the one," Lana says approvingly of the dress. "Get it, and if it's too much, I'll pay the difference," she says with a decisive nod.

"But—"

"Do this for Aiden. Remind him why he needs to reconsider his options," she says with a wicked smile. I roll my eyes but drape the dress over my arm anyway.

"I don't think a dress will change his mind. He has been waiting for word from his brother for ages, and I think he is tired of waiting." I sigh, and Lana gives me a sympathetic smile. I am tired of waiting for him. I am ready to be his wife. To be there for him in sickness and in health, in trials and joys. I want it all, but because I love him, I will be patient a little longer.

"You know he didn't have to wait for the border to open," she says quietly. "For the right price, there is always someone who can get you where you want to go or what you need."

"Right, but that was the problem; there was a price and he couldn't pay. You know how ruthless some of those gangs can be if someone is in their territory. He couldn't have gone without paying a guide." Those thoughts lead me to think about his upcoming journey. I wonder how dangerous it will be. Will the black market gangs still protect their border territories? Will he be safe if he stays on the main road? A lone traveler is hardly ever safe.

"Hey, stop worrying," she says with a hand on my shoulder. "The fact that he didn't try it tells us he is smart. He will be safe." I give her a grateful smile. Despite our differences, she has always been a great friend. "Come on, let's get that dress so you can remind him why he needs to come back to you," she says, bumping my shoulder and lightening the mood. We pay and wander into a few more shops.

"You should come to the festival opening with me," Lana says, looking at some scarves.

"It's always so crowded," I complain, shaking my head. I love the festival but hate the crowds, especially the first night.

"They are opening the lower courtyard this year, and guess who has an invitation?" she says in a singsong voice. I open my mouth to respond, but I have no words. The royals always start the festival, one of the reasons it is especially crowded on the opening day. The street between the palace and the Royal Temple of The Eternal is filled with vendors and entertainers as people wait for the royal family. They stand on the podium in front of the palace, facing the temple. I wonder why the change.

"They are hosting the opening ceremony in the courtyard this year?" I ask, interested. The royals normally have no problem being out and about with their people.

"Yes," she says, leaning in close and whispering, "There are rumors that there is a renewed threat to the crown princess's life."

"Where did you hear that?" I ask just as quietly, my eyes darting around to make sure we aren't overheard.

"I have my ways," she says casually, but I know what that means.

"You were listening in on a conversation at the inn again. You are going to get yourself in trouble one of these days," I hiss quietly at her. Her father's inn is a meeting point for many important men in the country. They go there because they know they can conduct business safely.

"It's not my fault they choose to have these conversations in places they could be overheard," she says, not looking at me. I purse my lips and narrow my gaze at her until she meets my eye. "It's not like I spread my knowledge around. I only tell you because I know I can trust you."

"You can, but you have to be careful. One of these days, you are going to hear something that will get you killed," I say, giving her a stern look, but she just smiles at me instead.

"Ah, but only if I get caught, and that is unlikely to happen." With a wink, she turns to cross the road to the next shop. Silently cursing her and her mischievous ways, I hurry after her.

"Fine," I say, stepping up to her side. "We will go, but only to keep you out of trouble." With a squeal, she gives me a hug and a cheeky smile.

"Trust me. You won't regret it."

The street is crowded as we make our way to the palace. People are packed together, and I have to use my elbows to keep from getting swallowed up in the crowds. *Why did I let Lana convince me to come?* The main street is wide enough to allow for sizable crowds, but with the vendors, it feels narrow. The street smells of fried dough and sizzling meat, making my mouth water.

The setting sun shines on the palace, causing the glass windows to sparkle. The gray stone shines like silver, and with the cliffs on the other side, it looks like the palace is floating on the ocean. The surrounding buildings match its splendor, the architecture the best the city has to offer. I love the countryside, but our capital is something to be proud of.

"And why did we need to come to the opening ceremony again?" Aiden asks as he pulls me through the crowd. He looks handsome in his simple white tunic with a leather vest over it and soft cotton pants, and I'm not the only one to notice. Several women eye him as we make our way through the crowd, but he doesn't even notice. I wore my new dress today with my brown hair half-braided back and little white flowers in the braids. I feel beautiful and lucky to be by his side.

"Because Lana invited us, and I just know she is going to get in trouble if she were to go by herself." I have to raise my voice above the noise of the vendors calling out their wares. A vendor to our left catches my eye selling savory-smelling handheld pies. My stomach reminds me we haven't eaten yet. I would love to stop and try one, but I promised Lana we would meet her by the palace steps at sunset.

"Yes, but we could have just come the second night of the festival, like we usually do, and brought her with us. Gareth could have been her date," he says, and I smile at the thought. They would make a pretty couple, but unless Gareth made more than he did as a caravan guard, Lana would hardly give him a second look.

"She has an invitation to the courtyard. The opening ceremony is more exclusive this year," I say, spotting my cousin by the wall talking to a tall blond-haired man. She is dressed to impress in a beautiful lavender cloak. I look down at my simple brown one and feel underdressed. It's well made—a gift from Aiden on my last birthday—but it is nothing like what the upper-class ladies will be wearing. Maybe this idea was worse than I realized.

"I didn't think you cared about that sort of stuff," Aiden says, leading us in her direction. Being taller than me, he had probably seen her first.

"I don't, but I care about my cousin." Lana looks up and smiles, giving us a wave as her companion disappears into the crowd.

"Who was that, and where is your escort?" I ask as we arrive, looking around for her brother Matti.

"Just an acquaintance, and I didn't bring one since I figured you and Aiden would be enough," she says, looping her arm through mine. I look up at Aiden on my other side and give him my best I-told-you-so expression.

"You know you are like a walking target," Aiden says bluntly, earning himself a frown from my cousin.

"I'm not an idiot," she says, scowling at him. "Matti and I walked here together, and then he saw some friends. I knew you would be here soon, so I sent him on his way." She leads us up the steps before producing our invitation to the guards, who let us in. The noise dies down as we enter the less crowded lower courtyard of the palace. It's bigger than I realized.

Tables are set up with food and drinks, and there is an area set up for entertainers. Steps lead up to the smaller upper courtyard, where I can see a fountain bubbling before the doors of what I assume leads to the Great Hall of the palace.

Before the fountain are two thrones with three less elaborate chairs, one on the right and two on the left, where the royal family will sit to start the festival. Groups of people from all different classes mingle, and a troupe of performers is setting up where the royals will be able to see them.

"Is this what all your parties look like?" I ask, taking in all the splendor.

"Of course not, silly. This is the first party at the palace I've ever been to. The only reason I have an invitation is that one of Daddy's clients gifted it to him. The ball is for the nobility, but this is supposed to be for the wealthy merchants and palace servants," she says, looking around before pulling us towards the treats.

I notice that while there are many dressed in finery, there are some groups gathered around and talking that are dressed more simply like me, and it allows me to relax a little. I take a bite of a puffed pastry filled with figs and powdered with white sugar. Aiden laughs as the sugar dusts my face. He helps me wipe it off before giving me a quick kiss. Lana just rolls her eyes, but I catch her smile as she turns away.

"Help me look for a wealthy beau," she says, licking her fingers clean of the sticky sugar and eyeing the crowd. "I've heard Machiavelli and his son should be here. If we can find them, I want you to introduce me," she says to Aiden.

"Oh, I see. That's why you wanted us to come," Aiden says, looking down at her while looping an arm around my waist. "We aren't that good of acquaintances, you know," he says with a skeptical look. "Plus, his son is, like, a good ten years older than you."

"I see no problem with that. If he is decent-looking and wealthy, we can make it work," she says with a mischievous wink before walking off to circle the courtyard. I laugh at Aiden's befuddled look before pulling him along to follow her. We don't make it far before trumpets sound and cheers are heard as the royal family steps out of the sparkling palace.

First out are the king and queen in fur-lined blue cloaks. The royal couple wear matching gold crowns set with blue sapphires, looking regal. They have an air about them that commands respect. Behind them walks Crown Princess Marina. Tall, black-haired, and blue-eyed, she is a beauty. Her eyes look over the crowd as she takes her place beside the king, a young guard following in her wake. Next is the youngest, Princess Coraline. About the same age as I, she has a softer bearing than her sister, a little smaller but with the same black hair and blue eyes. She smiles excitedly at the crowd, and I almost want to laugh at her eager expression. It makes me want to join in her excitement. She takes the seat next to the queen, leaving an empty seat beside her. The prince is not here.

"I've heard the prince is patroling with the city guard tonight," Lana says, coming up beside me, making me jump.

"Where do you hear all these rumors?" I ask, trying to hide my surprise, but her smirk tells me it doesn't work.

"The guards were talking about it while I waited outside for you guys," she says quietly as the king steps forward and a hush falls over the courtyard.

"My people," he calls in a loud voice, "I welcome you to the start of our Founders Days festival." His words are met with cheers and whistles, and the king gives a joyful smile to match his younger daughter's. When the noise dies down, he continues, "This festival is held each year so that we might remember our origins, that our great nation of Ileria was given to us by The Great Eternal, and we are ever blessed by His hand." He pauses, and I can feel the anticipation in the air. Many are anxious for the festival to begin.

"We remember the wars and hardships that preceded the founding of our great country and the tragedies that our ancestors faced to create our great nation. While we celebrate these next few days, let us take a moment of remembrance and reflection for them so that we may use their wisdom and sacrifice to better ourselves and our country. May we continue to be the great nation of Ileria, the heart of the Luminary Lands!"

The cheers are deafening, and I reach up to cover my ears. As they die down, music starts to play, and the crowd breaks out to enjoy the festival. Some servants wander out of the open gate into the main festival areas, and I am tempted to join them. An area opens up, and dancing begins.

"Quick, I see Machiavelli. You must introduce me before the next set," Lana says, pulling us in his direction. Machiavelli greets us kindly when we are near, recognizing Aiden from meetings with Rupert. He introduces us to his son, Robert, who asks Lana to dance. Aiden asks me, and soon we are spinning across the dance floor. I am grateful they are playing the country dances instead of the fancy dances of the nobility. We are having too much fun to notice when the royal family leaves the courtyard.

After a couple of dances, I am thirsty and ready for a break, so we make our way to the side of the courtyard. Aiden leaves me in front of the entertainers performing an old play about a long-ago prince, The Last Prince of Coati. It's a popular one, and I watch as I wait for him to come back.

"My mother used to tell me this story before bed when I was young," he says, coming up behind me suddenly. I can feel the warmth of his body behind me as his breath tickles my ear. He hands me my drink but stays behind me, wrapping his arms around me to keep me warm as we watch.

"I thought this was an Ilerian tale," I say as I watch the prince in the play sail across the sea in a little wooden boat that the actors pull across the stage. It's a historical tragedy about the last line of the Coati monarchy. The Crown Prince of Coati sails out on a diplomatic mission, only for his ship to be sabotaged by his jealous brother, who then runs the country into the ground. The impoverished queen with no heirs marries into the rich kingdom of Ileria, dissolving the country of Coati.

"The Lost Heir is a tale we have in Alberon as well. In our version, the prince washes up on shore, but he loses his memory. The beautiful princess finds him and nurses him back to health. They fall in love, but because no one knows he is a prince, their love is forbidden. The princess marries him anyway and is banished. They live out the rest of their lives in poverty, but they are happy because they have each other, and that is enough."

"That sounds lovely," I say as I watch the tragedy unfold. The prince sinks off stage, and new actors come on in colorful costumes representing the Coati court.

"I think it was just a story that we told in rebel camps to keep up hope," Aiden says, drawing my attention away from the play again. "You know, like a lesson—we may be poor, but we are with the people who matter—sort of thing." I look up at him, but he seems far away, lost in memories. "I think some people truly believed the tale and hoped that there were descendants of the prince and princess still alive."

"Do you think that is how they picked the new king?" I ask, fully turning in his arms to look at him.

"How would I know?" he says with a teasing glint in his eye and pulls me close. "I've been here with you."

"But I'm sure you're curious," I say, not letting the topic drop.

"Of course I am. I want to see this new king that my people have fought for. See if he really is as good as they say," he says, his eyes looking around the courtyard. "Hey, why don't we grab Lana and get out of here? Go explore the rest of the festival. We may not normally come on opening night, but since we are here, let's check it out." He lets go of me, taking my hand and pulling me closer to my cousin. He is done talking about Alberon, but I know the topic isn't over. We still have a lot to discuss before he leaves on his trip.

Chapter 4

The third day of the Founders' Festival is the Day of Remembrance. Many people use this day to remember their loved ones who have passed, and we are no exception. The Royal Temple of the Eternal is the most popular in the city, but Papa prefers to attend our neighborhood temple. It is not lavish, with no white marble featuring veins of gold, but the simplicity suits us. It is the normal gray stone used in many city buildings. The windows are plain glass, but the tapestries covering the walls are beautiful.

I don't attend often, but when I do, my eyes are drawn to the tapestry of a faceless man who represents The Eternal. He is floating in the sky, clad in white robes with a halo of light behind his head, gazing down at all his creations. The artistry in the weaving and colors, in just the right lighting, makes him seem like he is glowing. It's magic, and I often feel that if I could just reach out and touch it, I could be filled with his glow as well.

Mama would love it if she could see it. A wave of grief floods over me, and I suck in a breath. My hand creeps up and presses against my chest to stifle the sudden throb of longing for her. I miss her so much. I think of my life and how far removed it is from the life that I lived with her. Would she even recognize who I am now?

I suck in another rattling breath and wipe away a tear. My father, sitting next to me, takes my hand as the priest finishes his sermon. "I miss her too," he whispers, patting my hand. "Every day. I pray that The Eternal keeps her soul safe, and that she is waiting for us in the next life."

"Me too, Papa," I whisper back, but I don't know if I truly believe it. I still wrestle with why He took her from me when I still needed her. The people in the sermon line up for blessings, offered especially during the festival session. They each wish for good health and prosperity in the new year. I am contemplating whether I should join them when Aiden slides onto the bench beside me.

"I'm sorry I'm late. I ended up standing in the back," he says, taking my other hand and smiling at my father. I stare down at my lap, both of my hands held there by the two most important people in my life. My mother may be gone, but at least I have them.

"Are you going to get a blessing?" Aiden asks quietly, looking at the dwindling line. I start to shake my head—I never get blessings—but a sudden impulse stops me.

"I think you should get one for your travels," I say, looking up at him. He looks hesitant, though, so I push forward. "It would make me feel better." I flutter my lashes up at him, and he breaks into a smile at my antics.

"I will if you will," he says, and I agree, pulling him up. Papa stands slowly, shooting me a questioning but hopeful look. I shrug my shoulders and start to walk toward the line, but his hand on my arm stops me.

"I'll meet you at home," he says, leaning down and kissing me on the forehead. "You are the only blessing I need." He gives me a soft, tender smile and a little squeeze before walking out. I watch him for a moment before joining Aiden at the back of the line.

"What do you think your blessing will say?" I ask to pass the time. I'm nervous and glance to see how many people are left. There are only a couple ahead of us, but who knows how long they will take? Some people take the blessing very seriously and others as only a formality.

"Probably a normal blessing; the priest will put his hand on my forehead and ask The Eternal to bless me with safety in my journeys this year," he says, rubbing my shoulders. "It can't hurt, especially since I am going to be traveling a lot this year."

I nod my head instead of replying, rubbing my hands together in front of me. I am anxious about his travels too. "When do you leave again?" I ask quietly.

"I actually have some news in that regard," he says, and I look up at him. He looks so excited to be going. "Rupert wants me to travel with him in the first caravan to Alberon. From there, I can leave and search for my brother. I have a few people I'm sure I can contact who will know something," he says, smiling down at me.

"I'm glad you won't be traveling alone." My voice sounds small, so I try to smile at him, but he sees right through me and slips his arms down to give me a firm hug.

"This is good. It means that I will have people there to help me, and I won't be gone long. In fact," he says with a pause, "maybe to keep yourself busy while I am gone, you can plan for our wedding."

I turn quickly in his arms to look at his face. "Are you sure?" I ask, not quite believing it.

"Yes," he says, leaning in for a kiss, but the priest interrupts us.

"Would you like a blessing today?" he asks, and I blush, embarrassed, before I walk up the brief steps to him and kneel on a worn cushion.

"What blessing are you looking for this year?" he asks with a twinkle in his eye.

"How about whatever you think is best?" I whisper, not sure what the standard blessings are. Maybe he will give me a blessing of love or marriage after that display. I close my eyes, and he presses his fingers of his right hand to my forehead.

"Oh Eternal, I ask a blessing for this, your child," he starts before pausing. I wait for his next words, but the silence continues long enough to make me wonder if something has gone wrong. Cracking an eye open, I see the frown on his face and open my mouth to ask what is wrong, but his expression smooths and he smiles again. I close my eyes again, and he continues.

"As thou wilt," he says quietly, like he was having a conversation, then more loudly, "I have a special gift for you." My eyes snap open, and I let out a little gasp. He doesn't pay me any mind, though, and continues as if nothing out of the ordinary has happened. "I bestow not just a blessing but a gift on this child of yours. Your child will receive the gift of guidance. That she may have Your holy light shine over her as she journeys through her life. Let her feel Your light and guidance and know that You see her and have been aware of her even before she was born." A startling warmth flows into my veins, and I glance at the windows, sure that the sun must be shining on me, but the temple is the same.

"Let her seek thee when she needs help and have a surety of thy will. In this, we ask about this festival day. Let it be so." The warmth slowly recedes as the priest takes his hand from my head and smiles down at me.

"What was that?" I whisper, not wanting to disrupt the peace of the moment.

"I suggest you remember that feeling," he says as he offers his hand to help me up. "Don't hesitate to come see me if you need to." He gives me a tender smile and a pat on the hand before gesturing for Aiden to come up the steps for his blessing.

Our hands brush as we pass, but I am too busy with my thoughts to give them much attention. That was not the blessing I was expecting. *I have a special gift for you.* How could he have known the exact words my mother heard? The exact words my mother said to me before she died?

It's all too much, and I decide to speak about it with my father later. I'm sure he will have an explanation. I watch as Aiden kneels before the priest. His fingers press against Aiden's forehead. I'm sure the priest will bless his travels, but his words are too quiet for me to hear. It seems normal, but as the priest helps Aiden stand, they have a discussion that causes Aiden to frown.

"What is wrong?" I ask when he joins me. He furrows his brow in thought, but doesn't answer. He just takes my hand and leads me outside. I loop my arm through his as we stroll down the street. I allow him his silence, sure he will tell me when he is ready.

"How was your blessing?" he asks, surprising me.

"It was... a little strange," I say, pausing to think about it again. I raise my hand to my heart, from where the feelings radiate. "He said some things that reminded me of my mother, and then he blessed me with guidance. What does that even mean?" I ask, wondering if maybe Aiden has some insight of his own.

"Guidance?" he says thoughtfully, rubbing his chin. "Well, maybe you will be making a lot of decisions this year."

"Maybe," I say, but I think there is more to it than that.

"You've already made one big decision today, so I'm sure you will have more to make as well," he says with a mischievous curve of his lips.

I look at him, confused for a moment, but then I remember. I can't believe the blessing made me forget. "I have to plan our wedding," I say, delighted.

"Come," he says, kissing my hand before leading me home. "Let's go tell your father the good news."

"Join me over here," my father says, patting the seat next to him as I close the door after saying good night to Aiden. I cautiously walk over and sit down next to him, letting him take one of my hands in his. I notice that they are stiff and grab the ointment we keep on the side table and start rubbing it into his hands.

"You are a good girl," he says, drawing my eyes up to him. "You always take care of me."

"Of course I do, Papa," I say, finishing with the ointment and putting it away. "You are my family. We take care of each other."

Gathering my hand once again, he pats it for a moment before saying quietly, "Your mother would be so proud of the woman you have become." His words fill me with warmth, and I am reminded of the blessing earlier. *I have a gift for you.*

"Papa, may I ask you something?"

"Anything."

"Today, I received a peculiar blessing—no, a gift. The priest gave me the gift of guidance. Do you know what that means?" I ask. Ever since Mama passed away, Papa has become more fascinated with the old text of The Eternal, so I am sure he knows more than me.

"Guidance, you say? Interesting," he says, and I sit forward, ready to hear his wisdom, but he doesn't continue.

"Papa, what is a gift of guidance?" I ask again after his silence.

"Well, it is a type of gift," he says and then laughs at my expression. "Let's start by seeing what you already know. What do you know about blessings?"

"I know the priest gives them during festival days. Often, people ask for specific blessings like luck in travels or good fortune, or a blessed harvest; those types of things. They are whatever you wish for or want for the following year." *That is why I thought I would be receiving a blessing of prosperity in love and marriage.*

"Yes and no," he says, confusing me even more.

"I don't understand."

"Let me give you an example. Will you bring me the Holy Text?" he asks, and I go fetch his copy. It is a compilation of writings from kings and priests of old passed down from generation to generation. It contains stories and communications from The Eternal. Most families have one in their home, but I doubt they are as well loved as ours.

He takes the text and opens it somewhere in the middle. "Do you remember the story of the boy king?" The memory comes to mind in the vaguest of terms.

"He was a peasant boy of Parisa who became their king, correct?" I ask, recalling the story from my childhood.

"Yes, the Parisans' king had no heir and was dying. The country was in turmoil, split between the houses of nobles who were trying to rule. Their high priest prayed for guidance and found the peasant boy. The boy was wise and good and sought the will of The Eternal. The priest brought the boy to the temple and crowned him. Using his gift of guidance, he was able to stabilize the country, and it became the most profitable country of the time."

The gift of guidance, I thought. I knew of gifts like patience and healing, but these were always bestowed upon people in stories, resulting in miracles. I was just a girl who barely believed. I had just received a regular blessing—hadn't I?

"The gift of guidance is a divine gift from The Eternal. The Holy Text is full of these instances," my father says with a frown, his expression troubled.

"Then why me?" I ask, but he just shakes his head.

"I'm sorry I don't know, but I trust Him. If you do, too, I'm sure he will lead you down an amazing path," he says with reverence, but now it's my turn to shake my head. I don't want this. I just want to live happily ever after with Aiden in a normal life.

"Just think about it. Your choices are still your own," he says, patting my hand before wishing me good night. I sit out on the sofa till the fire dies down, thinking. My father's words bring me comfort; my choices are still my own, but if the divine comes to call, can I truly turn it down?

Chapter 5

"Three cheers to the happy couple!" Gareth yells, clinking his drink against his neighbor's before taking a big gulp. I smile and take a sip of my cider, enjoying the party, but there is also a bitter note to it. Aiden is leaving again. The whole patrol is here to celebrate before they head out to Alberon. Aiden agreed to travel the first part of the journey with them before splitting off on his own.

Tonight, we celebrate our engagement and his departure. I want to cry and pout and beg him to stay, but I know he needs to do this. If I don't let him go, he will always resent me. I try to stifle a yawn, but Aiden sees it. The party has been going on for hours, and it is now late into the night.

"We should probably get you home," he says, putting an arm around me and pulling me close. "I'm sure a few of these guys will stay here for another hour and have splitting headaches on the march tomorrow," he says with a smirk. I don't want to leave, though. If I leave, then tomorrow comes sooner, and he leaves.

"I want to stay and spend every second with you I can," I whisper, looking up at him.

He leans in close and whispers, "If we leave here, though, I can give you a proper goodbye." I close my eyes and take a long, slow breath before smiling up at him.

"Okay."

We stand, and he leads me to the door, but before he can take me home, Rupert comes in. "Aiden, I'm glad I found you. We need to meet before tomorrow," he says, looking around and locating Gareth as well. "Aloura," he says to me with a nod of his head.

"I need to take her home," Aiden says, looking at Rupert. His gaze is serious, and I know this is no simple meeting. Turning to Aiden, I place my hand on his arm to get his attention.

"I can wait," I say, but Rupert shakes his head.

"No, this meeting might last well into the night. It's sensitive in nature," he says, communicating with Aiden with his eyes. Aiden stiffens for a split second before reluctantly looking at me.

"Okay, I will walk her quickly and then—"

"It's fine. I can walk myself home," I say, ready to have a good cry as I do.

"No, it's dark," he says, but I interrupt him. I am ready to give in to my emotions, and I don't want to do it here.

"It's not far, and the lamps are lit," I say. I can see his resistance, but another look at Rupert and he nods his head.

"Okay, I will check in on you later if I can, but if not, meet me at the warehouse tomorrow morning. We leave at dawn, and I want to give you a proper goodbye," he says quietly. I give a nod before slipping out.

The night is darker and colder than I thought it would be, the moon barely a sliver in the sky. *I'm close to home*, I tell myself, the dark night making me wary. I repeat in my mind to keep away the doubts in my mind. *I could probably walk back blindfolded.* The doubt creeps in still, and I try to keep to the street lamps in the more populated areas, even if it means a longer walk in the cold.

I pull the collar up on my coat to hide my face as I think back on Aiden to keep my mind occupied as I walk. It's a bad idea, and I quickly lose the battle with my emotions. Tears leak down my face, but it hasn't turned into sobs yet. I will save those for my pillow.

A salty breeze tugs a few shorter strands of hair out of my braid, plastering them to my wet face. I brush them from my face and realize that I have taken a wrong turn. I'm not far from the tavern still and turn to make my way back to a familiar path, but a noise to my right startles me.

I turn my head, looking down the dark alley between two buildings. I know I should keep moving to a better-lit area, but my racing heart causes me to freeze. Something in the alley moves, and finally, I take a step, ready to bolt. A figure shuffles toward me before stumbling to the mouth of the alley. I turn to run, but a hand latches onto my wrist, and I let out a frightened scream. The figure just laughs.

"Aloura," a familiar voice says as the face of my assailant comes into focus. My stomach drops. I try to wiggle my wrist out of his grasp, but I can't break it. The smell wafting off of him tells me he is drunk, but he is still strong.

"Please let go, John." I want to sound strong, but my voice trembles as it comes out.

"Now, now, I don't mean you any harm," he says, pulling me closer to him. "I would like to offer you my personal congratulations. Where is your fiancé?" he asks, looking around. "I'm surprised he let you out of his sight. It is getting late, and a lady like you shouldn't be out here in the dark." His words sound friendly, but his tone is mocking, and I once again try to pull my arm out of his grasp.

"He had to meet someone and is going to catch up in a moment." Technically, he said he would stop by after his meeting, but I know it's not a good idea to let John know I am completely alone. It will be a while before anyone misses me.

I look around, trying to see if there is anyone else around, but the street is empty. "My father is expecting me," I say, trying to pull away, but he tightens his grip, and I wince. There will most likely be a bruise there in the morning.

"Of course, but this isn't your typical way home, is it?" he asks, and a chill runs down my back. I don't like that he knows where I live. A feeling of dread comes over me, and I know I need to get out of here.

"I just got a little turned around in the dark. Aiden will be along in a moment to finish walking me home." I'm desperately looking for something to break his hold. Maybe I need to scream again.

"Poor little Aloura," he taunts, "so lost. You know Aiden is leaving tomorrow, and he might not come back. What would you do then?" He leans in close, a cruel grin stretching his lips. I close my eyes against the foul smell of his breath. I won't answer him. I give a big yank to free my arm, but he lets go, throwing me off balance. He uses this to his advantage and grabs me, turning me to pin me to a wall.

I let out a whimper as his body leans against mine, keeping me in place. I shove, but he grabs my hands and pins them above me. "Poor, pathetic Aloura, pretty but no brain," he taunts. "She thinks she can have him, but she is nothing."

I close my eyes and turn my head away, but his hand comes down and grips my chin tightly, making me face him. "He won't come back for you," he says, voicing one of my biggest fears. I'm not just worried that he might die, but what if he finds his brother and won't leave Alberon?

Tears leak from my eyes, and I try to shake my head. "He loves me," I whisper. One of my hands is free with his holding my chin, and I push at him, trying to get him off of me. My breath comes out in quick gasps, and I feel like I can't breathe.

"Poor little Aloura," he says again, backing off finally. "So naive." He smiles wickedly at me, and I back away but trip and land on the ground in a heap. He laughs again as he walks closer, crouching down next to me, and I scramble to get away, but my heel gets caught in my skirt.

He bends down close to me and whispers, "I don't want to hurt you, Aloura. Not yet. But when you are heartbroken, when you realize he is not coming back, I'll come to see you."

"No," I cry, hating his threat. "I'll tell Aiden. I'll tell Rupert. I'll report you," I say, trying to get up again, but his hand launches around my throat and squeezes. "No!" I scream as loud as I can before the pressure on my throat cuts me off.

"Shut up, you stupid girl!" he snarls, shaking me. "You won't tell anyone, or I won't let you live to see tomorrow!" I claw at his hand that tightens around my throat, cutting off my air. He shakes me again but then lets go as we hear boots running closer.

"Halt! You are under arrest for the assault of that woman!" a voice commands, but John doesn't wait, taking off at a run. He doesn't get far before a guard tackles him, pinning him to the ground. "Take him to jail and lock him up. No bail," a tall man says to his companion. John curses and struggles against his captor, but another uniformed officer joins the first to drag him away. The tall man, the leader, approaches me. He squats down, and I glimpse dark hair and pale skin in the dim light.

"Are you okay?" he asks, and I notice his piercing blue eyes. His voice is deep and soft, but his face is stoic. He doesn't reach out to touch me, just looks me over as if assessing me for injury. I must take too long to answer because he starts asking more questions, "Are you hurt? Can you move?"

"I can move," I mutter quietly. My throat hurts, but he didn't crush it, luckily. My wrist will also bruise, and the places that hit the ground when I fell, but overall, that could have ended much worse. The man stands and offers a hand to help me up.

I wipe my wet eyes with the collar of my coat before taking his hand and allowing him to pull me to my feet. I let out an involuntary "Oh" as I realize just how tall he is now that we are standing. Aiden is decently tall, just under six feet, but this guy probably has him by a few inches. His black-and-blue uniform and blue-trimmed cloak marked him as a royal guard instead of the plain black uniform of the city guard. He must be important, I realize as I fiddle with my skirts, wondering if I should bow or something. I decide simply to say, "Thank you," my voice slightly raspy from my encounter.

"May I see?" he asks gently, looking at my throat. Feeling embarrassed, I give my consent, and he lifts a hand and ever so gently tilts my chin up to get a better look at my throat. I swallow and then flush, feeling foolish. This is my fault for being stupid. I should have just let Aiden take me home, even if he saw me cry for him.

"You will have some bruising," the guard says, stepping back politely and placing his hands behind his back, "but I don't think there should be any lasting damage." He looks around before making eye contact with me. "Is there a safe place we can escort you?"

Startled, I realize that there are two more guards standing by us on the street. "Oh, um," I start, not sure where to go. *Do I go back to the tavern? Or do I ask them to take me home?* My thoughts are sporadic, so I latch onto my last destination. "I was on my way home," I say slowly, testing out the answer. It feels right, and I am ready to be in my bed. But then I think of Aiden. I'm not ready to see him yet. He would be upset that I insisted on walking home alone and got myself into trouble.

"Of course," he says, raising a hand, indicating that I should lead the way. I head back the way I came, very aware of the guards trailing me. It makes me feel silly. I am sorry to inconvenience them. The leader walks at my side, and I turn to him as we reach a more lit street.

"I can walk by myself from here," I say, not wanting to take any more of their time. After the words leave my mouth, I blush and look away. That is the same reasoning that left me vulnerable. Still, these men don't owe me anything, and I don't want to be a bother.

"I would feel better if we saw you home safely," the leader says, beckoning one of the other guards forward. They exchange quiet words, and he takes off toward the tavern at a quick pace. I am making them late for something.

I just want to get home and nurse my wounds in peace. "I really can..." I start again, already taking a step towards home, but he interrupts.

"Miss, I can't let you go without seeing you to a safe place. Please, for my peace of mind." I meet his eyes, and I can't say no. His gaze is kind, and I start walking toward home, and he keeps pace easily with me.

"It's not your fault, you know." His voice is quiet, sympathetic, but I don't know how to respond, so I stay quiet. "It's easy to blame yourself for these situations, to think back and wonder if you made different decisions, if anything would have changed."

"Can you read minds?" I ask, wincing at the slight pain in my throat.

"No, but I've been in some pretty scary situations myself. Someone very dear to me suffered an attack, and for a long time, I replayed what-if scenarios in my head, but that couldn't change the past. Instead, I realized that the only thing I could do was make sure I prepared so it couldn't happen again." The conviction in his voice is strong, and I admire it.

"Is that why you joined the guard?"

"Yes," he says. We walk quietly after that, reaching my home quickly.

"Miss," he says with a little bow before walking off as I make my way through the courtyard and up the stairs. Papa is in his room already, so I make my way quietly to my room and prepare for bed. As I lie down, the tears come. I miss Aiden and wish he could hold me. Finally, all my tears are gone, and as I fall asleep, I realize I never got the guard's name.

Chapter 6

I groan as a knock pounds on my door. "Aloura, you are going to miss Aiden if you don't hurry!" my father's voice calls through the door, and I bolt upright. I quickly get dressed, pulling on a dress, and rapidly combing my hair, leaving it down.

Bursting out of my room, I grab my coat, tossing it on. I'm sore, and there is a bruise on my wrist for sure. I haven't checked my neck yet, but it still hurts to swallow. All of this is not important compared to making it in time to see Aiden.

"Wait up," my father laughs at my haste, coming over to grab his own coat. "I'll come with you." He smiles at me, but it fades as he takes me in. The bruising must be worse than I thought. "Aloura," he says, reaching forward but not quite touching my neck. My eyes meet his, and I can see the questions in them.

"I'll tell you as we walk," I say, opening the door. Sure, he would rather have answers right away, but I refuse to miss Aiden. I hear his boots clomping down the stairs behind me, relieved that he didn't protest.

As we start walking, I loop my arm through his. "I'm fine, Papa," I start, wanting to reassure him that I truly am okay. "Aiden had a last-minute meeting about the trip, and I assured him that I could make my way home alone." I look up to see my father scowling. "I know that was dumb."

"It was dumb of Aiden to let you go," he grumbles under his breath.

"Really, I insisted. I was distraught at his leaving. Not paying attention, I turned down the wrong street and ran into John, who was drunk…" I stop there. I always knew he didn't like me, but I didn't realize it was that strong.

"Aloura?" my father says, pulling me back out of my thoughts.

"I froze," I whisper, "He grabbed me, and I couldn't get away. He threatened me, but he didn't truly hurt me until I threatened him back. I told him I would tell Aiden and Rupert, and he got really mad…" My voice trails off again as I get lost in the memories. I hate feeling so helpless. The guard's words from last night come to mind. Maybe I need to do something to make sure I'm never in that position again.

Papa gently squeezes my hand, which rests on his arm, prompting me to continue. "The city guard showed up and took him away before making sure I made it home," I say, finishing my story. We walk in silence for a bit, making our way down to the warehouses that Aiden's group will leave from.

"Does Aiden know?" Papa finally asks, and I shake my head. He is not going to be happy about it at all. The thought flits across my mind that maybe this will help him want to stay. That he wouldn't leave if he was worried about me, but I quickly dismiss the thought. I don't want to get my hopes up.

As we reach the waterfront, I snuggle into my coat. A chilly spring breeze wafts up from the water, pulling at my hair and making me wish I had brought a scarf. If only it were strong enough to blow away the fog that sits heavy in the air. I can hardly see two feet in front of me, making me worry we have missed them. I listen closely for any noise—the call of a man, the grunt of a laborer, the clank or clink of a wagon—but the fog dampens everything, and it isn't until we are almost upon them that I finally hear them.

A pair of horses slowly materializes from the fog, and then the wagon. The shadowy forms of men turn into faces that I recognize. Finally, I see him, and my heart leaps as I take him in. Aiden carries a board with paper and a charcoal pencil, marking off items on a list and directing men as they prepare for their journey.

He is confident and commanding and looks like he is where he belongs, and that thought sends a pang through my heart. I don't want him to travel, but as I see him here, I know I can't let my fear hold him back.

Aiden looks over and spots us, squinting to see us through the fog, but I can tell when he recognizes me because he shoves his supplies in Gareth's hands and rushes over. I open my arms to let him sweep me into his arms. He kisses my face before setting me down and smiling, but just like my father, that smile fades as he takes me in. I need to look in the mirror.

"What happened?" he asks as he moves my collar to see my neck better. "Are there more injuries?" He looks me over, and I hold up my wrist. Besides those, I'm mostly just sore. "Who did this to you?" he demands.

"I'm sorry," I whisper, feeling like a fool again. "I was upset about you leaving, and I walked the wrong way," I say as he pulls me into his chest. He and Papa make eye contact over my head.

"What happened?" he asks again.

"It was John," Papa says, explaining my story so I don't have to. Aiden lets out a curse before gently removing himself from me. "When the Captain was late yesterday, he mentioned an incident..." he says, looking around and finding Rupert before motioning him over.

"John attacked Aloura," Aiden tells him as soon as he arrives, "That's why he isn't here." He is fuming. I want to reach out to help cool his anger, but a small part of me is glad to see his anger. It feels like proof that he cares for me.

"Are you okay, lass?" Rupert asks, and I give him a soft smile.

"Yes, they sent him to jail without bail. I'm not sure what will happen next, but I hope to never see him again," I say with a shiver. He can't get me, but I am grateful my father walked with me this morning. I'm not sure I will be going out on my own anytime soon.

"This changes things," Rupert says, turning to Aiden. "Maybe you should…" Aiden shakes his head sharply, cutting him off.

"No!" he says forcefully, making me jump. "No, I can't wait. I need to…" He trails off and looks at me, and the hope I didn't realize I was harboring dies. He is still leaving me.

"Can I have a moment?" he asks, looking at my father and Rupert.

"I will just be over here looking at the sea. It's been a while, and I need some new inspiration," Papa says, stepping away. The fog is too thick to truly see the water, but I appreciate the thought anyway.

"I'll join you," Rupert says, following him. I can hear the quiet hum of their voices, and I am sure they are talking about the situation.

Aiden faces me, taking my hands, but he won't meet my eye. I take a deep breath and square my shoulders, but I know whatever he is going to say will hurt. "Aloura…" He stares down at our hands, playing with my fingers. I wait for him to break his silence, but he can't seem to find the words.

"I know," I say quietly before he can find false words of comfort.

"I have to try," he says, looking broken. I pull him into a hug. This is hard for both of us, but I will respect his choice, even if it hurts.

"I know," I repeat, tucking my head under his chin so he doesn't see the doubt in my expression. It wouldn't do any good to express it again. He is still determined to go.

"Start planning the wedding," he says, rubbing up and down my back. "Then, when we are reunited, we will be married." I want to believe him, but I pull away.

Papa rejoins us, stepping up and giving Aiden a pat on the back. "Please be careful, son," he says, just loud enough for me to hear as well. Aiden swallows and looks away for a moment before he resumes a soft smile. He respects Papa, and I hope that one day we will be a family and he will be a true son to my father.

"I have to go, but thank you for coming to see me," he says, slowly walking backward. Before he gets too far, though, I run up and throw my arms around him one more time, kissing him long and hard even though we have an audience. "I will be safe, and I will return to you," he promises me quietly.

I nod, taking a shaky breath, and try to smile at him before he turns and walks away. I hardly notice as Papa walks back to my side, sliding an arm around me. We stay like that, watching until the wagon finally rolls out of view, and then, with tears falling down my face, we walk home.

It is always difficult when Aiden is gone, and this time is worse because I don't know when he is coming back. The past few weeks have seemed to drag on, each day a repetitious routine. I wake up, help Papa with the shop, and then we spend the evening together. There is nothing interesting to take my mind off of Aiden and his mission. Did they arrive in Alberon okay? Did he already split from the group? Did he find his brother?

Frequent letters are normal while he is on merchant runs, but I don't know what to expect now. This is unfamiliar territory. I bend over the counter, propping my chin on my hand as I look at the books for the shop, adding up expenses versus income to pass the time. We are doing okay, but the slow decrease in our revenue stands out as Papa cannot take as many commissions as he used to. I need to talk to him again about an apprentice.

I am contemplating how to convince him when the bell jingles over the door, drawing my attention.

"Hello, darling," Lana calls, sweeping into the shop, bringing with her the scent of rosewater and pastries. Her dress is yellow today with too many ruffles for my taste. It complements her olive tone and brown hair, though. "I had a feeling you were lonely, so I brought you a treat. Plus, we need to start planning your wedding," she says with a mischievous twinkle in her eye.

"I will gladly take a pastry," I say, taking the basket from her and putting it on the counter. It smells good, like sugar and fresh-baked cookies. "What did you bring me?" I ask, taking a peek inside.

"Robin was baking again today, trying something new. I think they are cherry tarts with a sugar cookie base. I don't know," she says with a shrug. "He was all excited about the new recipe. I had no clue what he was saying, but it was cute, and he gave me a few extra for free," she says with a mischievous smile. I roll my eyes but peek into the basket anyway. I'm not going to turn down free treats.

I reach into the basket and take one, the scent of warm sugar and fruit causing my mouth to water. I take a big bite, and my eyes flutter shut as I taste a mixture of sweet dough with the tartness of cherries. "Next time you see him, you have to tell him that they are amazing," I say through a full mouth, causing Lana to laugh.

"I'll tell him," she says with a smile as she takes a bite of her treat.

"So, what have you already planned for your wedding?" she says, eyeing my dress. "If we get you fitted soon, we can probably come up with something lovely, maybe a light blue silk. Prices are coming down. Have you noticed?"

"I have, but I don't need anything as fancy as what you wear. It wouldn't be practical," I say, thinking of our finances.

"But it's your wedding!" she says, looking at me sharply, her mouth pulled into a frown.

Her brows furrow at the thought of me getting married in a simple dress, but that's what I want. A simple ceremony with friends, followed by dinner and drinks at the tavern. Nothing elaborate or fancy, even if that is the style nowadays.

"It's not like I even know when my wedding will be. It could be in a few weeks or a couple of months," I say with a sigh and a shrug. "When it does happen, it will be simple with me in one of my mother's old dresses." That remark earns me a frown from Lana, causing me to laugh.

"That's not funny," she says, crossing her arms. "Fashion is nothing to joke about, especially on such an important occasion."

"To be honest, I would marry him in his dusty armor as soon as he gets back, if I could."

"No, no. You will want to get new clothes made for him too," she says, holding up a hand to hold back any protest I may have. I just roll my eyes and take another tart.

"What was this called again?" I say after I finish my bite. "I have to share these with Aiden when he gets back."

"They are cherry tarts," she says, taking another one as well. "How is Aiden, by the way? I miss seeing his handsome face." She must read the answer on my face, though, because she quickly moves on. "Did you hear the latest news?" she says, already knowing that I most likely haven't. Most of my gossip comes from her.

"Do tell me what is going on in the glittering world of the elite," I tease, but she doesn't take the bait immediately, launching into the latest scandal at court. Most of the information doesn't matter to me, but I still listen like I understand who she is talking about. A few names, mostly those on the king's council, stand out, but there are so many noble houses it's hard to keep track of them all.

"Of course, Duke Segnal wants Crown Princess Marina to marry his son Luke. So far, she has not shown favor to anyone, which is a point of contention for the council. They feel that it is past time she takes finding a consort seriously as she has now turned twenty-one."

"Does she have to be married at a certain age?" I ask. I will listen to anything to distract myself from worrying about Aiden.

"No, but the council is putting pressure on her, insisting that she cannot rule effectively without a powerful man by her side," she says, rolling her eyes. "Many of them still wish Prince Jude was the heir and ignore the good that the princess is doing."

I think of the proud woman from the festival standing tall by her father. She commanded authority, and I know from market gossip she has been instrumental in renegotiating trade tax now that trade has increased with Alberon.

"Any word about what the prince is doing?" I ask, trying to keep the conversation going.

"He has been doing patrols and taking an interest in all aspects of the guard and military. He is a captain now, and despite urging to join council meetings, he wants to work his way there and earn it."

"That's very noble of him," I say, not even questioning how my cousin gets her information. It's a little scary, to be honest.

Suddenly, Lana sits forward, dropping her voice to a strategic whisper. "I almost forgot the most interesting news I've heard recently, but this one can't be repeated," she says, meeting my eyes.

"Then maybe you shouldn't tell me," I say equally quietly, wary of this information. One day, she is going to get in trouble for what she overhears, and I don't want to be dragged down with her.

"It will be public knowledge soon, but not yet, so just don't be the one to spread it," she says, pointing her finger at me before breaking into a grin. She knows she doesn't have to worry about me spreading gossip.

"Just tell me," I say with a sigh.

"I heard that the new king of Alberon has put in an offer for Marina's hand in marriage," she says dramatically.

"Is that even allowed?" I ask, confused. My knowledge of politics is sorely lacking, but even I know that would be a sticky situation.

"There are no laws against it, but succession would be part of the marriage contract. In the offer he gave, he said that the first child would rule one country and the second child would rule the other," she says with a shrug, licking the sugar off her fingers.

"But what is the benefit of a marriage alliance?" I ask, still confused. My lack of knowledge is showing, but Lana gives me a conspiratorial grin. I know she doesn't mind explaining.

"He claims that he has new systems in place that will strengthen Ileria, help demolish the poor, and all that." I nod because I have already heard of his efforts. They were being talked about positively by many people.

"But the weird part," she says, leaning closer, "is that he claims through his lineage he has the birthright and obligation from The Eternal to rule the entire continent."

"Excuse me?" I ask, not sure I heard correctly. "What does that even mean?"

"Well, all monarchs are supposedly descendants of the Divine Family, who were first called by The Eternal to unite the lands of Lumina. I'm surprised you don't know this. I thought your father was pretty devout." Her brow furrows as she looks at me.

"No, I remember now, but I still don't understand. If he claims that he is part of the Divine Family, what gives him the right to rule the entire continent over the other monarchs?"

"Because The Eternal wills it, I guess," she says with a shrug. "Our priests haven't had any sort of sign that he is blessed, so the council claims he must be lying. They say he has gotten a taste of power and now wants more." Her eyes are full of excitement at the drama unfolding between the two countries, but I can't share in her joy. *Oh, Aiden, stay safe.*

"They are thinking of sending an ambassador, though, to meet him and see about his plans," Lana says, drawing my attention back to her. "They want to find proof of his lineage and make sure he is not raising an army against us. Alberon is practically a new country and a scary one at that, considering how the war was won. No one wants a war, but we can't let him take over."

"How did he win the Civil War?" I ask curiously. I'm sure Aiden talked about it, but now I can't remember.

"No one quite knows," Lana says. "There are rumors, of course. Some say he single-handedly took over. Others say it was with the power of The Eternal. All we know is that the rebels were making no progress, and then

King David took over, and suddenly they were winning. I think he has the council scared."

"All I've heard about the new king is positive."

"Of course! The people love him. He is smart, handsome, generous, and kind. His people think he is a saint, but claiming to have the right to rule everybody?" She says with her eyebrow raised as she sits back, letting her question hang in the air.

A chill runs down my spine, and I glance outside at the people walking around without a care. The air feels dangerous in here, full of secrets that we are not meant to know. My mind goes back to Aiden like it always does. Is he safe in this new Alberon with the dangerous and clever king? His brother was part of the rebels, as was everyone he knew. Are they dangerous too?

"I'm sure he is fine," Lana says, placing a hand on my arm. "I'm sorry, that was a bad topic of conversation. I was just trying to entertain you with interesting information, not scare you," she says, and I give her a weak smile.

"I know," I say, searching for a new topic. "So... if I were to get a new dress, you think blue silk would suit me?" With a grateful smile, Lana latches on to the topic, going on about current fashions until it is time for her to leave. I listen with a pleasant smile, but underneath, the worry never leaves.

Chapter 7

Don't borrow trouble, I tell myself the next day as I work like normal, but my conversation with Lana still runs through my head. None of them are things that I have control over or even a say in, but still, I worry. How does this affect Aiden? Will this end up in war? Husband or not, Aiden would be fighting in it, and then...whose side would he fight on?

Suddenly, I'm spiraling. Aiden and I have never seriously talked about the future. Where will we live? Will we still live in Ileria, or will he want to return to Alberon now that it is more stable? Where does that leave Papa? These are all things that we should have been talking about, but I was so focused on marriage, and Aiden avoided it.

Feeling stupid, I decide to go visit Papa in his workshop. Maybe he can talk some sense into me. I run up to our apartment to grab him some lunch. Knowing him, he probably worked through it again.

I walk down the stairs, through our small dirt courtyard, to the workshop at the back of our property. Today, the large doors of the workshop are open to let in the fresh air and light. I watch as Papa bends over his latest creation, adding a few last details before it is ready to be picked up.

"Come over here and take a look at this," he says, eyes still on the dresser he just finished. It is beautiful dark wood, polished till gleaming, with intricate carvings of leaves and roses down the sides. I am in awe of his artistry and proud of his work.

"Wow, Papa." I trail my hand delicately over a carving of an elk. "Another work of art," I say, smiling up at him. It is a wonder that more people don't seek him out. He could be charging a fortune for his work. He really needs to find someone to train.

He looks at his work, assessing it for anything that may still need his touch, but I can tell he is satisfied with this piece. My gaze catches on his hands as he looks. He is rubbing them, massaging them in a way that tells me they still ache. He catches me staring and gives me a soft smile. "I know what you are going to say."

"Oh, really?" I ask, placing my hands on my hips and narrowing my eyes at him. "Tell me then." I turn my head and present my ear, ready to hear his ability to read my mind. He just laughs at me, causing me to smile. He looks down at his hands again before glancing back at his masterpiece. My smile fades as I watch his shoulders cave in just a little. I hate to see him so defeated.

"I have been thinking about it," he says quietly, looking around his workshop. "Once you marry Aiden and find a place to live, then I will have an empty room that I can offer an apprentice, and then I won't have to live here alone," he says, looking at me from the corner of his eye. Smiling, I throw my arms around him and give him a tight hug.

"Papa, even when I marry Aiden, you won't be left alone. You know that, right?" I look up into his face and see him smiling down at me. After Mother's passing, we both hold each other dear.

"I know, but it won't be the same as having you under my roof," he says, bringing back my worries.

"Papa," I say hesitantly. I want to marry Aiden, but I'm suddenly scared of the reality of that and how unprepared I really am. "I don't even know where we are going to live," I admit, defeated, as tears come to my eyes.

"Oh, my dear," he says, gathering me into his arms. I burrow my face into his chest as tears leak out and my thoughts race.

"I just... I feel like marriage has always been the goal for me," I sniffle out. "Now that he asked and told me to plan the wedding, I've started thinking about all the other things that we have never talked about, and he is not even here to help me."

My doubts overwhelm me, and my silent tears turn into sobs. Papa just holds me, rubbing my back until my sobs turn into hiccups. Finally, Papa decides to speak. "Do you love him?" I want to laugh. What kind of question is that?

"Yes." I look up at him, confused. "I've loved him since I was old enough to realize that's what it was."

"Then you will figure it out," he says simply.

"What?" I pull back out of his arms, my brows furrowed. I was expecting fountains of wisdom. A story or something. "Just that simple?"

"Yes." Papa laughs at my surprise, and I frown back at him. Maybe he is not taking my worries seriously. "Let me explain," he says, leading us over to his workbench to have a seat. "Your mother always hated the city. I had grown up here, but I moved out to a little village just a day's ride away to do my apprenticeship. Your grandmother knew someone out there who knew of a carpenter who was willing to take an apprentice, and so I went. There I met your mama, and it was love at first sight. I would do anything for her." He pauses, lost in the memory, before continuing.

"I had always had the intention of coming back here and making a name for myself. Your mother agreed, but then the most wonderful thing happened. Your mother became pregnant with you. She wanted you to have the same simple upbringing she had and changed her mind. She would not go. She didn't want to raise a child in the city. We fought, and I left to visit my family for a bit."

"Papa!" I gasp, staring at him with wide eyes. "She never told me that part!"

"That was kind of her. She wasn't so kind back then. It was selfish of me to run away like that, and your mama let me know it when I got back a day later," he says with a laugh. "See, I thought I could go find proof that city living wasn't bad, but as soon as I got there, I realized how foolish I was being. I loved your mother, and where we lived didn't matter. I could provide for you just as well out in the country as I could in the city, and if she was happy, then I could be happy."

"And we were happy, Papa," I say, thinking of my mother. She would have been fine in the city, but she thrived in the country.

"You and Aiden love each other. You will figure it out. Maybe that is what your gift of guidance is for," he says, taking my hand. I look down at them, trying not to squirm at the mention of my "gift."

"I don't even know how to use it," I say. I'm not even sure I was truly given a gift. Maybe it was just a kind wish from an old man.

"Have you tried asking The Eternal?" he asks with a quirk of his eyebrow, making me look away. I don't answer, instead withdrawing my hand, and I stand up. I am ready to leave Papa to his work, but his hand on my arm stops me. "Maybe talk to the priest next time we are at temple. He might have some advice for you."

I don't wait until the next temple day to take my father's advice. I sit in the back of the chapel, waiting for the best time to approach the front. It's not a busy day, but there are a few petitioners in prayer. The priest is in quiet conversation with someone, but I'm sure he can feel my eyes on him. He is the same one who gave me the blessing.

His eyes meet mine, and he smiles, letting me know he sees me. I'm tempted to leave. Maybe this was a silly idea. I stand to leave when he approaches me, motioning for me to sit back down.

"Hello," he says in a soft voice, taking the seat next to me. "I've been wondering when I would see you back here." Both eyebrows raise as I sit up straight.

"You've been expecting me?"

"I give many blessings, especially during festival days, but it's not every day I give a blessing like yours," he says, a twinkle in his eye. My brows furrow at his amusement.

"I don't understand. What made my blessing different?" I ask, even though I suspect what he might say.

"Yours came with a gifting," he says, and I nod. It's what my father said.

"And what does that mean?" I try to keep my voice soft, but it comes out too forceful in this quiet place.

"Gifts are given by The Eternal to help His children. They are not uncommon, and we can find examples of them in the Holy Text," he says, repeating what my father has already told me. I clasp my hands in my lap as I listen to him, hoping for more. "When I placed my hands on your head to give you your blessing, I knew you were something special.

He gave me the words to speak to you. I felt His presence strongly, and I bet you did too," he says.

My eyes drift close as I think back to the experience. Unconsciously, my hand lifts to my chest and presses against my heart. The warmth that filled my veins before is simmering there again, and I open my eyes to meet those of the priest. "Yes, you feel it."

"You told me to remember that feeling."

"This feeling will help you come to know and understand your gift," he says reverently. His words make the feeling grow stronger, but leave me with more questions.

"How do I use my gift?" I ask, sitting forward eagerly, ready to learn.

"There is no one way for your gift to work. Just as each person is unique, so are their gifts," he says, looking at the room and each other, the depictions of The Eternal. My eyes are drawn to my favorite one, and they trace the threads of color as I try to hide my disappointment. The priest must notice my slumped shoulders, though, because he reaches out and places a hand on one of them.

"A good place to start is by asking questions," he says, earning a skeptical look.

"What questions should I ask?" I have plenty of questions. *Maybe I haven't been asking the right ones.*

"I think you mean who. Who should you ask?" he says with a teasing smile, earning an eye roll. He laughs quietly before squeezing my shoulder and letting go. "It's not the questions that matter so much as the intent behind them. Do you believe that The Eternal will answer your questions?" I am quiet for a moment in contemplation. I believe in The Eternal, but I think I need to have more faith that He is aware of me.

With a gentle smile, the priest continues, "When you ask Him, seek that feeling. It will help you know if you are headed in the right direction." He stands, giving me a nod before leaving me alone to ponder his words.

I look down at my hands and interlace my fingers, rubbing my thumbs together for a moment. I look up and glance around the chapel, noticing the few patrons here. A few women light candles in hopes that the light will help guide their prayers to The Eternal. A man sits with his head bowed in prayer.

I bow my head as well, but the words don't come. I look up at the tapestry of the faceless man. I take him in slowly, starting with the halo of light behind his head and his white robes. I look at his outstretched arms, hands reaching down toward his creations. I see how the light touches them as they all reach back toward him. I close my eyes.

Oh, Eternal, I think, since that is how the priest prays in service. *I have no idea what I'm doing or if you can even hear me, but I need help and direction. I want to marry Aiden, but there is so much I don't know. Where are we to live? What is our life going to look like? He's not even here to help me. Do we even have a future? Is he safe?* I pause, not sure what else to say. *Please help me.*

I sit quietly for a moment, waiting for some sign that He has heard me or an answer to my questions, but nothing comes. Feeling silly, I get up and head home. Maybe I'll try again later, or maybe not, but either way, I'm still just as uncertain as when I came here in the first place and my worry for Aiden's safety has only intensified.

Chapter 8

I'm on a roof overlooking the city. I can't remember how I got here. It is dusk, and the salty breeze blowing through my hair masks the smells of the city, bringing attention to the tear streaks on my cheeks. I've been crying. The ocean glitters next to the palace. I'm not high up, but high enough to see a good portion of the city. My heart races, and I realize I'm scared. *Why am I scared?* I look around again and notice that I am far from home. *I'm lost.*

"Hello," a voice says, startling me. It's a boy, a few years older than me. His clothes are too small, dirty, and patched. I take a step back but lose my balance, and he darts forward, grabbing my arm to keep me from falling. "Careful!" he says, pulling me to safety.

I look up into his familiar bright-green eyes and realize I am dreaming. *The first time we met,* my conscience registers as the scene plays out, just like it did years ago. Dream Aiden smiles at me. Even with his dirty curls, he is handsome.

He laughs, taking in my simple but well-made dress and tear-stained face. "You don't look like you normally climb on roofs," he teases, causing me to look away, blushing.

"I ...I'm not," I stammer out. "I'm lost."

"Lost?" He said the word like it's an adventure, bringing my eyes back to his. "It's a good thing that you found me. I'm the master of this city. I know where everything is," he boasts, puffing out his chest.

"Tell me, pretty one," he says, coming closer to me. "Where are you trying to go?"

"I don't know," I say, deviating from the script. I'm no longer eleven but nineteen, and Aiden turns into my Aiden.

"Hmm, that is a problem," he says, leading me to sit on the edge of the roof. "How are you supposed to go anywhere if you don't know where you're going?"

"I miss you so much," I say, throwing my arms around him and burying my face in his neck. His arms come around me, and he holds me close, resting his head against mine. "I am lost without you."

"Aloura, you are not lost," he says gently, rubbing my back. "You know what you need to do."

"I don't!" I say, pulling back and sitting up straight, "I'm lost without you." I look up into his eyes, pleading for him to give me the answer, any sort of direction to hold on to. He smiles before getting up and stepping away from me.

"No!" I call, scrambling to my feet, reaching out for him. "Don't leave me."

He turns and smiles again, holding out his hand, but no matter how hard I try, I can't reach him. My feet are moving, but I can never get closer.

"Come with me, Aloura," he says, but he just gets farther and farther away.

"I'm coming!" I cry desperately, clawing toward him. "I will bring you home." My fingers almost grasp his, but before I can grab hold of him once more, I wake up.

"NO!" I shout, sitting up. I frantically look around, but I am back in my bedroom, no Aiden in sight. I curl up into a ball and burst into tears. It felt so real, as if I could just reach him, everything would be okay.

My sobs quiet as an idea starts to form. He asked me to come to him. I sit up again and pull my hands to my mouth. *Maybe this is a bad idea.* But it has taken hold, and I can't shake it. I could go to Aiden. *Don't be impulsive, Aloura,* I tell myself getting up to pace my room.

He said he didn't want me to travel with him. It would be a dangerous journey. I would have to find someone to take me. *You don't even know where he is,* my mind tells me, but it doesn't matter. I sit back down again and shake my head. I can't do it. This is crazy.

I lie back down and try to go to sleep but my mind won't let go of the idea. I think of his hand reaching out towards me in the dream and a warmth starts to grow in me. *Maybe it was a sign.* I have to find him. The warmth spreads through my veins the more I think about it. This plan is reckless, but if he is my future, I need to be with him.

It's time for me to take action and not just wait for him to choose me. I need to show him that I choose him and am willing to sacrifice for him. I will go to him because together is where we need to be.

Plans take time. I have to remind myself as I work the next day, and the day after that, and for the next week. My first order of business will be to talk to Papa. I could never just leave without talking to him. It would break his heart.

My best shot at convincing him, though, is to present him with a well-thought-out plan. *How dangerous is it to cross the border on my own?* I ask myself as I attend to my chores. I would never actually do it, but I have to admit the idea is appealing. Being able to travel at my own pace and leave when I want. I shake my head at my preposterous thoughts and get back to dusting. I may be desperate, but I'm not stupid.

Maybe I could get hired at a caravan, I think, pausing again. The idea has merit. Now that the border is open, a lot of traders are crossing the border. Surely someone will have room for me, and I just happen to know people who work in caravans. Feeling pretty good about that idea, I get back to my work, a new bounce in my step. It is time to present my plans to Papa.

I wait until that evening to present my plan over dinner. I make apple tarts from some apples I canned in the fall and his favorite meal with fresh bread. The smell of the freshly baked treats makes my mouth water, and I smile. Everything is in order.

"You seem to be in a good mood today," Papa remarks as he watches me move around the kitchen. "Any particular reason?"

"I feel inspired," I say, sitting down to the meal and taking his hands to offer a prayer.

"About anything in particular?" he asks, watching me take a bite. His smile has turned suspicious, and he watches me with narrowed eyes.

"Let us just enjoy this meal and then I will tell you," I say, taking an exaggerated bite to encourage him to take his own. He does, but still watches me with concern. I try not to let it get to me, but nerves creep up at his continued stare. Finally, it is time for dessert.

"So," I begin. Now that it is time, I'm not sure how to bring it up. Papa sets down his utensil, giving me his full attention. I glance down at my dessert, pushing it around on my plate as I gather my thoughts and courage.

"I've been doing a lot of thinking since our last conversation," I say, looking back up at him. "I went to the temple and sought the guidance of The Eternal." I open my mouth to tell him about my dream, but close it again. He doesn't need to know about that. "I have concluded that if Aiden is my future, then I need to be with him."

"Hmm," Papa says, rubbing his chin with his hand before responding. I place my fork down, abandoning the rest of my food, my appetite gone. Papa sits back and folds his arms before speaking. "Have you heard from Aiden since he left?" he asks. His words are kind, but a pang of hurt flickers through me. I have not heard from Aiden since he left. I went to Machiavelli's warehouse, where the secretary took pity on me and told me that they had made it to Locura, Alberon's main trading capital, but there was no letter from Aiden.

"No," I tell him, glancing down, letting my frustration fuel my next words. "But what am I supposed to do? Sit and wait until he decides to contact me? Finally give up on him, and realize that his brother is more important than me? That he chose him?" I look up at him with a challenge. His mouth is drawn down in a frown as he looks at me.

"Do you truly think that Aiden chose his brother over you? That he is never coming back?" he asks with his brows pulled down. I sit back and cross my arms, mirroring his pose, but I won't look at him. Not after I've finally voiced some of my deepest fears.

"Aloura," he says, prompting me to look back at him. He sits forward, his gaze softening. "Do you think that Aiden would ask you to marry him and then just disappear? I have known him for years, and that doesn't sound like him."

"I know," I say, letting my arms relax their tight fold and looking back down at my lap. "But Alberon and his brother have always been his dream. He wants to marry me, but what does that look like? Does he expect me to move there? Live here with his brother? I have so many questions that need answers," I say, running a hand over my braid and looking up at my father. "I need to be with him. If he is my future, then we need to make that future together, not apart."

"And a letter won't suffice?" he asks, but in his tone, he already knows my answer. I slowly shake my head.

"He hasn't written me, and I wouldn't even know where to send it. I need to go find him," I say, standing up and clearing the table. This conversation has made me restless.

"Because you are afraid he won't come back," my father says, watching me as I do my work. He sits quietly as I stack the dishes and cover the leftovers, placing them in a cupboard for later. Papa stops me when I try to take his untouched dessert. Finally, there is nothing else for me to do, so I sit back down and let him take my hand.

"I am scared," I admit, looking down at his hand covering mine. "I'm scared that for as much as I love him, it won't be enough. Scared that his vision of his future doesn't match what I thought, and the best way to figure that out is to go to him."

Papa sits quietly for a moment, looking down at our hands before he slowly nods. "I understand your reasons, but let's talk this through," he says. My shoulders sag as they lose their tension, and I give him a soft smile. He is taking this seriously and not dismissing my idea right away. "So let us say you go to Alberon. How are you supposed to get there?"

"I will go with a caravan. I'm sure I could be hired to cook or something," I say, leaning forward. My energy is restored now that I have a chance to share my plans. "I'm sure if I talk to Rupert, then I can even go with one of his caravans. We know the guards and that they will be respectful to me." I smile at my father. It's a good plan, and Rupert will make sure I'm well taken care of. Convincing him to let me go, though, will be another challenge for another day.

"I'm sure Aiden has not been sneaking around unnoticed. I'll ask around and find him," I say with all the confidence I don't have. This is the part that I'm a little less confident about. It might seem strange to have a woman on her own asking about a man, but I'm sure people will understand that I'm doing it for love.

"And when you find him?" Papa asks, with his eyebrow raised. He hasn't shot down my plan yet.

"Then we will have an honest conversation about the future."

"And if it's not what you want it to be?" he asks the last part quietly.

"Then I come home with a broken heart, but ready to move on." I swallow the building feelings at even the thought of losing Aiden, but I'm ready to take the risk. Papa is quiet as he thinks, probably praying. Finally, he squeezes my hand, drawing my attention back to him.

"Might I make a suggestion, my love?" Papa asks, and I nod. I could use a little bit of wisdom right now, and Papa is one of the smartest men I know. "I suggest that you be patient and don't rush into anything," he says. My brow furrows in objection. I don't want to wait. I have a plan and want to get moving on it. I have waited long enough as it is for Aiden. I open my mouth to argue, but he stops me. "I know this is not the advice that you want to hear, but these are big decisions, and I want you to be safe, not run away on some adventure that could get you hurt." I pull my hand away from his and cross my arms again.

"I've been praying."

"So have I," he says with a sad smile. "It's the only reason I am even considering letting you do this. You know without a doubt that this is what you are supposed to do?" I blow out a breath. I was so sure the other night after my dream, but doubts have started to creep in. "Don't let emotions cloud your judgment," Papa says without waiting for an answer. "Turn to The Eternal, and He will bring you peace and possibly clarity while you wait for more news."

"I've told you I've prayed. I am supposed to go to him." I meet his stare, willing him to believe me, to believe in me. Finally, he sits back, picking up his fork to eat his now-cold pie.

"I can see there is no changing your mind. At least wait until Rupert comes back. Talk to him and see if he will let you travel with a caravan," he says, taking a bite.

That night, as I lie in bed, I think about his advice and commit to waiting to talk to Rupert before just leaving on my own. A warm feeling enters my heart for a moment, and I know I am making the right choice. I will find Aiden, and then we will figure it out and be married. I will show him that I am strong and capable, and nothing will stand between us.

Chapter 9

The next two weeks are probably the longest of my life. I am impatient to talk to Rupert and often find myself walking to the waterfront at lunch to see if the caravan is back early. It's unlikely, but each day, I spend a little more time there, just in case. The men on guard at the warehouse know me and keep me updated with any news that comes in. They are not scheduled to arrive before the first of the month, but I still hope.

Spring has begun to give way to summer, and sweat slowly drips down my back as I squint out at the water, lost in thoughts of Aiden. I still have not heard a word from him, and I can't help but imagine that the worst has happened. Did he find his brother only to find him in danger? Are they locked in a dungeon or stranded without means to contact me? Did he find out his brother is dead and is now languishing alone in his sorrow?

I shake my head, trying to dislodge the terrible thought. *Focus on the happy times.* I close my eyes against the glare of the sun and listen to the waves. I picture Aiden and the smile he has just for me, soft and a little higher on the left side. I try to remember the feeling of his arms around me, his lips on mine. *Everything is fine,* I tell myself. *He is fine.*

I breathe out and open my eyes, raising a hand to shield them from the sun. It's time to go home. The shop won't run itself. *It's only a few more days until they will be here*, I remind myself, but instead of turning the way I should, I wander closer to Machiavelli's warehouses.

I only ever walk around during the day now, after John's attack. It's not like I have a reason to go out at night anyway without Aiden. My mind wanders back to the attack and shudders. John had always set me on edge with his leering glances and dismissing remarks, but that was beyond what I thought he would ever do.

Even now, it is all so hazy. The physical assault stands out the most, but occasionally, at night when my brain is torturing me with thoughts of Aiden, it replays the attack and John's threats to get me once Aiden is gone. "I'm safe," I say out loud to remind myself that John is locked away.

Lost in my thoughts, it takes me a moment to realize the ruckus outside Machiavelli's. Three big wagons sit outside the merchandise warehouse, and men shout, unloading the last of the newest cargo. I wander closer, looking for a familiar tall, red-and-white-haired head. I look toward the front of the building, but have to pull up short as a big man steps in front of me, causing me to flinch.

"What'cha doing out here, girl?" a deep voice rumbles, and I blink, looking up slowly at the towering form of Rupert. He looks down at me with arms crossed and an eyebrow raised. I give him a sheepish smile. I normally don't hang around unless I'm looking for Aiden.

"Looking for you," I respond with a bright smile, lacing my hands in front of me. His dark-blue eyes look tired as they assess me. "You made good time," I remark awkwardly, rolling onto the balls of my feet. I want to leap right into questions about Aiden, but don't want to seem too eager.

"Yes," he says slowly, looking over at the wagons before looking back down at me. "We felt some extra pressure, and it put an oomph in our steps," he says, his eyes narrowing at me. He shifts his weight as I swing my hands, neither one of us talking. I don't want to be the one to bring up Aiden, but Rupert seems content to wait.

"He was well when you left?" I glance down, rolling onto the balls of my feet and back again, trying to seem unaffected. I peek up, though, to see his eyes soften and his crossed arms loosen as he smiles down at me.

"He was fine when we left him," he says, taking in my eager expression. I am a dog begging for any morsel of information he can give me. With a sigh, he pulls me into a hug. My entire frame is engulfed by his. I stand stiffly, not sure how to respond. Rupert is not a hug person.

"I'm sorry," he says softly, and I jerk out of his arms.

"About what? Did something happen to Aiden?" I start to breathe fast as the panic sets in.

"No, no!" he says, holding up his hands to ward off my panic, eyes wide. "I just mean, I'm sorry Aiden isn't here. Last time I saw him, he was fine," he says quickly, looking around frantically.

I take a deep breath, trying to calm down as I glare at a sheepish-looking Rupert. Maybe this will help my cause, though, as I make my request. He will feel so bad for making me panic that he will say yes.

"Hello, beautiful!" Gareth comes up, throwing an arm around me. "Come to see me since... Oh no, what's wrong?" he says, taking a step back at my frown.

"I may have made her think something was wrong with Aiden," Rupert says, rubbing the back of his neck.

"I'm fine," I say, getting my breath back under control. "Really. It's all good."

"Well, that's good," Gareth says, back to smiling. "Aiden would kill me if you were in trouble and I did nothing to help."

"He's well then?" I ask both men, who share a quick look.

"Yes, he is well. He got word about his brother and headed to the capital," Gareth says. His words are slow, carefully chosen. He is keeping something from me. I stare at him, eyebrow cocked, challenging him to hold to his resolve. He wipes the sweat from his brow and refuses to look at me.

"He found his brother?" I ask, keeping my expression in place. Gareth glances up and swallows. He is starting to crumble, and I have to keep a grin off my face. He is too much of a softy. He opens his mouth to speak, but Rupert puts a hand on his shoulder.

"Listen, lass," Rupert says softly, and I turn my glare back on him. I'm not going to like what he has to say. "Aiden is dealing with a lot right now. It's not that we want to withhold information from you, but it is his place to tell you. When he is ready, he will."

"So he didn't send you with anything for me?" I ask, my shoulders slumping. I wrap my arms around myself, and my eyes fill with tears. I blink rapidly to try to hold them back, looking away from the men. *At least he is well*, I tell myself but hearing that and knowing that he hasn't tried to contact me stings.

"He loves you," Gareth says, taking my hand. "He talked about you and your wedding while we traveled. He is excited about marrying you. Just give him time to adjust to having his brother back again." His words should reassure me, but I can't help it as a tear leaks out. I quickly wipe it with the back of my hand, drawing myself up to my full height. Gareth's words only strengthen my resolve to go to him. I turn to Rupert, ready to plead my case.

"Rupert, there is something that I need to ask you," I say, trying to keep my voice steady and strong despite feeling the weight of the favor I am about to ask. I know he will be against it, but there is no way around it. If I want to find Aiden safely, then I have to ask.

"Of course, lass, what is it?" he says, and I know he wants to make up for panicking me earlier.

I am silent for a moment, deciding how to ask before concluding that straightforward is the best way to go. "I need to get to Alberon, and I need your help to do it." I look up at him, trying to hold myself confidently, but I know my pleading eyes don't look as strong and sure as I want.

"No." Both of them answer quickly and firmly, causing me to take a step back. Not ready to give up, though, I square my shoulders and press forward. This is the best way to make my plan work, and if I can't convince Rupert to put me on a caravan, then it becomes much harder to get to Aiden.

"I know it seems foolish, but this is something that I have to do. Aiden and I need to be together."

"Aiden would kill me if I let you go running off to Alberon to find him," Rupert says firmly, his arms crossed and a stern expression on his face. "You would be in danger just traveling there, and Aiden is in the midst of a big change in his life. The best place for you to be is here. Wait for a letter. I'm sure he will contact you before anyone else."

I scowl. My reason for wanting to go sounds unreasonable, but my mind is made up. I will not give up so easily. "Listen, I need to be with Aiden. He is not just deciding his future; he is deciding *our* future, and he can't make those decisions without me," I declare, resisting stomping my foot to make my point. It would only make me look childish.

I make eye contact with Gareth. "You said Aiden loves me and wants to marry me, right?" I ask, allowing him only a head nod before continuing. "So then I should have a say in our future. He needs me there! Our fates are intertwined!"

Gareth and Rupert once again share a look before Gareth answers. "I know you are probably feeling unsure of your future when Aiden hasn't reached out..." he says, holding up his hands and reaching for me, but I won't take it.

"No," I say firmly, swiping at him. I take a deep breath, trying not to let my emotions get out of control. "I have been sitting waiting with no news for too long already!" My voice comes out a bit whiny at the end, and I take a breath before softening it to a gentle plea, "Please, Rupert," I turn to him, begging him with my eyes. "I need to be there with him. I need to do something,"

Rupert stares down at me with narrowed eyes, our wills battling against each other. I hold myself tall and determined, trying to show him that I am strong and capable. His jaw clenches. He is not ready to budge. I play my trump card.

"I'm going whether you help me or not." My voice is quiet but strong. I raise my eyebrows, challenging him to deny my request. He doesn't move, but something flickers in his eyes—a crack of doubt. He's starting to understand the situation. I will go whether he helps me or not. I have had enough of sitting. It is time for action.

"Fine," he growls, and I bounce on the balls of my feet, my smile stretching wide in victory. I have to resist throwing my arms around him. I have a feeling he wouldn't appreciate it at the moment.

"Oh, thank you!" I exclaim.

"Don't thank me yet," he grumbles. "I promise I will think about it and look into who is traveling in the next little bit, but it might take some time," he warns, but it falls on deaf ears.

"I'll be in touch," I call, turning and walking quickly away. My body relaxes now that I have won one battle. I am one step closer to being back with Aiden.

Gareth hurries to catch up with me, pausing me with a hand on my arm. He glances back before turning to me and leaning in. "If Rupert can't take you, then I will."

"What?" I ask, raising my eyebrows. His eyes on mine are steady and unblinking, no trace of humor. He is serious. "If Rupert can't get you safely on a caravan, then I will take you. Actually, I'm going either way. I don't like Aiden being alone any more than you do, and I don't think it's right that he hasn't reached out to you at all." I can't resist and throw my arms around him in a hug.

"You're a good friend," I say as I pull away. His wide eyes crinkle at the corners as his surprise morphs into a smile.

"Yeah, well, I should get back to work," he says with a little wave before striding off. I watch him go for a moment with a glow in my heart. Things are looking up. Soon, I will be by Aiden's side, where I belong.

Chapter 10

A few days later, I am bent over the counter at the shop looking at the books when the door chimes. I look up and watch as Rupert walks in. The tension in his shoulders and his furrowed brows tell me that he is not excited about the news he has come to deliver. I swallow, straightening up from my stooped position over the counter, and smooth my dress.

He approaches the counter, stopping a couple of steps away, and crosses his arms. I should walk around the counter and meet him head-on, but I prefer the barrier of the counter between us. I breathe deeply in through my nerves, glue my mouth shut, and we just stare at each other for a moment before he opens his mouth.

"You have an interview at the palace today at four bells past noon," he informs me, not beating around the bush. I was expecting disappointment, so it takes a moment to process what he just said.

"An interview? At the palace? For what?" I inquire. I was expecting a departure date with a caravan. I have no desire to be stuck at the palace catering to the nobility.

"I don't understand," I say, coming out from behind the counter. "I want to go to Alberon, not the palace." Rupert tracks my movements, taking a deep breath that he lets out with a sigh, and leans against the counter, his arms folded.

"The Monarchy has decided to send a delegation to Alberon. It will be a small group of trusted advisors who are going to assess the situation in Alberon and report back to the king," he states before pausing and looking at me again, assessing. I try to wait patiently, but can't help slightly bouncing on the balls of my feet in anticipation. My hands clasp in front of my chest as my smile grows. Rupert shakes his head, but I can see a slight smile of amusement on his face as he continues.

"Since I recently traveled the route, His Royal Highness, Captain Gardenia, who will be leading the delegation, has asked me to be the guide on their travels." I nod, signaling him to continue. This is looking promising, and if I am with a royal party, it will make it that much easier to ask around after Aiden. They will even help me get to the capital city without a problem.

"He has entrusted me to help him pick our traveling companions," he continues, pulling me from my thoughts. "There was an opening in the party that I felt you could fill, and they are interested in interviewing you."

"Oh, thank you, Rupert!" I launch into him, throwing my arms around his waist and almost knock him over in my enthusiasm. He pats my back awkwardly before I let go, and he clears his throat.

"Yes. Well, I still wish you would stay here, but I figured traveling with me and royalty would be the safest way to travel if you are still insisting on going."

"I am," I say before my mind latches on to the fact that I have an interview, and my anxiety takes over. "Will I have to speak Alberonian? I don't know as much as I should. It's been far too long since I practiced," I say out loud, looking at Rupert. I'm worried that that is one of my selling points, and if I don't meet their expectations, I will not be allowed to accompany them.

"You will be fine," Rupert says, awkwardly patting my shoulder again. "I will meet you at the palace gates this afternoon. Be sure not to be late. I won't wait around for you." He gives me a stern look, but I have a feeling he will wait even if I'm late. Nevertheless, I nod, and he departs, leaving me to prepare for my interview. I would be there no matter what.

I nervously smooth my dress as we walk down the street. It's quiet today. The weather is pleasant—not too hot with a breeze—but I can't enjoy it. The palace looms ahead of us, the sun shining off the glass windows.

"You look beautiful, my dear," Papa says as he walks beside me. I smile, but it's not very convincing.

I look down at my dress. It is my best one, a robin's egg blue color. White trim and flowers embroider the three-quarter length sleeves and square neckline. I often wear it at festivals or special events. I feel like it makes my light gray eyes seem bluer and my light brown hair richer. Papa says that when I wear it I remind him of my mother, but I'm pretty sure he is biased.

"Truly, Aloura. You will be brilliant," Papa says again, and my smile is more genuine this time. His words of encouragement convey his love. I reach over, link arms with him, and lean my head against his shoulder.

"Thank you, Papa." Just knowing he is here, gives me strength. He was not too enthusiastic when I told him about the interview. He asked me to reconsider again, but when I would not be swayed, he insisted on walking me to the palace gate.

I take deep breaths as we near the palace, trying to calm my nerves that are making me nauseous. I close my eyes for a moment and listen to the sound of the waves crashing against the cliffs on the other side of the palace. My nerves give way to excitement as we near. *I'm really doing this.*

Rupert waits up ahead at the palace gates. He must hear us coming because he turns his head and meets Papa's eye. He nods at him, and I glance between the two, taking in their matching resigned expressions. They think I am foolish for wanting this, but neither one will stop me.

"Well, lass, are you ready?" Rupert asks as we near, and I quickly kiss Papa on the cheek before walking to Rupert's side.

"Yes," I respond, glancing up at him before facing the servant's gate, squaring my shoulders and standing straight to convince myself I'm more ready than I feel. Papa bids me farewell, saying that he will wait down by the shore till we are done. I hardly hear him; the pounding of my heart is so loud.

I look up at the looming gate as we approach. It is not nearly as grand as the main gate by the sea that opens to the courtyard where we attended the festival, but even this is amazing. I feel small as we approach. The guards nod at Rupert, and then we are in the courtyard, surrounded by bustling activity.

The courtyard we enter is bigger than I thought it would be. Wagons unload supplies, and different artisans work in little alcoves along the sides. With all the people hustling around, it reminds me of a market square. I stop to marvel at the sights but quickly realize that I will be left behind.

Rupert knows exactly where we are going. His confident stride leads us toward a side entrance set into the main palace building. I have to take quick steps to keep up, but as I walk, my head swivels from side to side, taking it all in. I knew that the palace was a large operation, but I had never realized how much it is its own city.

Rupert enters through an ornate door, and I almost stop in awe. The door is easily ten feet tall, curving at the top. It's painted navy blue to match the royal color of loyalty. The trim surrounding it is carved into the stone with swirls and seashells to mimic the sea. I can hardly believe the opulence. I know this is the servants' domain, but it is still so elegant. The walls are simple, the same stone the outside of the palace is made of, with an occasional painting along them. The carpets are soft and match the blue of the door outside. The quality is more than we will ever be able to afford.

Distracted, I hardly notice when we reach the central office. I want to stay and explore, to check and see if any of the well-made furniture is from my father. I don't get the chance, though. There is already a servant waiting for us. He is dressed in royal livery, a simple blue coat with light tan pants. He bows and leads us to a sitting room nearby.

I am nervous and excited, which makes me fidgety. The room is small but lovely. I sit on a beautiful but simple sofa. I run my hands over the dark-red fabric. It goes well with the dark wood, probably walnut. It matches the other two seats in the room. I look around the rest of the room, taking in the details. Everything is high quality, but there is no extra ornamentation on the furniture. None of them is my father's design; his are always carved with animals or plants. The walls are mostly bare, a simple pink color, but there are flowers in vases and a window that looks into a garden.

I smooth my dress again, feeling shabby even in this servants' sitting room. I want to make a good impression. I know that this will probably be my only chance to get to Alberon and find Aiden. I stand quickly, unable to sit still any longer, and walk around the room for a moment before deciding to sit again and smooth out my dress once more.

"Calm down." The quiet command is gentle, and I glance over to Rupert, who has taken up watch by the window. I attempt a smile at him and resist standing up to pace again. He just sighs before saying, "You're going to be fine. Honestly, with me vouching for you, this is just a formality."

Only a formality? I think all of a sudden, reassessing the situation. I thought he didn't want me to go on this adventure at all, and I was expecting to have to earn my way onto it. I open my mouth to ask more about what he means when a frazzled-looking older woman breezes into the room and sits down across from me.

"Alright, dear," she says, hardly glancing up from her clipboard in front of her. "We have no time to spare, so let's get right to it." She glances up at me, taking me in quickly before launching into questions. I stumble through the first few answers about my experience with laundry, fabrics, and hair. Then she asks about my etiquette.

"Show me how you would address a duke," she says, looking up, waiting for me to comply. I scramble up and give a deep curtsy, mumbling, "Your Grace" with my head down.

"Bend your knees a little less and make sure you speak clearly," she says before continuing her questions.

What sort of job is this? I wonder as I walk across the room, and back, trying to keep my steps even and steady. I cling to the hope in Rupert's words that this is just a formality. It feels pretty intense to me. Finally, it feels like the interview is wrapping up.

"Are you willing to work hard and be adaptable?" the lady asks, looking up to see my reaction, giving me the feeling that the answer to this question is important.

"I will do anything asked: fetch, serve, carry. I want to be in this caravan. I will pull my weight and do what is needed." I hope she can feel my sincerity. I worry that I haven't said enough or that I said too much. Maybe sharing my strong desire to go was the wrong move.

She watches me for a moment before glancing at Rupert, who has stood as a silent sentinel by the window this whole time. She jots something on her clipboard and then smiles at me. "Well then, you are hired."

"Just like that?" I ask, still surprised even though Rupert told me I was going.

"I'll be honest," she says, "we are leaving in a week, and I am desperate to put together a team. I can't just pull everyone from the palace and their jobs. Plus, you have some pretty strong recommendations working for you," she says, glancing at Rupert again.

"We are leaving that soon?" Rupert's deep voice makes me jump. My nerves and his quiet presence almost made me forget he was there. I glance over at him and see the worry on his face. For some reason, this has unsettled him.

"Yes," she says, her brows furrowed as she looks at Rupert. "Plans have changed rather suddenly, and Their Highnesses want to leave as soon as possible. There was a missive sent, but you must have missed it."

"I'll be right back," Rupert says as he walks abruptly out of the room. I watch him go, wondering what distressed him, before I realize he has left me here alone. I was so busy gawking at the decor on the way that I now have no idea how to get out. Before my mind can dwell on that too long, the woman starts talking, reminding me that she is there.

"You will be a lady's maid and companion for the princess. The men will take care of themselves. You will mostly be staying at inns along the way, but be available to help where needed," she says, right back to business.

"I promise I will do all I can to help." Excitement and nerves swell in my chest as I realize this is happening. I am going to Alberon.

"Please be here bright and early tomorrow, just before the sun rises," she says, standing, and I follow suit, smoothing down my dress once again. Her eyes follow, and I can't decide if she approves of my appearance or not. I clasp my hands in front of me before she starts speaking again. "I will introduce you to Maggie, who is the lady's maid for the princess. She will instruct you in what you need to do and introduce you to the princess."

"Right," I say in response, but my nerves roar to life once again. I will be serving the princess. I will meet the princess tomorrow.

"You will have a day or two of training here at the palace with Maggie, and we will supply an extra dress as well. Report to the servant's entrance. Maggie will be there to meet you." With a nod, she leaves the room, leaving me alone in the palace.

Chapter 11

A half hour is a long time to wait when you aren't sure the person you are waiting for is coming back. I've been sitting in the window seat watching the light change in the garden outside. Papa is waiting for me. *It can't be that hard to get back outside*, I decide.

Striding over to the door, I step out into the hallway and turn toward what I am sure is the direction to the office. The hallway is strangely empty as I wander, but that doesn't deter me. I come to an intersection. *Maybe this wasn't such a good idea*. I look left and right, biting my lip. There is no indication of which way is the right one. I look back and can't even identify which door I came from.

Papa is still waiting at the gate... if I can find it, I tell myself, shaking out the tension in my shoulders. *I can do this*. I look around again and decide to head back the way I came. I thought we were right outside the servants' offices, but as I wander and peek around the next corner, I sigh, defeated. I missed it somehow, and now I am all turned around.

I listen for voices, hoping I can find someone to direct me to an exit, but there is no such luck to be had. It's still quiet. I decide to take a left, keeping an eye out for a window to help me reorient myself. When I reach a staircase, I know I've really messed up. We did not take any stairs on our way in.

Without a better idea, I decide to take the stairs, making my way to the next level. As I walk down the hallway, windows start to appear. They are covered in beautiful velvet and various gold-framed paintings. I wander over to a window and look out to find another garden. Was this the one from the parlor window? It doesn't matter. Anywhere outside will be more helpful than being stuck in this labyrinth.

The next opportunity I have, I turn toward an outside door, taking a deep breath of the salty air. It helps relieve my anxiety a little to at least be outside. The garden is beautiful, covered in large plants with a variety of colorful flowers. I smell a sweet pink blossom as I walk past and can't help but wish I knew a bit more about the flora and fauna of the area.

I follow the path around the outside of the garden, headed toward what I think might be an outside palace wall. Unfortunately, I come across a hedge blocking the way after only a few minutes. I pause again to try to decide which way to turn when I hear voices coming from behind the hedge. My shoulders sag in relief, and I smile. Hopefully, it's someone who can help me.

I walk until I find a break in the hedge and peek around the corner. I catch a glimpse of sparkling jewels and dainty gloves before I immediately pull my head back, eyes wide. I can't ask this group for help. I don't move, not sure what direction to head next. I can't walk past the gap and risk being seen, but I don't think turning around would help me either.

A light laugh sounds from behind the hedge, and I can't resist the pull to glance again at the assembled group. The ladies of the nobility are enjoying their afternoon tea outside, although I'm sure they will retire soon to prepare for their dinner. The air is still warm enough, but I can tell it will be cold once the sun sets.

It's a little early for the court to be in session, so the group of ladies is small, probably mostly those who are in the capital year-round and maybe a few southern nobles whose warmer climate makes traveling easier.

"You must be so excited to be going to Alberon," one of the young ladies says, and I immediately recognize the young Princess Coraline—the princess I will soon be serving. I should leave, but I am delighted with this opportunity to study her.

The first thing I notice is that Coraline is young, probably only a year or two younger than me. She has royal bright-blue eyes and pale white skin that contrast with her dark, almost black, hair. I watch her as she sits, back straight, head high and hands in her lap. She is trying to look poised and elegant, but it doesn't look natural. It's like she is trying to look like the perfect princess under the attention of the other ladies. "It is an honor to represent my people," she responds softly.

"Aren't you scared to be amid those barbarians?" another young lady loudly whispers, glancing over at the matrons of the group. Whatever they are talking about, it must be the current gossip going around the court. Everyone knows the Alberonians are not barbarians.

"Oh, but they are not barbarians," the princess graciously responds again in a humble and elegant voice. She straightens up in her chair like a star pupil being called on to answer in class. She is excited to share her knowledge of Alberon. Or wanting to show off.

As the third royal child, her role is to oversee the diplomatic relations of the country under the direction of her sister, the crown princess. I'm sure she has been tutored in all sorts of countries and customs.

"They may seem strange to us because they have different cultures and customs than us, but that doesn't make them uncivilized," she says, looking around at the group to make sure she has their attention. "Even some of those are changing under the new government. King David is very modern, and our reports say that the people are happy," she continues with a spark in her eye. Her voice is a little more excited now as she gets going. "He is trying to help the people with the transition. He grew up among them and understands them better than the old monarchy did, or so the reports claim. In fact..." she says before looking around at her audience. Her shoulders round a little as her excitement dies off. "There is a lot we can learn from him."

"I've heard he killed a lot of the old court when they didn't want to give up the old ways," a young lady says, earning her a few scandalized looks that turn into giggles as more absurd gossip is shared. The young princess doesn't join in, though. She looks wilted now as she fidgets with her dress, all pretenses of elegance now gone.

"A monarch must do what is best for their country," another young lady says, drawing all attention to her. I was so busy watching the younger princess I didn't notice she was there. A slight smirk graces her lips as she looks around the group, taking in their slightly abashed expressions. Her coloring matches her sister's exactly, but the crown princess holds a natural poise that, once noticed, can't be ignored.

"Of course, Your Highness," the one who spoke mumbles with her head bowed.

"A takeover is messy business. When the new king says free the slaves, and his nobles don't obey, he has to make an example," she says, looking down her nose at the other ladies with a slight smile. She looks like she is about ready to use them to set an example, but that image lessens as she shares a teasing look with her sister. Princess Coraline covers her mouth like she is trying not to laugh before she continues talking about some of the things she is looking forward to on her trip, her mood lighter.

The younger ladies must have gotten the message the older princess was sending and fawn over her, asking more questions about Alberon and the customs and cultures of the country. I listen, but most of the information is things that I've learned from Aiden.

I should leave, I remind myself, but my eyes are drawn to the matrons on the other side of the little garden patio. The queen is leading her court of ladies, her head held high and a simple crown on her head. I can't hear what they are talking about, but a loud squeal from the younger group draws their attention. I have to work to hold back my snickers at the manners of some of the young ladies. While the royals hold themselves with clear decorum, some of the noble ladies could be village girls giggling over the blacksmith.

"We are so proud of our Coraline and her diligence in her studies," the queen says loudly, drawing all attention to her and ending the giggles. "We are glad that she now has this chance to put that knowledge into practice. I know you will do a fine job, Coraline," she says, sending her daughter a kind smile, but it doesn't look like it reaches her eyes. Instead, her slightly raised brows send a message to her daughters, and they both sit taller under her gaze. "Especially with your brother to guide you." She turns toward the older ladies again, placing a delicate hand over her bosom. "It is so hard to let your children spread their wings, but I know Coraline needs this opportunity to gain more experience."

The queen continues talking about the difficulty of letting children become their own people, but my attention is drawn to the young princess. As her mother keeps talking, the princess's shoulders cave in a little, her posture slumping ever so slightly, and although there is still a smile on her lips, it doesn't reflect in her eyes. Movement draws my eye as the crown princess shifts closer to her sister, taking her hand.

At a break in the conversation, she raises her voice and clearly says, "We are so proud of the work Caroline has put into knowing the customs and goings-on of Alberon. There is no one more dedicated to creating harmony within the kingdoms that we could send to undertake this mission."

A few of the younger ladies nod their heads, and Princess Coraline's smile softens a little as she glances around at her sister and her friends. I silently nod my head as well. From the little I gathered, the princess takes her duty seriously, and I have a feeling she will be an asset to the country.

I glance up at the sky and notice the late hour. Papa will start to worry, and I'm sure Rupert has noticed I'm missing by now. I start to turn when a hand lands on my shoulder, eliciting from me a quiet yelp. I look back into the stern face of a guard. Immediately, I feel guilty about being caught eavesdropping even though I didn't truly do anything wrong.

"I don't want to make a scene, so please come with me quietly," he says with a hand on my shoulder uncomfortably tight. I can't even protest before he is leading me away from the garden and into a hallway nearby. I decide it is in my best interest to comply. I allow him to escort me quickly and quietly, hoping it will help, but my stomach is in knots. I worry I am in more trouble than I realize.

With a bruising grip, the guard leads me through the maze of hallways until we come to a stop in what must be the guard wing of the castle. He peeks around some doors before gesturing for me to take a seat on the bench outside what I assume to be an office. I sit down slowly, taking in the hallway. It is still nice, just like the rest of the palace, but plain like the servants' quarters. The bench is hard under me, and I wring my hands in my lap.

"Why were you spying on the royal ladies?" he demands, making me jump. *I thought we would wait for whoever's office this was, but instead it seems I will be interrogated here.*

"Who are you, and what are your intentions?" He looms over me on my bench, and I want to stand. I don't like feeling small, but I worry he will take it as a sign of resistance.

"That wasn't my intention to spy," I start to explain quickly, rushing to get out my explanation before he interrupts me like I'm sure he wants to do. "I got lost after my interview. I've been hired to travel with the envoy to Alberon." I keep it short, hoping that information will help, but I squirm in my seat both from his gaze and my own guilt at not turning around as soon as I realized I had come upon the nobility.

The guard opens his mouth to reply, but the sound of footsteps stalls him. I glance to the side to see another guard approaching. He is tall with dark hair, and looks vaguely familiar. "If you would just help me find Rupert," I ask, turning back to my interrogator. "I'll be able to..." He is no longer paying attention to me. He salutes the man, who has now come close enough for me to see his features, and I recognize him.

I slowly rise and look down at my feet as his familiar deep voice says, "Ah, you are the one Rupert was worried about." When I glance up, his face is as stoic as the last time he rescued me, but his voice is coated in amusement. His bright-blue eyes take me in, and I know he recognizes me, too. The captain who saved me from John.

"I'll take it from here," he says, dismissing the other guard, who hesitates for a moment, glancing at me before giving a brief bow and walking away. I watch his retreating back for a moment, glad to be out of his hands, before glancing back at the captain.

He is watching me, and heat creeps up my neck. I don't look away, though. I stand my ground and look him in the eye. I will not be ashamed. The only thing I did wrong was not staying put and waiting for Rupert.

He is just as tall as I remembered, a little taller than Aiden. With his dark hair and those startling blue eyes, most women would consider him handsome. *Just because you're engaged to Aiden doesn't mean you are blind,* my mind reminds me, causing my cheeks to turn red. His face shows little emotion as we stare, but then I see the corner of his mouth lift in the smallest of smirks. The spell is broken, and I look away.

"You seem to end up in trouble a lot, don't you? Come, I'll take you to Rupert," he says, gesturing for me to walk with him. We walk silently for a few minutes before I finally find words to say.

"I really don't," I say quickly, breaking the silence. "Get in trouble, that is." I wait for him to comment or reply as we walk side by side, his hands clasped behind him and mine at my sides, fisted in my dress. I almost miss the faintest hum like he doesn't believe me but is too much of a gentleman to call me out.

"It has only been twice in the last few months that I have been in any serious trouble, if this encounter even counts as serious trouble, which I don't think it does," I say defensively, folding my arms. "It just so happens that you have been here both times." I am huffing now, and I don't know if it is because of anger or because of trying to keep up with his long strides. I drop my hands back down to my sides and resolve to refrain from talking to him. *I don't care what he thinks anyway,* I remind myself.

He is quiet long enough that his voice surprises me when he decides to respond. "So I shouldn't save you next time." It's a statement, not a question, and my eyes shoot to his face. Once again, that slight amusement. I open my mouth to respond but realize I have nothing to say. I close my mouth again and face forward, resolved to just walk in silence.

My anger dissipates quickly though as we walk. Instead, guilt starts to settle in. I've been ungrateful for his help. *Father would be so disappointed in me. If I am honest with myself, I know I wouldn't be here without him after my attack from John.* I shiver slightly at the memory, drawing his attention.

"I do appreciate your help," I blurt out, breaking the silence once again. "I'm grateful for the assistance both times. Especially last time." I whisper the last part, not even wanting to think what would have happened if he hadn't gotten there on time. My mind tries to bring it forward, and I shake my head as if that could make it all go away. Luckily, he clears his throat, drawing my attention back to him.

"I actually have some news about that," the captain says, slowly drawing my eye. He glances down at me before looking away and resuming his mask. He slows to a stop, and I stop next to him as apprehension fills me. He won't meet my eye, his gaze staring over my head, and I know the news is not good. I force myself to take deep breaths so I don't panic.

"I'm sorry," he says, finally meeting my eyes. "I am afraid that the man who attacked you has disappeared."

"What?" I gasp, my voice quiet in my shock. I surely did not hear him correctly. My heart rate picks up, and my breathing becomes shallow. His brow furrows, but he continues.

"He was being transported from the jail to a more permanent location," he says, his voice emotionless like he is giving a report, but his hand is ever so slightly extended, like he is worried I am going to faint. He is not wrong. I might faint.

"The wagon broke a wheel. He overpowered the two guards overseeing the transport and got away." My heart pounds in my ears, and I can hardly hear his words. "After looking at the wagon, we believe it was sabotage to help him escape. Maybe an accomplice."

Feeling lightheaded, I reach out and grasp his arm, and his other reaches out to cup my elbow, giving me additional support. "When was this?" I ask, my voice coming out strangled.

"It has been a few weeks. We had patrols in the area where he attacked you to make sure that he didn't show up again, but we weren't ready to contact you to let you know he was out. All accounts point to him headed toward Alberon's border."

My mind is spinning, my head is spinning, and I start to sag, my legs losing all strength. Aiden is gone, John is missing, and I am about to embark on a journey far away from home and anything familiar. I really might faint.

"Are you okay?" the captain asks, his brows furrowed in what I hope is concern and not annoyance. His hand on my elbow slips around my waist until I am almost in his embrace, holding me up. "Here, come sit down and take a few deep breaths."

He leads me to a bench and sits down with me, his arm still around my back and his other still held tight in my grasp. "Here, breathe with me," he says, taking a long, slow breath before holding and letting it out. We do it a few more times together while he rubs my back until my hand relaxes on his arm.

"I promise we are doing everything we can to make sure the streets are safe. You don't have to worry. Furthermore, I will be going with the envoy," he says, looking down at me, his face softening a little as we make eye contact. "If I understand correctly, so are you. So you see, you have nothing to worry about. I will keep an eye on you." My eyebrows arch up in surprise at the declaration. He is staring at me intensely, and I feel a blush creeping onto my cheeks.

"Thank you," I whisper before looking away. I admittedly feel better now that I know he will be there with me, and then I blush again at the thought. *I am going to find Aiden,* I remind myself, *not make eyes at pretty guards.*

"Of course," he says, looking away down the corridor. I follow his gaze and see light at the end of the passage. We must be close to the courtyard. I stand on shaky legs, let go of his arm, and lift my chin. I am strong, and I can do this.

We start walking again, and he speaks up, "I will have some of my most trusted men with us, and they will keep you safe," he says before adding, "Plus, it's good you are going. Who else will save you next time you are in trouble?"

I want to laugh at his statement but don't want to give him the satisfaction of knowing I think he is funny. Instead, I shoot him a playful scowl and catch the smirk he sends my way. He is kind to try to distract me. We approach a doorway, and light momentarily blinds me as I step into the courtyard. The sun is setting, the last rays hitting the palace. Despite the late hour, the courtyard is still busy.

I follow the captain as he heads toward a side gate and watch as his stoic mask slips back into place, all traces of humor gone. Back is the guard captain, serious in his duty. My eyes slide to the courtyard, and I scan our surroundings, noticing Rupert waiting for us.

"There ya are, lass. I'm sorry I left ya, but if ya would have stayed put, I would have come back," he reprimands me gently as we approach. When we get close, he places a comforting hand on my shoulder. It brings a smile to my face, and I feel better next to this gentle giant of a man.

"I'm sorry. I thought I could find my way back," I say, ready to explain more, but the captain beats me to it.

"She had walked in the wrong direction and ended up in the west garden." His tone is amused again despite the bland expression on his face. It brings another flush to my face, but I have to admit to myself that I am glad I did not end up in more trouble for my wanderings.

"Yes, well, thank you for yer help, Your Highness. I'll be in touch," Rupert says, bowing his head to the man who has saved me from trouble twice now, the man who apparently is not a simple captain.

"Your Highness?" I squeak out, startled, before silently calling myself an idiot. I step back, looking him over, and realize he looks just like his sisters, the same black hair and straight nose. Even if he didn't, the blue eyes should have given him away. The bright blue is unique to those from the royal line.

"Yes," he says almost hesitantly, almost shyly, before he stands tall. "Prince Judian Gardenia at your service," he says, giving me a formal bow. "While we travel, though, I am just 'captain,'" he says, but I don't know if I can be that informal now that I know he is a prince. *The prince.*

Automatically, I curtsy, almost falling over from my rush. "Your Highness," I say, still looking at the ground. *I'm sure I look like an idiot, but what is one supposed to do when one has been blindsided by royalty?*

A throat clears, and I glance up at the prince, who looks down at me almost awkwardly. "Please rise..." he says, pausing, and I realize we have never introduced ourselves. "Aloura," I say, bobbing another curtsy and then blushing.

"Right. Well, I will see you around, Aloura," he says with another bow to me and Rupert before he turns and walks back into the palace. I watch him go.

"That was the prince?" I ask, staring after him, not really sure if I'm asking or stating. Rupert chuckles and squeezes my shoulder before turning me towards the gate.

"Yes, and ya better get used to it, lass; you will be seeing him and his sister around while we are traveling, so close that gaping mouth. Let's getcha home."

Chapter 12

If I thought the sun setting on the palace was beautiful, it has nothing on the sun rising behind it. All I can see is the outline as I approach the side gate. From here, I can see the ocean sparkling, almost blinding me with its brilliance, like a sea of diamonds. I always thought I was more of a night owl, but if I could wake up to these views, I would be up every day to watch the sunrise.

The guards let me in after I show them a letter from Rupert granting me entry for the next few days. I enter the same courtyard as yesterday. The hustle and bustle is a little slower this morning, but it is still filled with people as they begin their day's work. I make my way around the edges of the courtyard, not sure where to go. Finally, a woman with ginger hair spots me and waves me over. She is young and pretty, and I'm guessing she must be Maggie.

"Over here, I have a dress for you to change into," she says, getting straight to business. She shoves a bundle of clothes into my arms before turning to go inside. I try not to drop the dress as I hurry to follow her. "It won't really matter what you wear on the road, but here in the palace we have a strict dress code," she says, leading me down a few hallways before coming to a stop in front of a small room.

"You can change in here and leave your stuff. It will be returned to you before you leave," she says, ushering me into a small bedroom. I wonder if it's her room as I quickly change and leave my folded dress on the bed. The dress is royal blue, plain but made of fine material. I find a white apron as well and tie it on. I look down at my dusty shoes and try to brush them off, but they will have to do.

"Oh no," Maggie says, noticing them immediately. "Come, let's go to the cobbler and find you some proper slippers." She leads me along the labyrinth of hallways, knowing exactly where to turn at each intersection. I have no idea how she doesn't get lost. "It's a good thing the princesses sleep in, or we would be late. It should be fine for now, but we must hurry if we are to be on time for breakfast."

"How long have you worked here?" I ask as we walk quickly down the hallway. I'm glad she is not taller because I am already having a hard time keeping up.

"My whole life, but I have been the princesses' maid for a few years now. Here we are," she says, stopping at another door. The room is filled with fabrics and leather and two sleepy apprentices working. "Donovan, we need a pair of maid slippers for Aloura here. She is to help me with the princesses for the next few days," she says to someone I can't see in the room while looking at some green fabric.

An older man emerges from the depths of the room, looking me over as he stares at my hair and slowly moves down to my boots. I want to hide them under my skirts, but they hit just at my ankle to make sure I don't trip while serving. "Pen, go grab the black slippers over there in that pile," he says, not taking his eyes off of me. One of the boys hops up to comply. "So, the princesses, you say?" he says, turning to Maggie, who looks back at him, her brows raised in challenge.

"That is the only bit of gossip you will get from me," she says, staring him down. "Whatever conclusions you come up with on your own, please keep me out of it. You know I will not spread gossip, and that's how I keep my job." Her mouth curves up in a polite but distant smile. I want to ask questions, but her eyes dart to me with a warning, and I hold my tongue.

The boy reappears with some slippers, and I quickly take off my boots and put them on. They feel like clouds. I obviously can't hide my admiration for them because the cobbler smiles.

"I know. I'm good at what I do. Now we will fix your boots and send them to..." he trails off, looking at Maggie.

"Mrs. Goodwin's office," she says tartly, obviously not thrilled to share even that much more information.

"Right. They will be waiting there for you," he says with a mischievous smile as Maggie ushers me out the door.

"Horrible gossip," she says before stopping, suddenly turning to face me. "If I can give you one piece of advice, be careful who you trust." She stares into my eyes, her face serious.

"What do you mean?" I ask, confused. He seemed nice enough, but Maggie obviously didn't trust him.

"When you work closely for royalty, it puts you in a position of trust. You are close to them and hear things that are not meant for others. If you trust the wrong person, they can learn things they are not supposed to know," she says, her eyes narrowing as she looks at me, as if she can look hard enough to see into my soul. I slowly fold my arms in front of myself and look away from the intensity of her stare. "I don't know why you were given this position because you have not earned it, but it is not my decision," she says, resuming our walk.

I don't know what to say to her, so I keep my mouth shut, but I think about it. Rupert must have a lot of sway if I was given this position. Especially since we are traveling to a foreign court where servants could be used to spy.

"Quickly grab some breakfast, and then we will take trays to the princesses," Maggie says, taking a pastry for herself and a hard-boiled egg.

"You serve both of them?" I ask, serving myself from the spread. I am amazed at how well the servants eat here.

"For now," she says vaguely, and I debate whether to press for more. She has already made it clear she doesn't gossip. She watches me as she eats, waiting for me to ask. I decide not to, and we quickly finish our meal in silence. It seems I passed a test, because she smiles as she passes me a tray.

"Today you will focus on Princess Coraline while I take care of the crown princess," she says, leading me from the kitchen and up the stairs. Many, many stairs. "The princess likes to eat outside on her balcony, so set up the tray out there, then knock on her door. If she answers, let her know breakfast is ready. If she doesn't, then enter and open the drapes before going and waiting for her to wake up."

"Okay," I reply, my head reeling with the instructions and concentrating on not dropping the tray that seems to get heavier with every step. How does she do this every day?

"After I get the crown princess ready, I will join you and teach you how to prepare Coraline for the day. She is pretty easygoing and very kind, but the queen has high standards for her daughters, and it's part of our job to make sure they are met," she says, finally slowing down. We must be getting close. There are guards along this hallway spaced every so often, so I know we are in a more secure area.

"Here we are," she says, stopping in front of a beautifully carved door. "Go on in," she says before making her way farther down the hall. Carefully, I reach out and open the door. The suite is bigger than Papa's shop, and I have to stop my jaw from dropping as I walk in. The curtains are still shut, so the room is dim, but even in the weak light, it is gorgeous. Light-blue fabrics cover the room, and lace and flower patterns give it a feminine touch.

Realizing I have stopped in the middle of the room, I quickly set the tray on a side table. I open the curtains to the balcony next and can't help stepping out to see the view. Words escape me as the sun sparkles out over the ocean. Today, there is no fog, and I can see for miles. I close my eyes for a moment and just breathe in the salt air and let the cool breeze revitalize me.

"Beautiful, isn't it?" A soft voice startles me, and I let out a little squeak. A laugh follows as I look over to see the princess sitting on a chair on the other side of the balcony.

"I'm so sorry," I say, curtsying and almost falling as I take a step backward. "I didn't realize you were out here." I glance over and notice a second door leading to the bedroom.

"It's okay," she says with a sweet smile before gesturing to the other seat. "Please come sit, and let's get to know each other." There is an excited gleam in her eyes, but I hesitate. It feels wrong to sit in front of royalty.

"I really should..." I start to say, backing up, not even sure how I am going to finish the sentence, but the princess lets out a small laugh.

"Oh please, who is going to say anything? I'm the boss, aren't I?" she teases. "Grab the breakfast tray and join me. We are to be traveling companions, and I would like to get to know you better." She settles her robe around her and looks at me expectantly. Not sure what else to do, I do as she asks.

"Tell me about your family!" she says as soon as I'm sitting down, grabbing a roll off the tray. Hesitantly, I tell her about Papa and his shop. "That must be wonderful to create such beautiful things with your hands," she says dreamily after I tell her about his carvings. "You must be so proud of him."

"I am." I smile out at the ocean, thinking of him. I really was blessed with a wonderful papa.

"Do you have a beau?" she asks mischievously, interrupting my thoughts. I laugh in surprise at her eagerness as she sits forward, watching me. "You do, don't you! Tell me about him!"

"We met when we were quite young, but I knew right away he was special. Before he left for Alberon, he asked me to marry him." My smile should be grand, but it dims as I am reminded of why I am here.

"He is in Alberon?" the princess says, bringing me back to the conversation before I can follow that line of thinking too far.

"Yes," I respond lightly. "He is looking for his brother, but he refused to take me. I think, though, that he needs my support, so I asked Rupert to help me get to him."

"So that is how you got the job!" she says, clapping her hands in delight, like she has just solved a great puzzle. "After the whole incident with Marina's maid and Maggie having to take her place, I was at a loss as to who would accompany me. I'm sure there will be many girls jealous of your position, but then again, after Abby, I don't know if anyone wanted the position."

"What do you mean?" Maggie hinted that something had happened, but she wouldn't elaborate. The princess bites her lip, obviously doubting if she should tell me or not. I sit quietly watching her before she gives a decisive nod and leans closer, talking quietly.

"It's all very hush-hush, so don't tell anyone," she says, and I suddenly wonder if this is a bad idea. Maybe I shouldn't know. "Can I trust you?" she asks quietly, staring intensely into my eyes. This is a test. I could say no, and she would keep the information to herself, and that is that. We would have a professional relationship.

But if I say yes...

I look into the princess's eyes, and suddenly I know that she will need a friend in the upcoming days, and I can be that for her. I lean ever so slightly forward and match her intensity, and I say, "Yes."

Smiling, she sits back, popping a grape into her mouth before speaking. "Marina's maid was poisoned."

"What?" I sit back, stunned.

"It was wine left in her room. Abby was cleaning. We don't know exactly what happened, but I think there must have been some dust that got caught in her throat. Anyway, she took a drink of the wine and then..." She trails off, leaving me to my own conclusion.

"Do you know who did it?" I ask quietly, looking around like an assassin is going to jump out from behind the curtain.

"No. There are suspects, but nothing solid. Poor Abby is so sick that she has barely gained consciousness enough to drink some weak broth. She is so weak she can't even speak," she says, her eyes starting to turn red, and she sniffles a little.

"She's not dead?" I ask, my eyes wide.

"Oh no! She is alive, but we weren't sure she was going to make it for a long time. Maggie and I heard her screaming and rushed into the room ... It's hard to talk about." She quickly wipes a tear from her face before looking out at the ocean once more. I can't even imagine how that could have been, and the fact that it was meant for her sister. A shiver travels down my spine.

"As you can imagine, we were astonished when some unknown girl was to be my maid on the trip," the princess continues, mustering a smile once more. "If Rupert requested you, that makes much more sense. Father has always trusted Rupert."

"He is a very loyal and capable man," I say, feeling bad now for practically blackmailing Rupert into letting me come. I'm sure it was not an easy decision with the princess's safety in mind. Warmth fills me at the realization that he trusts me enough to let me come on such an important mission.

"There you are!" Maggie walks out onto the balcony. With a curtsy to the princess, she takes my arm. "We will prepare your things for today," she says, pulling me to the door. The princess watches with an amused smile. I have a feeling that traveling with her will be anything but boring.

Chapter 13

The few days until our departure pass quickly in a flurry of learning and packing. After getting the princess ready that morning, I didn't see her again the rest of the day. It has left me little time to get to know her more. Instead, I spend my days with Maggie packing and receiving instructions on what dresses are appropriate for which situation and which accessories to use. My favorite part is learning how to do a few simple but elegant hairstyles, which I hope to replicate on my hair when I have time to practice.

Maggie is lovely but intensely focused. She has high standards for how everything is done. The clothes must be folded and pressed just so, and the hair must be pinned at just the right angle to keep it in during dances. I find my body aching and my mind so full of information at the end of my days that I am surprised I don't pass out from exhaustion every night. Instead, my mind keeps me up, worrying about whether I am making the right choice. Will my father be okay without me? Will Aiden be happy to see me? Does he think of me? Does he miss me?

Oh, Great One, I find myself praying. *Watch over my loved ones. Keep Aiden safe and help me get to him safely*. I'm still not sure He answers, but after voicing my thoughts to Him, I always find peace, helping me sleep better.

Today is different, though. There is no peace to be found because today I leave. My stomach is a riot of nerves as I pack my meager belongings and try to eat a little breakfast. Maggie is getting the princess ready so I can get my own things ready. I will meet her at the carriage when we are ready to depart. It doesn't take long before we are on our way. Papa holds my bag, an old but sturdy thing, that contains my few possessions as we walk side by side to the palace.

"I've placed an ad," Papa says, startling in the quiet of the morning. I look at him confused before I realize what he means. He is finally hiring an apprentice.

"That's wonderful!" I am glad that he will have companionship while I am gone. I know his sister is here, and Lana has promised to check in on him, but this is a good thing.

The walk isn't awkward even though we don't talk much. I soak in these last moments with my father, pushing back the foreboding feeling that everything is about to change. The gulls cry overhead, and the ocean crashes in the distance. I just want to freeze time and stay here just a second longer, but too soon we reach the palace gates.

We enter the main courtyard again, the one with the festival. I wish I were back there again, twirling in Aiden's arms. *That is why I am here now*, I remind myself. *I will find Aiden, and we will get our happily ever after.*

I try not to gawk at the beautiful carriage that sits at the foot of the stairs that lead to the main doors. I've never ridden in one before. *It's too late to be nervous now,* I try to tell myself, but it doesn't work. For such a small party, there are groups of people and many preparations happening in the courtyard.

Soldiers and attendants walk around securing trunks to the carriage and packs to saddles. Papa and I try not to get jostled as we slowly make our way toward the carriage, looking for someone to tell me where to go. Nobles mill about on the upper level, taking advantage of the benches and shade of the plants as they wait for a glimpse of the royal party.

A lady with a pinched expression turns to a lord with puffy blue pantaloons that clash with a burnt-orange doublet. She wears a turban from Alberon with a large feather sticking out of it, bobbing from the movement of her head. I smile at their outfits, stifling a laugh, and turn to comment on them. A sudden pang catches in my chest, stopping the remark. This is something I would do with Aiden—sit in the shopping district, making fun of the garish fashions of the court. I look around for a distraction and find it in the form of a friendly face.

Gareth stands in the courtyard adjusting his saddlebags and attaching a bedroll to the back of his saddle. I call his name, walking towards him.

"Hello, beautiful," he says, sweeping me up in a quick hug.

"I didn't realize you were coming!" Guilt creeps up on me as I realize what a terrible friend I've been. I have neglected someone who cares for Aiden almost as much as I do.

"And let you have all the fun?" He gives me an amiable smile, and I know he forgives me for my thoughtlessness. "I meant it when I told you I was going with you either way, but between you and me," he says, leaning closer like he is about to tell me a secret, "I am glad we are traveling with this lot. It took me a minute to convince Rupert to let me come, but I can be pretty persuasive." He puffs out his chest, hands on his hips, and a smirk on his face.

"What did you say?" I don't trust that look.

"Just that I could be helpful, especially when it comes to keeping an eye on a special little girl who insisted on going to Alberon," he says, teasing me.

"Hey!" I say, shoving him, "I am not a little girl!" He stands up straighter, towering over me, but before he can say anything, a voice interrupts us.

"Oh, good, you're here," Maggie says, looking me over. "You will be riding with the princess." She looks down at my bag at my father's feet. "Is that all you are bringing?"

"Yes..." I say awkwardly, looking down at the ugly thing. It only has a couple of changes of clothes and a brush. There was really nothing else to bring.

"Well, you can just take it with you into the carriage then." We all look over at the already overloaded carriage, and I can't help but think, maybe it's a good thing I have so little.

"Well," Maggie says, turning back to me and purposefully ignoring Gareth, who is trying to give her his most charming smile. "I have a few more things to check before the princess and her party arrive. Please make sure you are in your carriage soon." Maggie walks off, but I see her turn her head just slightly to catch a glimpse of Gareth's disappointed face. I swear I see a blush before she strides away.

"She didn't even look at me," he pouts, and I give a little laugh. I'm sure he is not used to rejection.

"I believe it is time for goodbyes," Papa prompts softly, and immediately tears spring to my eyes. Gareth is kind and leads his horse away, giving us some privacy. Reluctantly, I turn to Papa. I'm not ready for this.

A sad smile pulls at his lips. I know he is proud of me—he's told me enough— but his smile tells me he is not ready to let me go. I pull my shoulders back and try to stand tall and sure, but I don't know if I'm ready either. I don't know if anyone is truly ready, though, to leave the comfort of what they know for the unknown. But this is different. I am leaving Papa for the first time in my life. I let out a quiet sob as I fling myself into his arms, clinging to him tightly.

"I'm not ready for this," I whisper into his neck, my voice breaking with emotion, "but I have to." Pulling away, I look into his eyes and see the battle he is fighting. This is hard for him too. Following Mama's death, only we were left, and now even that will change.

"I know," he whispers back, his voice strained as well, and the tears stream harder down my face, "but that doesn't make letting you go any easier." He squeezes me tight again, and I can't help but laugh a little at the picture we probably make, both our faces wet with tears. "I am so proud of the woman you have become," he says, pulling back again. "I know your mother would feel the same way."

"Do you truly think so?" I ask quietly. Even after so many years, the grief hits as fresh as the day we lost her.

"Yes," he says, closing his eyes and placing his hand over his heart, "in moments like these, it is like she is still with us." Following his lead, I close my eyes and think of my mom. Warmth creeps through my veins, leaving goosebumps on my skin as it spreads to my fingers and toes. She is here—my guardian angel.

"We are proud of the strong woman you are," Father says into my ear, causing my eyes to startle open. I didn't realize he had stepped so close again. "Be careful," he says, giving me a last look before handing my bag to me. I take it and hurry to the carriage. I know if I look back, I will never get myself back under control.

I take refuge in the carriage, taking advantage of the quiet to get my head back on straight. Despite the discomfort of leaving my home and family, I am excited to go on this adventure. I am especially excited to see

Alberon. Even growing up in a war camp, Aiden talked about Alberon with fondness.

A commotion outside disrupts my peace, and I move aside the curtains of the carriage. The crowd outside gathers to watch as the large blue doors to the palace slowly swing open. A trumpet sounds, announcing the arrival of the royal family. I'm grateful for the vantage point the carriage gives me as I watch the parade of people who walk with them.

I feel a sense of déjà vu as the king and queen walk through the doors, followed by the crown princess with her guard. My princess, Coraline, is next walking arm in arm with the prince. Unlike the rest of their family, the last pair are dressed simply in travel clothes. Coraline's simple blue dress makes her blue eyes stand out. The prince wears a standard military travel uniform, the crown on the sleeve the only indication of his royal status.

I watch as they descend the steps, heads held high and backs straight. I watch as they all gather on the steps to the lower courtyard, all smiles and waves. This goodbye looks nothing like the tearful one I just shared with my father. Not one of them looks anything less than completely confident, if not a little bored with the whole situation. In a way, it comforts me that the royals are not visibly worried, but at the same time, it makes me feel silly for my previous display of emotion.

There is a hush as the king raises a hand to address his people. His hair may have a little more gray in it, but with the prince next to him, it is easy to see their similarities. All the children take after the king, and the effect is more noticeable seeing them all together like a matching set.

"We are so very pleased with the bravery and willingness of Princess Coraline. She has graciously agreed to travel to our neighboring country and seek out a friendship with their new monarch," the king says with a booming voice. "With her quick mind and her caring nature, she is sure to capture the hearts of Alberon, as she already holds our own."

At this, he turns and smiles down at his daughter, softening his demeanor and bringing a beaming smile to her face. The look makes me smile as I think of Papa. He gave me the same look today—the look of a father proud of his daughter.

"Although it is hard for this father's heart to part with his daughter, I know she is ready to do her duty to her people whom she loves." The crowd gives a big cheer. I have only known her for a few days now, but it is clear she is well loved.

"Of course, it helps that my valiant son, your prince, has agreed to accompany her and protect her," the king continues, sweeping a hand out to his son, who bows gracefully to the crowd. "He is swiftly moving up the ranks and showing himself to be a wonderful soldier and strategist." He smiles fondly at his children. I've always thought the king was a decent man, but seeing his love for his children raises his esteem in my eyes.

The crowd, though, responds less enthusiastically. Several lords are silent as they watch the king with frowns on their faces. It is not a secret that most of them wish to work with a crown prince and not a princess. Their silent display of displeasure makes me think of the poisoning attempt on the princess, and I shiver. I am glad we will be away from their treachery, but I glance at the crown princess and hope she will be safe while her siblings are gone.

"I send my children off with all the advantages I can and ask a blessing on them. May The Eternal watch over and protect you all." The king continues as if nothing is amiss, ignoring the disrespect of his nobles. The crowd cheers again, and in short order, the princess joins me in the carriage.

"Can you believe it's finally time?" she says, waving out the window to those seeing us off. "Oh, I'm so excited!"

The carriage lurches into motion, and the princess almost falls out of her seat. It takes a surprising amount of time to get out of the city because of the crowds gathered to see us off. The princess leaves the windows open and waves, but I try to stay hidden in the corner. People aren't gathered to see me, and that's fine.

After we make it out of the city, the princess sits back with a tired sigh. "Do you mind if I nap?" she asks, already closing her eyes. "I could hardly sleep from excitement last night, and it is finally catching up with me."

"Of course," I say, as she settles herself into a comfortable position on the bench, but I can't bring myself to rest. I gaze out the window, enjoying the scenery, even if it is mostly fields with sparse forest. The men ride horses in front and behind the carriage, and I catch occasional glimpses of them. Gareth is behind, and Rupert is in front with the prince and a few more guards for safety.

Around midday, we stop for a quick lunch. There is a basket for the princess and me, and the men have food in their saddlebags. No matter how fancy the carriage, I am relieved for the break when we stop.

I stand and stretch, trying to loosen my aching back before I take the basket and find a place for us to sit and eat. I start to pull out the lunch provisions—some cheeses, bread, and leftover meats from the palace—when a deep voice calls my name. I turn to find Rupert walking up, a roll already in his hand stuffed with some meats and cheeses. I didn't get to see him before we left. Now, so far from home, it is nice to see a familiar face.

"How ya doing, lass?" he inquires as I finish laying out the food and help myself. I don't know if there is a protocol to wait for the princess to eat first, but she is talking to her brother, and I am hungry.

"It has been good. The carriage is nice, and the princess slept the whole way so far. Thank you again for this opportunity."

"She's a good lass," he says, taking a seat next to me. I glance around the clearing, enjoying the moment's break. This is a nice little grassy area set back from the road a bit. A gentle creek babbles in the background, faintly, somewhere in the forest behind us. A few guards stand watch as the royal siblings converse.

"It should be clear weather most of the trip," Rupert says, breaking the silence. "We will be staying at inns most of the way until we get closer to the border, where we will have a few days camping till we get to Locura."

I nod and continue to enjoy my food and the quiet. It has been a long time since I've been away from the noise of the city. After some more silence, I glance over and notice his furrowed brow.

"Is everything okay?" His gaze flickers to me before he gazes back toward the woods.

"Yes," he finally says, "I don't expect any trouble while we are deep in Ileria the roads are good and the people friendly. I am worried about the state of the border, though. There have been some problems, raiders or bandits attacking the trade caravans. We had a little skirmish on our last trip—nothing major—but I do worry."

"It is your job to worry and be prepared," I tell him. I want to reassure him that all will be well. It's hard to explain why, but I feel safe in our group. "I'm sure with your planning and expertise, we will be well prepared for anything we encounter."

"Just promise me you will be careful," he says, looking at me. It's an easy promise to make. I may be ready for an adventure, but I'm not a reckless person.

"I promise," I look him in the eye, hoping to convey my sincerity. "Plus, I think I have a dedicated bodyguard," I say, looking at Gareth laughing with a group of royal guards. He looks like he is having fun, but I see him glancing over every so often to check on me. I lift a hand to wave and am rewarded with a smile.

Rupert stands, drawing my attention, as the siblings walk over to us. I scramble up as well. "Sorry to share my burdens with you, Aloura, but I want you to stay vigilant," he says before walking to the prince, who stops to converse. The princess keeps walking until she joins me.

"Oh, I needed this break. Long carriage rides always make me sore," she says, sitting down gracefully before digging into the basket of food.

"Is there anything I can do for you, Your Highness?" I ask, lingering uncertainly by her side.

"Sit down and keep me company." She pats the ground next to her. I slowly lower back down and nibble on the remains of my lunch. I look around the clearing once more, awkward silence filling the space between us.

My eye meets the prince's gaze while he talks to Rupert, and I blush under the brief attention. His expression doesn't change; it looks almost bored, but I swear I can detect slight amusement radiating my way from him.

I look away, annoyed, busying myself with straightening my dress so I can resist the urge to glance back. When I look up, I notice the princess glancing between us with an eyebrow raised.

"So..." she says slyly, "Tell me about your fiancé."

I blush, looking down guiltily at my stray thoughts. I am here for Aiden, who I am going to marry. I have no business noticing an annoying prince. I'm grateful the princess refrains from remarking on it.

"He is kind and funny, loyal, and protective. He saved me, and I have stayed by his side ever since." *And by his side is where I'm meant to be,* I remind myself.

"How romantic," the princess sighs, looking dreamy.

"What about you?" I ask, ready to turn the conversation off of me. "Anyone catch your eye?" Too late, I realize I have no idea how dating works in court.

"No," the princess says sadly. "It is complicated. While relationships are not forbidden, I have to be careful who I choose to favor. Everything is a power play, even matters of the heart."

I can't help feeling sad for her. It is a privilege to be a princess, but with all the wealth and ease comes responsibility. I can't imagine a life where everyone's eyes are on me, and I can't trust people's motives.

"I am much too busy to pursue romantic relationships anyway," she says flippantly, like it doesn't matter to her, but she can't completely hide the loneliness in her voice.

"Time to go!" Gareth calls as he strolls happily over to us. He bows politely to the princess, who blushes at the handsome guard. "Captain wants to reach the Boar's Inn before nightfall, so no more stops till then," he informs us, reaching out a hand to assist us. I quickly put the leftovers back into the basket before scooping it up and following the princess back to the carriage.

As I settle in for our next stretch, I can't help but think maybe this won't be too bad. The princess and I get along well, and the rest of the group seems kind and capable. But as my mind starts to wander, my thoughts turn once again to Aiden and Rupert's words. I watch the woods as we drive along and can't help the small amount of anxiety that starts to bubble in my chest. It would be easy to give in and let myself spiral, but once again, I close my eyes and send up a prayer that we will be safe. Peace enters my mind, and I can relax.

Chapter 14

We reach the inn just before dark. It is busy but not too crowded. The dining room is cheery and warm. Even though it is the beginning of summer, the nights are still cool, and I am grateful we are sleeping inside.

Rupert insists on a private dining room for us. Our traveling party consists of the royal siblings, Rupert, and a small squadron of ten soldiers. The princess and I head straight into the private dining room once we leave the carriage. I never realized how sore a bottom could be after sitting for hours on end.

I look around the simple space. It is plain, but at least it is clean. The innkeeper comes to greet us with his wife. A daughter, I assume, starts bringing in food, and my stomach rumbles at the sight. My companions take a seat, and I awkwardly follow suit, not sure what protocol is in this situation. I am supposed to be a servant, but so far I have been treated very casually.

Rupert and the royal siblings start immediately talking logistics and travel speed. Not wanting to draw attention to myself, I hesitantly gather some food and eat while I listen. "With the smaller carriage and fewer guards, it should only take a couple of weeks to travel to the capital," Rupert says to the prince.

"And you're sure sending the decoy carriage through Coati to the coast is the right thing to do?" The prince asks.

"They won't be expecting it, and I expect we will reach there about the same time," Rupert says. "We will get a boat once we reach their main trading port, Locura, and that should speed up travel."

The conversation dies, and I realize they are all exchanging glances, their eyes darting to look at me before looking back at each other. There is some silent communication they are having, and I have a feeling I am at the center of it.

"Will you go prepare our room for bed?" the princess asks me, and I realize they are trying to get rid of me. Probably ready to discuss secret information that I am not allowed to have.

"Of course!" I say, hopping up and heading out of the room quickly. It's only after I step into the public room that I realize I have no idea where our room is. Looking around for the innkeeper, my eyes land on a familiar, charming smile. It's Gareth.

He beckons me over, and I decide I can spare a minute to talk to him. He is sitting with several guards from our party, and they make room for me at the table as I walk over.

"I was wondering where you were," I say, squeezing myself next to my friend. The low murmur of voices, with a joyful laugh every once in a while, is surprisingly soothing. Sitting next to Gareth reminds me of evenings spent in the tavern with Aiden and his company.

"I don't have too much time. The princess asked me to prepare her room," I say, looking at the table. I haven't met any of the guards officially yet, but they all seem nice. They have to be of the highest standing to be in the Royal Guard.

"Relax. The princess seems nice. I'm sure she will be fine if you take a moment to visit," Gareth says, taking a bite of food. "Oh, right! Introductions!" he says after an awkward silence. Twelve men are traveling with us, but only a few sit at our table. "These are Ethan, Jacob, and Jared."

"Please let us know if you need anything, Miss Aloura," Ethan says, and I smile before excusing myself to once again find the room. Without too much trouble, I locate the innkeeper and find the room. It's bigger than I expected, with a bed and a palette on the floor that I assume is for me. My bag and one of the princess's trunks take up the wall under the window, and a small table is pushed into the corner.

I look through the princess's trunk, finding a nightgown and her brush, which I lay on the bed. Looking around, trying to decide what else to do, I notice a pitcher on the table and walk over to look inside. It's empty, but I'm sure there is a well or a pump I could use to fill it. Picking it up, I head back downstairs.

Maybe I should ask the innkeeper's wife about the well. I'm sure there is a better way to fill this. I don't really want to wander out in the dark. I glance up and startle at someone waiting for me at the bottom of the stairs. My hand flies to my heart, and my voice comes out loud. "Goodness, you scared me. You should make a noise or something. I could have fallen down the stairs from fright!" I take a deep breath to calm my racing heart and focus on my silent companion. My eyes lock onto the bright-blue eyes of the prince. I can feel the heat in my cheeks as I attempt an awkward curtsy and almost lose my balance, my arms flailing.

"Careful!" he says, reaching a hand forward to steady me and almost getting rewarded with a pitcher to the head.

"Sorry!" I say, walking down the final few steps, putting us on even ground before I attempt a bow.

"No, stop," he says with a little laugh. "No need to bow," he says, smiling down at me. *Goodness, he is tall.* We stand in silence for a moment as I try to figure out what to say. *Maybe I should just go.* I open my mouth to excuse myself, but he beats me to it.

"I'm glad I ran into you," he says in a rush. "I wanted to make sure you are settling in okay." It may be the low lighting, but I swear a blush rises on his cheeks, and I want to laugh at the thought. I must be mistaken. The prince is not blushing.

"I'm fine," I say. "This is a nice inn." There is another pause. "I'm just going to go fill this," I say, holding up the empty jug, but the prince is in my way, and I can't go.

"Of course," he says, stepping aside, "I'm glad you are on this trip."

I stop, my eyebrows shooting up as I turn to look at him. "I thought I was trouble," I say, remembering our last encounter.

"No, you just find yourself in trouble a lot, but I'm glad you are here for my sister. She needs a friend on this trip, and you seem like you would be a good one." His tone seems sincere. I can tell from his eyes as they stare into mine, and now I am the one blushing.

"Thank you." I'm not sure what else to say. It's not every day that a prince compliments you.

"I, uh..." I stumble over the words that just aren't coming when we are interrupted by the princess. I let out a breath of relief as she joins us.

"Aloura," Coraline says with her usual cheer, looping an arm around mine. "Brother," she says with a nod to the prince. "I am surprised to find you still awake. I am quite ready for bed myself after a long day of travel. There is only so much rest to be had in a moving carriage." She looks between us for a moment and then makes eye contact with me. Her eyes seem to be asking if I'm okay, so I give a small nod.

"I ran into Aloura on my way up," the prince says, his tone formal, lacking some of the warmth and maybe vulnerability it had before.

"I was just getting us water," I say again, holding up the pitcher.

"Oh, wonderful! I will wait for you in the room," the princess says, letting go of my arms and turning to her brother. "Walk me up?" He holds out his arm in practiced formality, and they disappear up the stairs, leaving me alone to wonder what just happened.

We find our rhythm for the next two weeks of travel, alternating between staying at inns and camping. My duties are simple: help the princess dress in the morning, keep her company as we travel, bring her things as she needs them, and help her prepare for bed. The princess is not a demanding mistress, and most of the time she treats me like a companion rather than a servant. We get along well.

I see the prince every day, but we don't interact more than necessary. Like the princess, he is kind and never demanding. As the only other woman in our company, I usually eat with them in a private dining room and try to offer polite conversation, but I am more than happy to be ignored.

My favorite times are traveling in the carriage. The princess is more casual when it is just us, and we like to admire the sights of the passing landscape. The fields and forests have started to turn into a jungle as we near the border.

"Isn't it magical?" Coraline says, looking out the window. She has insisted that when it is just us, I call her by her name. "I always love watching this transition."

"My mother would have loved this," I say. The trees have gotten taller and thicker. Vines have begun to creep over the trees and the ground, and everything is green. Luckily, the path is clear from the trade caravans, so the ride is relatively smooth.

"Tell me about your mother," the princess says, turning to me.

"She was wonderful," I say quietly as I think about her. What would she say about this whole adventure? Thinking about her is painful, so I decide to change the subject.

"Do you want to play a game?" I ask suddenly, and the princess raises an eyebrow.

"What sort of game?" she asks, sitting forward.

"A game of stories." I am eager to play just like I used to with my mother, but the next moment, I feel silly. This is a childish game, and maybe the princess will think it is beneath her. I am about ready to change my mind when she answers.

"Sure," she says with a smile, and my excitement returns.

"Let's pretend this forest is magical," I start, "and we are traveling to visit a fae prince."

"Is the prince handsome?"

"Of course, but he is also wicked," I say with a mischievous grin.

"Oh dear!" she exclaims, giggling. "Why are we going to visit him then?"

"Maybe he is the only one who can break a curse," I say, searching my brain for a good curse.

"Or maybe my father made a bargain with him, protection from a curse for my hand in marriage," she says, and I am delighted at her participation in the game.

"Yes! But of course, he will be moved by your beauty."

"And he really has a noble heart, but he himself is under a curse by the evil fairy that haunts these woods. He refused to marry her, so she cursed him to remain a villain until his one true love appears," she says dreamily.

"Oh, but she still wants him for herself. We have to be careful because she is fond of making his brides disappear." Goosebumps run over my flesh as we peek outside at the guards riding with us. The guards are alert, ready for action, adding to our story.

Rupert has grown more tense as we get closer to the border, and with good reason. At the last inn we stayed at, there were rumors that a caravan passing through recently nearby had been attacked. All signs pointed to bandits in the area. As we set out this morning, everyone has been a little more on edge. Gareth wasn't as boisterous, either. Our game doesn't feel quite like a game anymore.

Following my gaze, the princess looks at Rupert as he rides next to us. "Tell me again how you met Rupert?"

"Aiden, Gareth, and I had been hanging out down by the docks, and it was growing late. A ship had come in, and the men were rowdy and had been drinking. On the way home, a group of men started bothering us, calling to me and such." I say with a shiver. "Their words had been nasty, but I wasn't afraid until Aiden decided to confront them. He wanted to defend my honor."

I shake my head with a small smile at the memory. "Gareth jumped in to help, of course, but we were still young, and these men were burly sailors. They were greatly outnumbered. For a moment, I had thought that I might lose Aiden. I had been yelling hysterically when Rupert came to the rescue. If it weren't for him, Aiden and even Gareth could have lost their lives, but instead, he took them in, gave them a job, and trained them. He has become very dear to all of us," I say with a smile.

"No wonder he vouched for you. We weren't sure who to trust after the poisoning, and I knew that Maggie had to stay with Marina, so when Rupert said he had someone... We knew we could trust him. He has been loyal for years. I'm so glad that you are here." Coraline reaches forward and hugs me, surprising me.

"I'm so worried I'm going to mess this up, and I hate leaving Marina in such a vulnerable position, but I am glad I have you as a companion," she says, drawing back.

I swallow hard against the lump that has risen in my throat and reach out and squeeze her hand. We stay like that for a little while, each of us lost in our thoughts. We don't talk until a break is called.

I reach my arms up as I climb out of the carriage. This break is needed. "Careful," I lean over and whisper to the princess. "The evil fairy may be watching us now." Her eyes widen, and she looks around before breaking into a laugh, earning us a few scowls from the guards.

The humid jungle buzzes with the sound of chirping insects and the distant calls of unseen creatures. Dappled sunlight filters through the thick canopy above, casting shifting patterns on the damp forest floor. It truly looks like another realm.

"Not too long till we reach the border," Rupert says, looking around the clearing. "I don't want to stop here long. I don't like the feeling I'm getting."

I shiver and look around. It seems quiet to me, but Rupert's words have me feeling like I'm being watched. I take a deep breath and shake my head. *You're being silly. It's just your game with Coraline that has you on edge. There are no evil fairies and plenty of guards to keep you safe.* I kneel by the stream to wash my hands. I splash some water on my face and cup some in my hands, taking a drink. The water is cool and fresh.

The stream must flow from the mountains north of here, runoff from the spring snows.

I dip my hands once more, bringing water to my neck as well, sending a little shiver down my back as the water wets the back of my dress. The humidity of the jungle has left me feeling warm and sticky, very aware of all the dirt in my crevices. I wish for a proper bath.

Aware of the unease of the men, I stand and turn to walk the short distance back toward the camp, but a prickly feeling creeps along my spine. I freeze and listen. The jungle, once alive with sound, is eerily silent.

"Aloura," Gareth calls, beckoning me back. "We need you and the princess back in the carriage." He is tense. I'm not the only one feeling the surrounding wrongness. I look around and notice most of the men on their horses, which shift nervously under them. I don't see Coraline.

"Where is the princess?" I ask as he takes my arm and walks me quickly to the carriage.

"Already in the carriage. Get inside," he says, helping me climb in and closing the door behind me quickly. Coraline sits on my side of the carriage, peeking out of the covered windows.

"Oh, good! You're back!" she says, sitting back and clasping my hands in hers as I sit beside her. "I think our game has me extra spooked," she says, pulling me close. "Rupert sent a few men ahead to scout, and Jude assures me that we are fine but they haven't come back yet. I think something is wrong."

"Do you think it's the evil fairy trying to keep us from getting to the prince?" I ask, trying to joke, but she just shudders.

"Oh no, let's play a different game to take my mind off my nerves," she says

"Okay, how about..." I start trying to think of something less scary to talk about.

A sharp whistle cuts through the air, and then shouts call out. I lean past Coraline and look out the window, and immediately draw back. A thump hits the carriage followed by a few more.

"What is it?" She asks, looking out the window herself. She draws back with a gasp, her frantic eyes finding mine. We are under attack. More thumps hit the carriage as arrows rain from above.

"They are in the trees," A man shouts before his cry is cut short. I glance back out again and look at the scene. Our men are well trained but the trees hide out attackers well and they are being picked off quickly.

"Get them out of here" the prince yells from nearby and I fall back as the carriage gets moving.

"What should we do?" I ask in a whisper, turning to the princesses. Surely she has had training in this sort of thing.

"I...I don't know," she says before we both let out a shout when the carriage is jostled. More shouts and the scream of horses meet our ears. Our carriage jolts again and Coraline and I shriek as we are tossed around the carriage. I land on the ground hard when the carriage comes to an abrupt halt, tilting to the side. The door closest to me flies open, and before we can even shout, rough hands yank us out. More masked figures charge from the undergrowth, yelling and shouting as they charge our protectors.

"Guards!" Coraline cries out, struggling against the iron grip of her kidnapper as he drags her back into the thick grove of trees. I struggle against the hands around my waist, but freeze when a dagger presses into my throat. My eyes widen as I see a guard charge after us only to be quickly struck down by a bandit. They have us greatly outnumbered.

"Make a sound, and she dies," a gravelly voice threatens in my ear. I glance over to see Coraline held at dagger point as well. Her wide eyes meet mine and dart back toward our protectors. I can't tell what she is trying to tell me, but the cold steel at my neck keeps me frozen. My breath comes in quick and shallow as we move further into the trees. We walk backward, and my eyes strain to try to catch a glimpse of any rescuers. Rupert's distinct voice reaches my ears, but it is faint. The bandit behind me stumbles, and I let out a hiss as his knife nicks me.

"I've got her!" Coraline's bandit calls to a companion I can't see. Coraline struggles again as she is shoved forward, falling on her hands and knees. The knife at my throat nicks me again, the blade pressing against my throat. I let out a whimper.

"Let her go!" Coraline demands, climbing to her feet, her eyes glaring fiercely at a foe I can't focus on. I close my eyes and try to take a deep breath, but tears leak out instead.

"I don't think so," a confident voice responds. I open my eyes to look around, but the blade at my throat keeps me from turning my head. My breaths are still too shallow, and my head is starting to feel like it is spinning. I close my eyes again, just wanting this nightmare to be over.

"I need your cooperation, and your friend will help us get that," the leader says. I blink my eyes open again, but the figures are blurry. I can't get enough air. I want to reach up and claw at phantom hands around my neck but there is only a sharp steel. I start to sway, and my captor tightens his grip on my waist to keep me up as my knees weaken.

"Let her go, and I will cooperate," Coraline says, but her voice sounds far away. "She is nothing to you." Shouts sound closer, and I can hear the clash of steel over the roaring in my ears. "Can you hear them? They are coming for us."

"We need to move," a thin, shaky voice says, one that sounds familiar, but I can't place it as I sway once more. My knees are weak, and I'm sure I'm going to faint.

"Move or your friend gets it!" the leader commands, but before any progress can be made, an arrow whistles through the air, and a cry sounds. Yelling and shouting follow, and my captor drops me. Chaos surrounds me before I pass out.

I wake slowly, disoriented. Shouts sound nearby, and someone is talking and touching my face. I blink, and Coraline comes into focus, bent over me. "Aloura, we have to move." Our eyes connect, and I can see the relief in her eyes. She climbs to her feet and reaches a hand out, helping me up. She doesn't let go once I am standing, instead pulling me behind her as she takes off. I stumble behind her, trying my best to keep up until I trip over a vine and land on my hands and knees. "Come on," Coraline says, pulling me up again, but I don't have to go far before a pair of arms scoops me up.

I look up into a pair of familiar, startling blue eyes. "You're safe," the prince says, striding towards the clearing where the rest of our company waits.

"You've saved me again," I say, looking up into his face. His mouth is set in a grim line, and his eyes sweep back and forth as he walks.

"Sorry, I said I wouldn't do that again, but it seems like you needed it," he says with a quick glance down at me. I think I must be in shock, though, because a laugh startles out of me, which leads to more crying.

"Thank you," I say through my tears. He frowns as he looks down at me, but before he can say anything, we have reached the clearing to a chorus of voices.

"Aloura!" Gareth calls as he rushes up to us while the prince sets me down. "You had me so worried!" he says, scooping me up into a hug. "They popped out of the bushes so fast, and there were so many of them," he says, pulling back. His eyes scan me for injuries as he continues. "We heard a scream, but I couldn't get away to follow you. I would never have forgiven myself." He gasps, his hands hovering at my neck. "You're hurt."

Rupert, Coraline, and the prince pause their conversation to glance over at us, but Gareth has it handled and summons bandages. I make eye contact with Coraline, who mouths sorry to me before turning back to her conversation. Gareth fusses over me like a little mother hen. "It probably looks worse than it is," I say as he leads me over to the stream to rinse it.

"Well, we are going to clean it and bandage it, and then you are going back in the carriage, maybe with a guard, to keep you and the princess safe," he says, wetting a cloth. I take it from him to wipe my neck, feeling faint again when I see the blood.

"Come on," he says, wrapping my neck. "Let's get you to the carriage, where you can rest."

Chapter 15

Gareth rides inside the carriage to keep a closer eye on us and to be more available in case of an emergency. We are lucky it wasn't damaged. I fall asleep quickly as the carriage starts moving. I am only waking up as the sky darkens.

"It's more complicated than that," Gareth says as I come to consciousness. I am lying down with my head on colorful skirts. Gentle hands stroke through my hair, almost putting me back to sleep. I am lying on Coraline's lap.

"But shouldn't she..." she replies, but I sit up, cutting off her response. "You're awake! How are you feeling?" she asks, reaching forward to touch my cheek. I smile but pull away. I hate being a burden, and my weakness makes me feel like the biggest liability here. Rupert must regret bringing me along.

"I'm fine," I respond, looking out the window. "Where are we?" It is darkening rapidly. The thick canopy overhead obscures the moonlight or any weak light the stars might offer. Torches flicker ahead, giving just enough light for those in the lead.

"Across the border in Alberon. We wanted to get away from the area as fast as we could, but we will probably stop soon. The attack delayed us from reaching the next town on time. I'm sure the prince would like to push through, but Rupert will advise us to stop," Gareth says, glancing outside at the jungle. I forget that he has traveled this route once before and wonder if any of it looks familiar.

True to his word, the carriage slows and pulls off to the side of the road soon after. The clearing is decently sized, and the torchlight reveals the remains of campfires. The men get busy quickly, lighting our own fire and spreading out bedrolls. Coraline is pulled aside by her brother, and I am left standing alone.

"This is where caravans will stop for the night on occasion," Rupert says, approaching me. "We should be safe enough here."

I give him a half-hearted smile but don't respond, and with a pat on my shoulder, he goes to help with setting up camp. *So this is Alberon,* I think, taking a deep breath. The very air feels different. I make my way over to the campfire one of the guards set up, while the rest of the party sees to the horses and sets up a tent for me and the princess. I should probably help, but instead I plop down on the ground in front of the fire and stare into it. Gareth comes and drapes a blanket over my shoulders.

Slowly, Coraline, the prince, and Rupert join me. Hard bread and jerky are passed out, but I hardly taste them. I keep going over the attack in my mind, but it's becoming muddled with the one that happened weeks ago. I am seeing John in both places.

"Let's talk about the attack," the prince says, drawing all eyes to him.

"What do we know?" he says, looking around at Rupert and the guards who have joined us.

"Well, they started by taking out our scouts. When we reached the clearing, they must have already been hiding in the trees," one of the guards, Bradford or something like that, says.

"Why didn't they attack while the princess was out of the carriage?" The prince asks, looking towards Rupert.

"They probably wanted to make sure there was something of value to steal, and then they wanted us to run into their ambush further down the road."

"Right, they lined the path with large stones that ran the carriage off course, and they had men waiting there ready to attack. They had these devices, ropes attached to rocks. They threw them at the horses' legs to take them down," Bradford continues.

"Do you think they knew it was the princess and not just some noble?" another guard says, gesturing to the princess.

"They knew exactly who I was," Coraline says. "The leader was wearing a mask, but he didn't look or sound familiar. He wasn't trying to kill me, though; he wanted my cooperation."

Rupert glances over at me from the corner of his eye before he shares his news. I can tell from his expression that it's not going to be good.

"I think I might have some insight into our attackers," he says, carefully glancing over at me again. "I thought I might have recognized one of the attackers. He was in the background and the first to flee. If it was who I think it was, this attack is bigger than we think."

"Who did you see?" the prince asks. Rupert glances at me again, and the little food in my stomach sours. I have a feeling that whoever he says is not a name I want to hear.

"It was a recently escaped prisoner, a man I've known as John of Alberon," he says with a sigh, looking over at the prince. My breath falters for a second when I hear his name, and a gentle grip squeezes my shoulder. I glance over and see the grimace of sympathy on Gareth's face.

"Are you sure it was him?" the prince asks Rupert. I force myself to pay attention instead of giving in to the desperate sobs I would rather indulge in.

"He stayed behind in the shadows. I saw him when I chased after a few of the men. I didn't want to believe it, but I've worked with the man for years. I would recognize his little rat face anywhere."

My breath picks up, and my heart starts to pound. A hand grabs my elbow, and I glance over at Coraline, who is looking at me concerned. Thoughts flash through my mind. *Was he here because of me? Did he follow me here to finish the job he started?*

A hand reaches out and touches mine gently, and I look up at the prince. "Deep breath in and then out," he says, guiding me through the breathing exercise he used earlier. I match my breaths up to his until I'm calm again. Unfortunately, I'm also aware enough to be embarrassed. I can feel the heat as it creeps up my neck and into my cheeks. I can't meet the prince's eyes.

"This changes things," the prince says, standing. He makes his way back over to his spot, looking toward Rupert in silent communication.

"I am confused," the princess says, glancing around the circle. "Who is John of Alberon?"

"Do you think he was here for me?" I ask instead of answering her question.

"John attacked Aloura and was arrested for it," Gareth whispers from the other side of me. "You think he was behind the attempt to kidnap the princess?" he asks, addressing the group.

"He might have had information that we would be traveling this way," Rupert says as he and the prince share another look. "I never quite trusted him. I always felt like he was watching me, trying to overhear my conversations. He wanted a hand in everything and was very outspoken. I always thought Machiavelli shouldn't have hired him."

"Why? Why would he want to kidnap me? What does his involvement mean?" the princess asks, looking at Rupert and her brother. She has taken my hand and holds it in her lap. I'm not sure if it is for her sake or mine, but I appreciate the comfort anyway.

The men glance at me again, and I am getting close to demanding answers. *I don't need to be coddled,* I want to shout. The shaking in my hands betrays me, though, and I keep my mouth shut for now.

"We are trying to figure out some vital pieces of information that will help enlighten us about the situation, but until we get to a town, we don't know anything for sure," the prince says cryptically before dismissing everyone to bed.

Coraline and I climb into our tent while the men bed down outside. The remaining guards will take shifts throughout the night. We lost quite a few good men, not that I knew them well, but it is hard to see our diminished numbers. Some are injured and will have to be left behind to travel at a slower pace and will hopefully meet us in Locura on our return trip.

"I'm sorry," Coraline says as we lie down on the bedrolls provided for us.

"For what?" I ask.

"For today, and what happened before. I can't imagine how traumatic this all must be," she whispers.

"You were kidnapped, too," I say quickly. I don't want pity or special treatment.

"But they weren't going to kill me. You had a blade at your throat. I tried to keep a brave face, but I was so scared they were going to do

something to you before our guards could get to us." She sniffs. I reach
out and take her hand.

"Well, we are okay," I say as my other hand fingers the bandage on my
neck. I repeat that quietly in my mind as the princess's hand in mine goes
limp and her breathing deepens into sleep. Unfortunately, I can't say the
same for myself.

My mind keeps running through the attack. Every time I close my
eyes, I feel the cold steel of the knife on my neck. I smell the foul breath
of my attacker. He morphs into John, and I fling my eyes open in terror.
I don't know how long I toss and turn before finally climbing out of bed
and wandering closer to the fire. The guards on duty nod to me as I sit
by the dying flames.

My mind goes through all the information I learned, and I wonder
why John could have been here. I turn my thoughts to The Eternal and
ask *what purpose could capturing the princess serve?* My mind flashes back
to John's attack. It's like a film has been lifted, and I can recall every detail
of that night. I have been so caught up in being scared that I have hardly
paid attention to his words, but now they run through my mind. *Aiden
is leaving, and he might not come back. She thinks she can have him, but
she is nothing.* He was drunk, and that's all I thought it was. Maybe he
knew something about Aiden that I didn't. Maybe Aiden didn't even
know. I feel like I'm on the verge of something when I'm interrupted.

"Can't sleep?" Rupert sits down next to me. I would be mad, but he
is just the person I need to talk to.

"Is Aiden involved in all of this?" I ask, needing to know. He doesn't
speak, but his silence tells me the truth. This is bigger than I realized.

He glances over at me and sighs, his shoulders slumping as he rests
his arms on his knees. "It's just a theory," he says. "I don't think he is

knowingly involved in anything, but he may be a more important player than we thought."

"Explain," I demand quietly, but he shakes his head.

"I can't tell you more yet. We need to know what we are dealing with first."

"I am wrapped up in this now," I say, ready to plead my case, but a thought suddenly enters my mind. "Is that why you let me come?" I watch him, but he continues staring into the fire.

"There are multiple reasons," he finally whispers, "but I thought you might be useful." Pain fills my chest, and I turn away from him. *How dare he*, I think, picking up a twig and throwing it into the fire. *Am I just a pawn to be used in whatever game he is playing?*

"I deserve to know what you have dragged me into," I say, glancing at him again, but when he doesn't start talking, I get up to leave.

"I can tell you some of my guesses," he says, stopping me. I glance down at him, and he extends a hand, inviting me to sit again. I want to leave on principle, but I'm too curious to turn down his olive branch.

"My guess is John joined the group of bandits that already lived here and convinced them to attack us. I also think he is taking orders from someone."

From what I remember about John, he was always all talk. He always seemed to be a man of little action, but it seems that has now changed.

"Who is giving him orders?" I ask.

"We have our guesses, but we will know more once we reach the trade port. There, they trade in more than just goods," he says with a raised brow. I want to ask more, but a yawn catches me off guard. Exhaustion from the day hits me with full force and I sag under its weight. "Go to bed, lass. We will watch over you."

I sleep fitfully and try to hold in my yawns as we break down camp the next day. I am grateful that I will be traveling in the carriage today and hope that I will be able to get some rest. I stretch and grab my pack, ready to go, but before I climb in the carriage, the prince stops me.

"I have been talking with Rupert, and we have come to the decision that you need self-defense training."

"Excuse me?" My eyebrows shoot up. "What gives you the right to decide that?" I demand. My lack of sleep makes me more irritable than usual.

"You were held at knifepoint, and if John is lurking around, you need a way to defend yourself."

"Fine," I say, crossing my arms. I'll agree to it, but I don't have to be happy about it.

With a slight smirk, he continues. "We don't have time to truly train you, but Rupert and I want you and Coraline to be able to get out of a dangerous situation if we end up in one."

"You mean when we end up in one," I grumble.

His eyes soften as he leans down, putting his face close to mine. "Don't let him win," he says before walking off, leaving me alone to deal with my confusing feelings.

Chapter 16

The morning light shines in my face, waking me up too early. It was late when we arrived at the inn, and I have my first training session this morning. I stretch and turn over to my side, trying not to fall back to sleep. My mind was troubled last night, circling around thoughts of secret plans and deception. It made it hard to fall asleep, and when I did, my longing for Aiden seeped into my dreams, stealing any rest I might have had.

What sort of thing could he unknowingly be involved in? I rack my mind for anything I might have missed about Aiden or his past. He was always so private about it that I only have a handful of information. His father was a leader and a brute of the resistance. He loved his brother. He loved his mother, but resents what she put him through, but none of that helps me understand what is happening and how he is involved. My only clue is his brother. He never talked about his part in the rebellion, but he was older than Aiden by a significant amount, and maybe he was more involved than I realized.

Coraline is up and dressing already, and I roll out of bed to slip on a simple dress. A shout from outside brings our attention to the fact that we are supposed to report to the courtyard of the inn for training. We are already late.

"You go on ahead," I tell Coraline, still pulling on my shoes.

I rush down the stairs when I am done, apologizing to a server as I dodge around her. I am the last one out in the courtyard. I quickly find Coraline and stand by her as we watch Gareth spar with one of the royal guards.

"He's good," she leans over and whispers to me. I notice a blush on her cheeks and smile. Gareth may have just won himself another admirer.

"Of course he's good. Rupert helped train him," I say.

"Maybe..." she says hesitantly, leaning close, but the prince spots us before she can get out the rest of her thought.

"Good. Now that we are all here, let's begin." He directs us to a small area to the side of the courtyard, away from the sparring men. It's just the four of us: Rupert, Coraline, the prince, and me.

"What I want to do today is teach you how to defend yourselves," the prince says, pacing around us like he is taking in our measure. I want to laugh a little at how seriously he is taking this. It feels a little excessive for a quick defense lesson that I will probably fail at, but I do have to admire his dedication. He is in his element here.

"We don't have much time to train before we arrive in Locura. It's only a day's journey to the capital from there. With that in mind, today we will work on how to surprise or incapacitate your opponent to give you time to get away." He glances over at me, and I feel the heat rising to my cheeks, feeling singled out. "With both of you being small with little experience in fighting, you are at a disadvantage. Your opponents will mostly be bigger and stronger than you, so using every advantage you can get will help you if you are in trouble."

It's too early for this. I fight a yawn as he continues. "We have the numbers to pair up and assess you individually so that we can help you find what tools you have." My shoulders tense up as I wait to hear my assigned partner. The thought of working with the prince makes me feel anxious, and I can't tell if it's in a good or bad way. *It's bad,* I tell myself, but I know that's not completely true. "I will work with my sister, and Rupert will work with Aloura."

I let out a sigh, and my shoulders lose their tension. *This is good. I will be working with Rupert, who is familiar and comfortable.* I don't pay attention to the little sliver of disappointment that runs through me at the announcement. We run through a few warm-up stretches and strength-building exercises together. By the end, I'm already breathing hard.

"Very good, lass," Rupert says as I barely finish a round of push-ups. I glare up at him, too tired to come up with a retort.

"Now don't give me that. I want you to do these exercises every morning. They will strengthen you and give you better mobility. Stand up, and let's talk about what to do if you are caught in a sticky situation." I stand, brushing off my hands before he walks me through the weaker parts of the body.

"Don't be afraid to fight dirty. You know from experience that these men will hurt you, so do whatever you can to incapacitate them so you can get away." I shiver at the reminder. The past two attacks I have survived so far on pure luck, but that ends now. I get ready as Rupert leads me through a drill. His arms come around me from behind, pinning my hands to my side, and I start to struggle. "Okay, lass, I want you to get out of my hold. Stomp on my foot, throw your head back, whatever you need to do."

His hold is tight, and my arms are completely useless. I try to stomp on his foot, but his boots are too thick. Panic starts to set in, and all his instructions fly out of my mind. My breath starts to come in gasps as I remember hands tight around my throat, a knife drawing blood.

"Let go!" I scream, and his hands let go quickly, letting me fall to my hands and knees on the ground. I stay there, unable to move, my breaths coming out too fast. A hand touches my back, and I flinch, but it doesn't move.

"Deep breath, Aloura. Just listen to my breaths and match mine. You are safe." The prince's familiar deep voice brings me back to the present, and my breathing quickly evens out. I sit back on my heels, scowling as the prince drops his hand. I want to cry and scream with frustration. Will I forever be handicapped by panic?

"I'm fine," I say when he reaches forward again to help me up. I don't want his hands on me. I'm embarrassed by my reaction, but I just want to be away.

Coraline hovers close by, her hands raised like she wants to comfort me. "Are you okay?" I nod as I get up, but I don't make eye contact with anyone. I just want to run away and be alone for a moment.

I accidentally meet Rupert's eyes as I look for an escape, and see the frown on his face. "I'm sorry, lass. I didn't realize it affected you so badly. It's not uncommon for soldiers to relive traumatic moments in times of stress. I should have realized that would have triggered you."

"It's not your fault," I say. "I just need a moment." I walk past everyone, keeping my head down so they don't see the tears.

"Finish up for today," the prince commands behind me, and everyone starts moving again. "We need to be ready to go in an hour." The sound fades as I rush up the stairs away from everyone. I close the door to our room softly before sinking down. I wrap my arms around my knees, resting my head on them, and let the tears fall.

The rest of the morning passes by quickly. Most people leave me alone, and I can't decide if I appreciate it or if I hate that it makes me feel fragile. Coraline is kind and tries to distract me with stories of her siblings.

"And then Jude pushed Marina into the pond!" she says with a laugh, bringing a smile to my face.

"He really pushed her in?" I ask, not believing it of the upright but kind prince.

"She may be the oldest, and he respects that, but he has never shied away from reminding her that she is not all-powerful." The fond smile on her face makes me ache for my family—Lana, Papa, and, of course, Aiden.

Soon after, we break for lunch. The guards are on edge as they eye the thinning jungle around. Gareth stands by me and the princess as we eat on a blanket, keeping watch over us.

"If everyone is so worried, why did we stop?" I ask him, taking a bite of an apple.

"We needed to water the horses and give them a break. We got a later start this morning than we meant to," he says with a glance at me. "We want to be sure to make it to the next inn before nightfall." I scowl at the implication that we left later because of me. He has been hovering, and I need a break. Almost like reading my mind, Coraline starts talking to him, and I sneak off to talk to Rupert while he is distracted.

Rupert and the prince are deep in conversation, but break off as I approach. We haven't talked since this morning, and they stand quietly waiting for me to be the first to speak. Rupert keeps looking at me and glancing away, arms crossed, and shifting his weight from one foot to the other. The prince keeps his arms at his side, but his eyes scan over my face like he is looking for something. "I am not a vase," I say, crossing my arms and scowling at them. "I won't break."

"We don't—" Rupert says, but I'm not finished.

"Everyone has been treating me like the slightest look will blow me over, and I'm sick of it. I am not that fragile!"

"No, you're not," the prince says, surprising me. He has been quiet so far. "You are strong and resilient, but you still need to give yourself time to heal," he says quietly, and I blush, realizing the whole clearing has gone quiet, listening to us.

"If you say I am strong," I say, stepping closer so our voices won't carry, "then don't leave me in the dark." His eyes give a flash of surprise behind his mask he has been wearing. "I know you have been keeping things from me."

He glances over at Rupert, who has made himself busy along with the rest of the clearing. The prince sighs before gently grabbing my arm and walking to the treeline. He stops before we are out of view, though. "Listen, I don't know what Rupert has told you, but we don't know much ourselves. We are walking into a dangerous situation."

"Surely you have ideas," I say.

"We have some ideas of what might be going on," he says slowly, as if he is trying to decide how much to tell me. "But we need just a little more information before we can come up with a plan. After we meet with our informants tomorrow, we will bring you in on the information that you need to know, including what your boyfriend is involved in."

My eyebrows furrow, and I put my hands on my hips, ready to demand answers, but he doesn't give me the chance. "I understand you are concerned about him," he says, holding up his hands, "but you have to remember I'm not just concerned about what situation we are walking into. I have to consider the impact it will have on our entire country and the countless lives that my decision will affect." He raises his eyebrow, waiting for my retort, but I have nothing to say. With a nod, he walks away, leaving me feeling guilty and selfish.

The next morning, I report to the inn courtyard after another sleepless night. The guilty feeling persisted after my talk with the prince yesterday. I felt selfish for only thinking about how this mission affected me. After my outburst as well, people continued giving me a wide breadth, so I was left with far too much time to think.

Coraline and I start warming up on our own as the men work on their sword fighting. I thought we were up early, but both days the guards were well into practice when we arrived. There is excitement in the air today, and everyone seems more motivated. It is probable that today we will arrive in Locura, where we will spend the night before boarding a boat to take us across the lake to the capital city. The knowledge that I am so close to Aiden helps me push through my exhaustion and soreness.

"It's worse today," I complain to Rupert as he joins me in my exercises. All my muscles feel like they are on fire, including ones I've never noticed before.

"It will get easier with time," he assures me with a laugh. As we finish up, I stand, mentally preparing myself to push through my panic and practice today. I start reviewing with Rupert about where to hit someone to make the most impact: eyes, throat, groin. We are about ready to start practicing when the prince steps up and puts a hand on Rupert's shoulder.

"I would like you to work with my sister today, and I will work with Aloura," he says, taking Rupert's place.

"Why?" I squeak as I watch Rupert walk away. My nerves shoot up as I take in his casual stance before me. He is stoic again, but at my obvious discomfort, the right side of his mouth ticks up in a smirk. My brow furrows, and I scowl at him as my nerves turn to annoyance.

"I didn't want him to treat you like a vase," he says, his smirk firmly in place now. He is making fun of me. I move into the beginning fighting stance Rupert showed me, feet apart and shoulders squared.

"I won't go easy on you even though you are the prince." I am not sure what to do next, though, as I wait for him to make the first move.

"Of course not," he says, stepping closer and circling me. "That would defeat the purpose of the exercise. Let's start from where you left off yesterday. You were going to practice breaking away from a hold with Rupert. I'm going to come up behind you and try the same hold. If you feel like you can't do it, just yell stop like you did yesterday, and I'll let go, okay?" he says, all teasing gone now.

I nod, trying to prepare myself mentally, but my fire has left again. As he wraps his arms around me, I can already feel my breath increase as my heart beats hard inside my chest. His arms are solid, but his grip is still loose enough that I don't feel like I'm suffocating.

"That's it. Just breathe for a moment," he says, his voice closer to my ear. A shiver runs down my back, and his arms tighten slightly. Goosebumps run up my arms, and I can't decide whether I hate his arms around me or like it a little too much. The thought scares me, so I do what I was instructed.

"Good," he says again as I start to struggle again, but this time, I am in control. "You are not powerless, Aloura," his voice encourages. "You can't use your arms, but you have other resources."

I take stock of the situation, noticing where his hands hold me and the strength of his arms. *Don't think about his arms,* I chide myself before deciding what to do. He is too tall for me to ram my head into with any accuracy to break his nose, so I go with the next best thing. I stomp on his foot. His arms loosen as he takes a hop back, and I lunge forward out of his grasp. I use too much power, though, and quickly lose my balance. The prince reaches forward to grab me before I hit the ground, but with his weight on one foot, we lose the battle with gravity and both go down.

I close my eyes, bracing for impact on the hard cobblestones, but the prince's hand on my arm slows me down. My knees still hit the ground hard enough to bruise. A quick "Oh no!" is all the warning I get before a heavy body squishes me.

I groan as the prince scrabbles off quickly, mumbling apologies. I roll over and look up at him, and he offers his hand to help me up. I can't help but notice his rosy cheeks, and he hasn't stopped apologizing. "Are you okay? I thought I had you," he says, rubbing a hand behind his head. He is so flustered. I can't help it, and a laugh slips out. The dam breaks, and before I know it, I am laughing hysterically. The prince's deep laugh joins mine as he pulls me to my feet.

"I'm fine," I assure him as I wipe the tears from my eyes. I can't remember the last time I laughed that hard.

"Well, besides losing your balance, you did well," he says, taking a step back and straightening himself again, but he has a smile on his face.

"It's a good start," I agree, but I can't keep the beaming smile off my face. I am not powerless. And with this training, I don't plan to be a victim ever again. "Let's go again."

Chapter 17

We make good time and arrive at Locura in the early evening. The days are stretching longer, and there is still plenty of sunlight left. I'm left to my own devices when we arrive at the inn. Coraline decides to rest, and the guards each have their tasks, such as securing passage on a boat to the Alberon capital city and meeting with their contacts. With nothing else to do, I decide to check out the local market.

"Where do you think you're going?" Gareth asks, following me out onto the street.

"Going exploring," I say, looking over at him as he falls into step with me. "What are you doing?"

"I guess I'm going exploring," he says, shooting me a grin. It will be nice to have company. Locura is a large city, the center of trade in Alberon. Being on the lake with a wide river to the sea puts it at an advantage for trade.

Our inn is near the center of town, so it doesn't take long before we encounter a market. I can hear it long before we arrive. The market is large and full of color and languages. It is a completely foreign feeling from the gray sky of the Ilerian markets. Life thrives here with the people. We wander the stalls looking at the brightly colored garments and indulging in some of the sweet treats. My favorite is a long fried pastry dipped in a sweet and spicy dust that makes a mess as we eat them. As we walk around, I can't help but notice the remains of war, although they don't look like what I expected.

The people look haggard, dressed in rags, but they smile. Soldiers wander through the crowd, but they are greeted like friends. In the distance, I can hear the sounds of construction as a new building is being raised. I wander closer, admiring the craftsmanship. Already, carvings on the outside take shape, depicting scenes from the Holy Text. It looks like a new temple to The Eternal, and a magnificent one at that.

"What do you think?" Gareth asks, smiling at my wide-eyed expression.

"It is not what I expected," I admit. "I expected hardened people, having fought for so long, but there is so much joy in the air."

"That's because we are in Locura. The new king is a champion of the people. The merchants love him now that trade is opening, and I've heard that his council now consists of guilds instead of nobility. You are going to find a lot of people who love him here," he says, glancing down at me. There is something in his eye that tells me there is more to what he is saying.

"But not everyone?"

"I think you will find that once we get to the capital, things will feel a little different. The remaining nobility and religious leaders... It's complicated." His voice is quiet as his eyes follow a pair of soldiers in Alberonian green uniforms as they pass by us. "We should probably wait to talk more about this later."

"But—" I start to protest as he turns me back toward the inn. "If you would just—" I try again, but he shakes his head, not looking at me. He has said as much as he plans to. I scowl as I stomp along next to him. No one will tell me anything.

Smirking, he slings an arm around my shoulders. "I promise you will know everything you need to soon."

"I'm so glad my frustration brings you amusement," I say, shrugging off his arm and walking ahead of him. I can hear his sigh behind me, but he lets me stay ahead of him as we walk.

I pout all the way back to the inn. It's childish, but I have the feeling I am about to walk into a complicated situation. I don't want to walk in blind and mess it up, but I can't do anything about it if I don't have all the information available.

"I was wondering when you were going to show up," Rupert says as we walk into the private dining room. Coraline and her brother are there as well. Rupert invites Gareth to join us, and we take our seats. The room is quiet, the only sound the clanking of silverware as we serve ourselves food. I can feel the tension in the room, and I just know they were talking about information that I need to know.

"Careful, brood like that too long and I might be tempted to write a ballad about you," Garth says, startling me out of my thoughts. "There once was a fair maiden who needed a nap... or maybe a snack?" he says, getting a giggle out of Coraline and a little smile out of me. Rupert rolls his eyes, and he continues. "She was looking for her boyfriend, who got caught in a trap. She yawned and she muttered, 'He best not have died,' then flopped on a log with a very loud sigh..."

"Gareth!" I say to everyone's laughter.

"Ya missed your calling, lad," Rupert chuckles, but I just scowl.

"That is not funny. What if Aiden really is caught in a trap or dead? I wouldn't know because none of you will tell me anything!" I say, getting up and shoving my chair away from the table. I've lost my appetite.

"Sit back down," Gareth says, grabbing my arm before I can get too far.

"No! I just want to know what is going on. We will be arriving tomorrow, and you are keeping information from me. I want to know, so I don't make a mistake." I say, looking around the table and finally meeting the prince's eyes. I know he is the one withholding the information.

Coraline looks at her brother, shifting uncomfortably in her chair. Rupert clears his throat and takes another bite of food. Gareth's fingers tighten on my arm as he looks between me and the prince. My heart beats faster, but I don't take my eyes off the prince. The air feels heavy, and I hold my breath. I can see the muscles tighten in his jaw, and I know that whatever information they have kept from me is big.

I'm not sure I can keep up our stare down much longer, but the prince breaks first, turning to look at Coraline. "It's your call. You are in charge from here on out." His voice is soft, but it feels loud in the quiet room.

"Only because you finally told me all the information," she says, arching her brow as she looks at her brother, lips pressed into a line. His eyes soften as he looks at her, and she sighs, turning to me. "I think we should start from the beginning," Coraline says, and I slowly sit back down in my chair. Coraline looks at Rupert, and with a nod, he begins.

"Alright, from the beginning then. To fully understand, I feel like we'd best start at the end of the civil war here in Alberon. For many years, the war went nowhere. The rebels never had a chance against the monarchy. They were scattered in camps, barely surviving. Aiden was born in one of those camps." I nod my head as I follow along. None of this is new information, but if Rupert says it is important, I will not interrupt.

"Aiden's mother, like many, decided to seek a better life in Ileria. She took Aiden and left his half brother behind with his father, a leader in the rebel band. When his father died, David rose in the ranks quickly. He had a vision or something and declared he was called to unite the people and replace the wicked king. He banded the people together and succeeded in taking over the monarchy."

Goosebumps start to cover my body as he speaks, and I slowly shake my head in disbelief. *Aiden's brother is the king?* I open my mouth several times to ask a question, but nothing comes out, and I close it. I look around the room, and everyone is watching me. None of them seem to be experiencing the same confusion I am. *They all knew,* I realize, and my confusion turns to anger.

"How long have you known?" I stand scowling at Rupert, not able to hold still anymore.

"I've suspected ever since the new king was crowned," Rupert says calmly, meeting my eye. "Aiden had been restless and kept asking when we would be going into Alberon. I had heard enough of his story over campfires to start piecing things together."

"I just assumed he wanted information on his brother," I say, looking away. There is pressure in my throat and a heat in my cheeks that tells me tears are not far off. I can't believe I didn't ask more about his thoughts and feelings after word arrived that the war was over. I was selfish though, more anxious that he was going to leave me than wondering why he was on edge.

"I didn't know for sure until we got to Alberon," Rupert continues. "There was a ship already waiting for him when we got here to take him to the capital."

"He left with hardly a goodbye," Gareth says, jumping in, and I see the flash of hurt in his eyes. "It was hardly even a day, though, until we heard the rumors about the king's brother. He had been spirited away by his mother against his father's wishes and only now had the ability to return."

"Oh..." I say, sinking back down into my seat. It is Aiden's story.

"We never heard his name, so we didn't have confirmation it was him until now. Our informants reported that the king has proclaimed his brother as Prince Aiden, and he has been taking over some duties of overseeing the reconstruction of the cities," Rupert says, folding his arms in front of him.

"Why didn't you tell me?" I ask again softly, looking between Gareth and Rupert.

"I didn't know how to tell you," Gareth says before looking to the prince. *And then the prince ordered you not to.* My eyes go to his, but I can't read any emotion in them. Does he feel sorry for keeping this information from me? *No*, I decide. *He was just doing his duty.*

"Now that you know, what are you going to do with the information?" the prince asks, his hands folded in front of him like he is holding a council meeting. I open my mouth, ready to give him a sassy remark, but then the question really sinks in. I was so mad about the information being withheld that I haven't considered what that means for me and Aiden.

Aiden is a prince. Can I marry a prince? Prince Jude waits patiently for my response, but I don't have one. I don't know what I'm going to do.

"What do you want me to do with the information?" I say carefully, looking at the prince. He remains silent, and it is a hesitant Coraline who answers me.

"I'm sorry, Aloura, but you just became an important player in whatever political game we are about to enter."

I nod slowly, still trying to process. I am engaged to a prince. *Am I engaged to a prince?* I wonder. This is the whole reason I wanted to come find Aiden, although now I glance towards Rupert and see the guilt in his face. He knew that I could be useful, and it hurt a little that he would use me like this. I can feel the flush on my cheeks. I've been a fool.

"What do you expect of me?" I ask, feeling drained. I need alone time to process all this, but I need to get through this meeting first. Coraline glances at me, her brow furrowed, but her brother prompts her to continue.

"When we arrive at the palace, we will be seeing Aiden, and he will be happy to see you," she says, smiling a little too brightly. I can't return it. I fear that he won't be happy to see me, and now our reunion will be public. I don't know if I could survive if he chooses to reject me.

"We are hoping that you will be a source of information for us," Coraline says, coming closer and taking a chair by mine, grabbing my hand. "We are hoping that the king has taken Aiden into his confidence." Her face is pleasant and full of hope, which contrasts with the growing unease in my stomach.

"And if we resume our relationship, he might tell me those confidences," I state. They want me to spy on him, to trick him into sharing his secrets.

Maybe sensing my reluctance, Coraline backtracks a bit. "Or at least invite you to situations where you could gather information we couldn't. Even being close to him can help."

"And you think that will work?" I ask, pulling my hand out of hers and standing up. I fold my arms and move away, pretending to look at a picture on the wall. Who even knows if Aiden will welcome me? The seed of doubt has been planted, and it's hard to move past it.

"You have a presence about you that makes you easy to trust," the prince says, drawing my attention. "It would not be hard for someone who already cares for you to share more with you if you probe." I scowl at him. How dare he, and just when I was hoping we had become friends.

"I won't lie to him," I snap. "I won't trick him. If Aiden welcomes me as his fiancée, I will not betray him like that," I say, looking at Rupert and Gareth. They know Aiden. They are his friends. How could they ask this of me?

"Until we understand what the situation at the palace is, we need any help we can get," the prince says, staring me down. I refuse to turn away. "King David is more dangerous than you realize, and we need to know his plans."

"Why is he so dangerous?" I ask. "All I've heard is how good he is. He ended the war, opened trade, and is healing his people. I don't think any of that is bad."

"His people think he is a saint because he claims to be a saint," the prince says, looking at me disapprovingly, and I look away. Why does that look make me feel so guilty? I have done nothing wrong.

Coraline speaks up again, gentler in her demeanor, and I realize why she is the one in charge of this mission. "He claims to have won the crown through being blessed by The Eternal. He is claiming divine rule through his lineage," she says softly. "He claims to be a descendant of the Coati line."

"Oh," I manage to say. That is a pretty big claim. A descendant of the family blessed by The Eternal to rule the whole continent. I vaguely remember my cousin mentioning that weeks ago.

"Listen," the prince says, interrupting my thoughts again. "We are not asking you to do anything that goes against your moral code. We can take it one step at a time. If you can at least help us gauge Aiden's loyalties, that will help us."

I slowly nod. The request isn't unreasonable, and I am ready for this conversation to be over. I hear the heavy tread of boots approach and know it is Rupert before his large hand lands on my shoulder.

"Come, lass. You need your rest," he says, helping me up and turning me toward the door.

I let him lead me, but I can't help but ask, "Do you think he has turned on us?"

"Aiden loves his brother, but he loves you too. No matter what happens tomorrow, I'm sure that boy will welcome you with open arms. At least if he has any sense in that pretty head of his." I laugh lightly at his attempt to cheer me up. I should have known he would see through my question. "I worry about him too, you know," Rupert says suddenly, more serious. "It will be good to see him tomorrow."

Tomorrow, I think to myself as I prepare for bed. Tomorrow, I will know the truth, if our love is as strong as I thought it was, or if he will cast me off now that he has everything he ever wanted.

Chapter 18

Today, I am going to see Aiden. I wasn't able to sleep with that thought running through my mind all night. I tried to focus on that and not all the other information battling for space in my brain. Not able to rest any longer, I get up and run through the exercises Rupert taught me. The movement helps calm my anxiety a little. I dress and head down to breakfast in the dining room. I am not the only one awake early. Surprisingly, I find Coraline and Gareth sitting together in conversation. While the two are not close, they have become friends as Gareth has assigned himself as my personal bodyguard.

I approach the pair warily. They lean towards each other, talking in rapid whispers. Coraline practically bounces in her seat. They look like they are up to trouble, and with the way their eyes light up when they see me, I have a feeling I'm not going to like what they have to say.

"We've had an idea," Coraline announces as I sit down beside them. "I do not doubt that Aiden will be thrilled to see you, but we think it might be best not to have you approach the palace looking like a servant. You are basically my companion anyway, so we need you to look like one."

"Not that he wouldn't be over the moon to see you," Gareth rushes in to say, "but it might help others see you as someone with status as well and make it easier to transition into his new circles."

A slow smile forms on my face as I take in her words. "That's actually a pretty good idea," I say. I didn't even realize how much it helps to be able to come to him feeling worthy of his new status instead of the little peasant girl left behind. "Oh, but how am I supposed to dress the part? I have no money to spend on a fine gown."

"Don't worry about it," Coraline says with a wave of her hand, like that can brush off my concern. "You will need more than one. Let's see, you will need day dresses, dinner dresses, probably a ball gown, and we can't forget accessories!" My anxiety is back.

"I'm sure we can get a few commissioned at the palace, but it would look strange for you to show up as my companion with only your one bag," she says. I can feel the flush come over my face at her words. She is not being mean, but the difference in our circumstances is significant. "Don't worry about it. We can do a crash course on your responsibilities on the boat. It won't be much different from what you are doing now," she says, but it's not as reassuring as she thinks.

"And my wardrobe?" I ask.

"Job provided," she says, and I reluctantly nod. It's not like I really have any other choice.

"Well then," Gareth says, rubbing his hands together like he just can't wait to get started on this shopping spree, "let's eat. We have a lot to get done before we get on the boat."

We eat quickly and rush out the door to spend the morning shopping. While searching through endless dresses and scarves, I quickly learned something I already knew: I have no sense of fashion. Surprisingly, Gareth does. He and Coraline find me a few dresses and accessories to help me pass as a princess's companion. In short order, we are gathered on the boat with a cabin full of new purchases.

The boat ride across the lake will only take a couple of hours, but I don't feel like that is nearly enough time to understand all the things that I need to fit in.

"I'm so glad the dresses fit," Coraline says, walking around me to make sure that everything is in order.

I blush and smooth my hands down my new dress, smiling a little at the fine fabric. It is a wonderful blue color that reminds me of the ocean back home on a sunny day. I haven't gotten a chance to look at myself in a mirror, but I have to admit, I feel more confident about meeting Aiden dressed in this finery.

"Thank you," I say, taking Coraline's hands as she comes back in front of me. "I know Gareth says that Aiden will be excited to see me, but so many things have changed. This just helps me feel like I have a better chance of a good outcome."

Coraline watches me for a moment before she pulls me into a hug. "I have to admit that I don't understand this kind of love, but I am grateful that it has brought me you." She pulls back, looking into my eyes. "Court doesn't allow for any true friends, and while Jude and Marina are wonderful siblings, they have always had each other. I haven't had many chances for a true friend. I know that I can trust you."

I clear my throat past the emotion. It would be silly to cry, but apart from Lana, I haven't had many girlfriends either. And now I have a princess. I laugh at the absurdity of the situation.

"Now let's fix your hair," she says, moving me to a chair. "It will be pretty simple, but my sister and I would sometimes help each other, so I can do something." She quickly unbraids my hair and runs a brush through it. I close my eyes and enjoy the feeling. I can't remember the last time someone brushed my hair for me. Soon she rebraids it, looping it around my head to form a braided crown. She pins it in place and steps back, looking at it. "That should do," she says with a nod before pulling me up. "Just wait, pretty soon you will get used to having people wait on you." She giggles as she pulls me out on deck.

"Oh, I don't think I will ever get used to this." The wind tugs at my newly braided hair, loosening a few strands. The view is amazing, jungle to one side and water as far as the eye can see on the other. I have never seen a lake so big.

"You'll have to get used to it; you are now part of the gentry," the prince says, coming up behind us. His eyes quickly take me in. I blush, but his face doesn't show whether he approves or not.

"No, I'm not, and everyone will know it because even if I look the part, I have no idea how to act," I respond, voicing my next worry.

"Don't worry too much," Coraline says, drawing my attention away from her brother. "Just be yourself," she says, smiling at me, but at my dismayed expression, she continues. "Just do what I do. Watch me, and you should be fine. If it helps, we can walk through a few things you should know. We have the time." She looks around and pulls a box over to sit down on. The prince remains standing, turning to rest his arms on the side of the ship. I expected him to wander away, but he stays, listening to my lesson.

"When we arrive, you will stand behind me. When we reach the king, keep your head bowed and make sure to give a deep curtsy like so." Coraline stands and gives an effortless dip of her knees, holding her skirt out to the sides. "Rise when he tells you to do so." She doesn't even give me a moment to practice before launching into the next thing.

"When we eat, you will probably be seated down the table from me, but as my companion, you will be invited to dinner. You will just have to wait to see what fork or spoon your companions take. I'm afraid we don't have the time or the means to go over all the etiquette for dining. And oh, the dances. We should practice one or two, just in case." I can see her start to get flustered as she takes in all the information I need to be taught.

My head starts spinning from just hearing the information. There is no way that I am going to be able to learn all this. I will make a fool of myself. "Oh, I make a terrible partner," Coraline mumbles to herself, obviously taking this job seriously.

"Coraline," the prince says, drawing her attention. "You are overwhelming her. We have time to work on some of these later," he says, turning to address me. "Why don't you start with the curtsy, since that is the first thing you will need. Coraline, will you demonstrate again?" he asks, taking command of my training. It's almost like he can't help it.

The princess shows me the curtsy again, and I stand, ready to try. It is more complicated than it looks. I slide one foot behind the other, grabbing the sides of my skirt and bowing my head before bending my knees. Of course, at that moment, the boat decides to dip, and I tumble out of my curtsy into the arms of the prince.

"Try again," he says, gently setting me on my feet as my cheeks burn with a blush. After a couple of tries, I successfully complete a curtsy to the royal siblings' satisfaction. "I think that is enough for now," the prince says before his sister can force any more lessons on me. I send him a grateful smile before excusing myself. I need a moment to breathe.

I walk to the bow of the boat, leaning against the railing. The lake is beautiful. If I close my eyes, I can almost pretend I am back home, walking by the ocean. I feel calm as I smell the salt in the air and the gentle breeze. In a situation so full of uncertainty, this familiarity centers me. Warmth and peace fill my heart as I take a deep breath.

Boots on the wood alert me to a companion, and it doesn't surprise me when the prince leans against the rail. I wait for him to speak, but he lets the silence stay between us. I want to enjoy it, but expectation sits in the air, and after a moment, I feel like I need to say something.

"Thank you for your help, Your Highness," I say.

"I feel like we can stop with the 'Your Highnesses' now," he says, turning toward me with his arms crossed as he leans against the railing.

"Prince Jude, then," I say awkwardly, not feeling ready to drop his title like I do with Coraline. He lets out the briefest chuckle. "My discomfort amuses you."

"Maybe a little," he responds with a gentle smile, surprising one out of me as well. I quickly turn back to the lake, keeping my eyes pointed towards the water, not sure how to respond. I can feel his eyes staring at me, but I refuse to look.

"I'm worried about you." His words startle me, bringing my eyes back to him.

"Why?" I ask. I am worried as well, but I have no idea why the prince would worry about a nobody like me.

"I might be overstepping my bounds with this, but I'm worried that you are not ready for the political game that you are about to get pulled into."

"Is this genuine concern for me or a worry that this pawn will put the safety of your country at risk?" I ask, my tone coming out a little sharp. I hate that he is right. I've tried not to think about it, but this is now bigger than just solidifying Aiden's and my future. "I understand what's at stake here," I say when he doesn't respond to my question.

"I don't think you do," he says. I glance over, and it's like his face has gone carefully blank, like he is trying to keep his emotions from me. He's good at it, and I hate it. I turn to go, but he catches my arm, keeping me there. "It would be a lie to say that all my decisions carry the weight of my title, but I genuinely want to know that you will be okay. I will not force you to do more than you are able. That would be cruel. I may not be one ruled by passion, but I am not cruel."

His words startle me, and I look sharply at him. "I don't think you are cruel, but I can't trust that you have my best interests at heart. You would sacrifice me for the sake of your country."

His lips press together in a tight line as he looks down at me. "I know where my loyalty belongs," he says, and I try to pull out of his grasp, but he tightens his grip, keeping me there. "You are about to enter a highly emotional situation where you have a high stake in the game. I worry that you are going to be tested in ways that you can't anticipate. You need to decide where your loyalty is, or you are going to be torn apart."

I glance over my shoulder at the water, trying to find calm as his words wash over me. Instead, they bring waves of dread. "Thank you for your thoughts, Your Highness," I finally say, dismissing him. I'm relieved when he complies and walks away, leaving me alone again to deal with my rising panic.

Chapter 19

Coraline was surprisingly adept at fitting my new clothes. We had to pin the hems up a little since I am short. With my hair pinned up, though, I look the part of a lady. "You look lovely," the princess assures me, patting my hand and looking out the window. A carriage met us at the docks when we arrived to take us to the palace.

I try my best not to fidget, but it's hard to keep my mind off my nerves. I intertwine my fingers in my lap, but my thumbs slowly circle each other as I look out the window. The city is lovely. Aiden had never lived here, but he said that the buildings looked like they were made of gold. With the tan stone they are made from, I can almost picture what it will look like as the sun sets. The palace up ahead is covered with windows that make it sparkle. It is not as tall as Ileria's, but the arches and domes are exotic. Perfect for an oasis city on the edge of the vast desert that covers a good portion of their country.

As we approach, my heart rate speeds up, threatening to beat out of my chest. If Aiden were with me now, he would pull me in close and try to soothe my emotions, probably sharing a joke or two. But he is the reason I am so nervous. I close my eyes and take a deep breath, trying to center myself until the carriage comes to a stop.

I try not to throw up as the door opens and the prince descends from the carriage, followed by Coraline. Before I know it, it is my turn. I take the hand offered to step down, keeping my eyes on my feet as I exit so I don't trip. Even when I am on solid ground, I keep them down. I'm too scared to look and see if he is there.

I expect the hand assisting to let go, but it doesn't right away, instead gently squeezing mine. I sharply look up into the eyes of the prince before looking away again. I can't tell if he is trying to be comforting or remind me of my job, but I'm too anxious to bother to find out.

I fall in line behind Coraline, and we stop at the bottom of a set of stairs that lead to a magnificent set of wooden doors covered in gold patterns. They are open wide enough to allow us a glimpse inside. I notice lots of plants and high arches before my eyes are drawn to the scene in front of us. A large group of courtiers gathers to welcome us, standing before the doors. Their clothing is shiny and colorful, but I can't make out individual faces before I follow Coraline's cue and dip into a curtsy. My knees tremble, but I don't fall. I wonder if Aiden is there and if he will recognize me.

After what feels like an eternity, a loud voice calls out, "Welcome, delegation from Ileria. We are so pleased you made it safely. Rise and join me so that we may get to know each other better."

We rise, and my eyes search the group until they find the king. I can hardly hold in my gasp. For a moment, he looks so much like Aiden that I lean forward, ready to fly into his arms, but there are differences. He is older, shorter, and more hardened. A scar crosses his face from one cheek to the other, and a golden crown sits on his head.

My eyes search the rest of the group, looking for the very man I have traveled all this way for, but he is nowhere to be found. Maybe he looks different now, dressed in finery like me, but as my eyes keep searching, they confirm what the king is announcing. His brother is not there.

"... from a hunting expedition but should be back in time for dinner. Now, let's get you settled, and then we can take a tour of the palace." The king has a smooth voice, not deep, but pleasant. He extends his arm to the princess, and we walk to join him as she takes his arm and leads us into the palace.

The palace is grand, made of tan stone with tall arches and open doorways. Each area we pass is filled with color and exotic plants. Alberon has always been a wealthy country, and it is clear that even though they are recovering from war, they still hold a lot of power. If I were less anxious, I'm sure I would gawk at the architecture and art that we pass, but as it is, I distractedly follow the royal party. I glance at every face we pass, trying to find the familiar handsome face I feel could appear at any moment.

"And here are your rooms," the king says, leading us through a set of doors that contain the guest wing. I look around, surprised we are here already. *How did I miss the whole tour?* "Tomorrow we can take you on a more extensive tour, but I'm sure you are tired from your journey. Rest, and I will send food up for you." The king leaves us to get settled. I watch his retreat. His resemblance to Aiden is eerie, and I want to chase after him. I want to ask him all sorts of questions, but the aura of power that surrounds him holds me back. He is not as approachable as Aiden.

I turn my attention to the room we have entered, and my jaw drops as I take it in. The guest wing we are giving has a common sitting room covered with rugs and couches with pillows and tables everywhere. Two hallways branch off on either side of the common room, housing individual rooms. Right across from the entrance, doors open up into a small courtyard with a fountain in the middle. I wander out and look at the colorful tiles lining the bottom.

"Aloura!" Coraline calls, drawing my attention to her. She beckons me over to one of the hallways. "Come pick your room," she says, pulling my hand. I look behind me to see the men disappearing down the opposite hallway.

"Are we the only ones on this side?" I ask as she peeks inside the first of six rooms in this hallway. It is covered in all shades of red. I scrunch my nose and shake my head. It's too dark for me.

"Yes. My brother and Rupert will stay on the other side with Gareth and a handful of guards. The others will be down in the barracks. Better for gathering intelligence," she says, leading me to another room. This one is done all in light blue. It's magical, and Coraline and I wander inside.

"Do you want this one?" She turns to look at me, but from the way she strokes the bed covering, I can tell she wants this one.

"No, I'll take the next one," I say, wandering out. Luckily, the next one is green. It reminds me of the jungle outside. I touch the silky fabric of the bedcovers and the gauzy feel of the curtains as I look out the window to the courtyard. I turn around and take in the room and feel out of place. *Who am I, pretending I can be a companion to a princess?* I wonder, shaking my head. It's all too much.

In a haze, I change into a new dress after my trunk is brought in. The lid creaks on new hinges as I open it. I pull out a dark-blue creation with off-the-shoulder sleeves that dip down to a triangle at my hands. A maid comes in and styles my hair before going to attend to Coraline. I wander into the communal sitting room, sinking onto a couch. I pull a pillow in front of me, hugging it as I wait for everyone else to get ready.

Rupert and the prince wander out first. "Ya look nice, lass," Rupert says, coming to sit in a chair by me. I give him a small smile but don't respond. My stomach has been a riot of nerves all afternoon, and it is getting worse as we approach dinnertime.

"He will be happy to see ya, lass," Rupert says, correctly interpreting my silence. "I've seen you two together now for years. He will not put you off, although don't be surprised if he doesn't recognize you right away. He isn't expecting you to show up, especially not looking as pretty as that."

"I know. Thank you," I say, but his words do little to relieve my worries.

Coraline sweeps into the room, a vision of blue and silver. Sapphires glitter at her ears and throat and sparkle on her bodice. I glance down at my much simpler dress and smile. Compared to the vision she is, I still look like me, just a touch more elegant. She drifts over to me and settles on the couch beside me. The prince walks over, and I notice we are all wearing the royal colors of Ileria, blue and silver. I'm glad I picked this dress.

"A quick update," the prince announces as he gets closer. "I sent Gareth with a few scouts into the city to see what information we can find about the state of things here in the capital. While everything might seem in order on the outside, I would like to remind you all to still be cautious and keep your eyes and ears open. King David is not someone to underestimate."

We all nod and stand ready to depart for dinner. Coraline turns to me with a friendly smile that I try to return. I worry I am going to be sick.

"Aiden is supposed to be at dinner," she says, looping her arm with mine and guiding me towards the door. "Our goal tonight, besides charming the courtiers, will be to get you to Aiden. It will all work out."

I nod my head again and try to swallow my fears as we follow a servant towards the dining room.

Tonight's dinner is supposed to be a smaller affair; a larger banquet will be held in a day or two, but there are still quite a few people who mingle around a table as long as two carriages. As an untitled guest, my seat is at the opposite end of the table from the King's seat. A perfect place to observe. The room is filled with the quiet buzz of conversation in both Ilerian and Alberonian. I look around for Aiden, but still no sign of him.

"He will probably enter with the king," Rupert reassures me, but when the king enters, he does so alone. We all take our seats, and my eyes focus on the empty one on the left hand of the king. On the other side sits the princess in the place of honor as the official head of our delegation. I try to make polite conversation with the man next to me in a mix of my rusty Alberonian and his sparse Ilerian, but we soon give up. I'm grateful, as my attention is still on the empty seat next to the king.

The food smells incredible: first a savory soup, followed by a spicy dish I don't have a name for, but I only pick at it. My appetite is almost nonexistent, and nerves keep my stomach in turmoil. We are well into the meal when there is a commotion, and a man strides into the room.

"Sorry I'm late," he says, taking a seat in the empty chair. "Ran into some trouble, and then I wanted to make sure I was presentable to our guests." He gives the room a familiar smile. I'm not even sure I'm breathing as I take him in.

He looks the same—unruly golden-brown hair, tan face, and green eyes—but he looks natural in his elegant clothes and confident in his place here. My heart pounds in my chest as I watch him so naturally fit in.

The king smiles at him, but his eyes narrow in a silent reprimand as he affectionately says, "I would like to hear of this trouble later. I had thought you would be more eager to return and talk to the countrymen of your host country these past years."

"Of course I want to meet them, but it's not like this is my only opportunity. We have time to get to know each other." He directs his smile across the table at the princess.

"Yes," the king draws the word out like he has more to say, but has decided to hold it for later. "Well, Princess Coraline, Prince Jude, let me introduce you to my brother, Prince Aiden."

The title hits me again, and I want to crawl under the table and hide before he notices me. This is no longer my Aiden. He is now a prince with a title and a crown, and I am still a carpenter's daughter playing pretend in a pretty dress.

"It is a pleasure to meet you," the princess says. "I do believe you are familiar with some of our companions," she says, indicating first Rupert, who is closer, and then me.

"Rupert!" Aiden exclaims, standing. He starts walking down the table, arms out to welcome his mentor, but they drop to his sides when his eyes snag on me. Our gazes meet, and the breath leaves my lungs.

"Aloura." My name is a whisper on his lips, and I am standing before my mind is even aware that I have moved. In a moment, he is striding around the table toward me, and then I am in his arms, his face buried in my hair.

"Aloura," he breathes, and then his lips are on mine. Tears sprang to my eyes as we fit together like we had never been apart. His lips are hard against mine at first, and my hand fists into his shirt, pulling him close. His arms are firm around me like he is trying to convince himself that I am truly there, but after a moment, his arms loosen, and the kiss softens.

"I can't believe you're here," he says, pulling back as one of his hands slides up my back and into my hair. I want to melt into him and lose myself in his touch, but the moment is lost when he pulls back even more, his hands now sliding down to hold my arms as he takes a step back to truly look at me. "How are you here?" he says as his eyebrows scrunch into a V above those bright-green eyes that are looking at me in total confusion, taking in my clothing. "Why are you here?"

I open my mouth to answer him, holding back a laugh at his adorable confusion, but we are interrupted by a throat clearing down the table. I feel a flush of embarrassment, remembering that our reunion has an audience.

"Aiden, will you please introduce me to your pretty friend?" the king says, indicating for us to join him. I try not to stumble after Aiden as he escorts me up to the king, but all the emotions flooding through me make me dizzy. My eyes dart to the princess as we approach, but she just gives me a tentative smile. The prince has his usual polite, bored expression, and I can't read the look in his eyes. I glance back at the king. His expression looks open and welcoming, but it feels fake to me, though I can't pinpoint why. I just hope he will accept my presence and not cast me off.

"Your Majesty," Aiden starts before his expression becomes softer, more intimate. "David, let me introduce you to Aloura, my best friend and love for many years now. If it were not for her kindness to a scruffy, poor boy, I would not be where I am today."

I blush again, both from pleasure at Aiden's comments and embarrassment at the attention, so I decide to put my practice to use and dip into a deep curtsy.

"Well met, Miss Aloura," the king says, and I stand. "You are most welcome here. I would love to get to know you more." The king stands, and the rest of the table follows.

"It seems we have an unexpected reunion. My brother and I will retire with all of our guests to my study, but the rest of you are welcome to finish out the dinner. Tomorrow night, we will have our official welcome banquet."

The king turns to leave, and Aiden tucks my hand in his elbow as we follow. I glance behind to see my party following us to the king's study. It's a large room covered in bookshelves of dark wood and filled with books and knickknacks. Any wall space is covered with maps. I want to explore, but my attention is quickly drawn to the king, who rounds a large desk and sits down. There are two chairs in front, and Aiden leads me to one before perching on the edge of his brother's desk. Coraline takes the other while Rupert takes up position behind my chair. I look around and find the prince standing by a window, although I don't know if he can see anything out in the dark. I glance at Aiden again, and his casual manner makes me smile. Maybe this won't be so bad.

"So this is Aloura," the king says, and my calm feeling evaporates. "I've heard so much about you." My eyes dart to Aiden, who is smiling at me. At least I know now he hadn't forgotten me.

"I've heard about you too," I say cautiously. I'm not really sure how to talk to the king. He may be Aiden's brother, but there is no doubt that this man is a leader. There is nothing warm and fuzzy about him.

"None of it is true," he says with a cool smile, like he is teasing, but the tone is not quite warm enough for that. "Especially if it came from Aiden." His smile turns affectionate as he looks at his brother. Aiden laughs, and my heart fills with joy to see him so happy, even if I am unsure about the whole situation.

"It is fortunate that you were able to travel with Their Royal Highnesses," the king continues as he looks between me and the princess, who has taken the other seat beside mine. The prince stands behind her with his hands behind his back.

"Yes," I say with a nervous swallow. I don't want to share all my doubts about my love life with the group, so I try to keep my answers minimal. I would love some alone time with Aiden to finally feel like my feet are on solid ground. "It's a long story. Let's just say there was a need, and Rupert thought that I might be a good fit."

"Thank you," Aiden says, standing and moving to the man standing behind my chair. They clasp hands like they are glad to see each other. Aiden has always looked up to Rupert. "I am delighted to see you both, although I would have sent for Aloura once I was more settled," he says, smiling down at me. I smile back, but questions erupt in my mind, and it is difficult to hold them back. Coraline speaks, though, before I can voice any of them.

"We were fortunate to have her with us," she says, smiling politely at me before turning back to the king. It doesn't quite reach her eyes. This must be her version of a political mask. She is still trying to get a feel for our welcome. "We had quite the adventure here, and Aloura has been the best companion, although I'm afraid we have put her in some danger. There was an attempted kidnapping along the way."

"I am so sorry that happened," he says, his brow furrowed and his lips pressed together. "I'm glad you both made it here safely, and I would like to assure you that you will be safe while you are here. Did you find out who tried to kidnap you?" the king inquires. He sounds sincere, but once again, something feels off.

"We are still looking into it," the prince answers calmly, like the information is not urgent.

"If I can be of any assistance, please let me know," the king says, and the prince bows his head in acknowledgment. "Well, I'm sure you are tired from your journey. We will all talk tomorrow, and I look forward to getting to know you more, Miss Aloura," the king says, dismissing us. Aiden stands to escort me out, but his brother stops him. "Come see me before you retire for the night," he says before allowing us to go.

As we walk to our rooms, the prince and princess quietly talk ahead of us while Rupert and Aiden make plans to spar in the morning. When we reach our rooms, everyone else disappears, leaving Aiden and I alone for the first time since we had been reunited.

Aiden takes advantage right away to kiss me, but as much as I want to lose myself in his touch, there are too many unanswered questions.

"Aiden," I say, pulling back and meeting his eyes. "We need to talk," I say, stepping out of his arms. "I'm sure you have questions for me, and I have a few questions myself."

"I do have a few questions," he says, looking down at me and crossing his arms. "The first of which is, why are you here? Don't get me wrong—it is good to see you, but this wasn't the plan." I hate his tone. It makes me feel like I've done something wrong by coming here for him.

"No," I say carefully, but my frustration is rising. "You left me alone in Ileria to plan a wedding and a future that it seems you knew was not going to happen." My voice rises as I talk, and I place my hands on my hips. "I was alone with no reassurance that you would come back, no timeline, and no idea of what you wanted our future to look like. You can't get mad at me for wanting to find you for a little reassurance." I'm pouting now, scowling at a chagrined-looking Aiden. At least he looks a little guilty. "I waited, but I didn't hear a word from you. Why didn't you write to let me know you were okay? Why didn't you tell me?"

"I'm sorry," he says, stepping close, cupping his hands around my elbows, and leaning down to speak into my ear. "You are right. I should have left you with more information. I just wasn't sure of what I was going to find here." I look up into his face, and my anger fades a little.

"Things here are busy, and my showing up has caused a bit of a stir," he continues, and I stare deep into his eyes. They are so full of longing that I want to kiss him, but I also need to hear what he has to say, so I hold back. "I am trying to get myself established, and then I was going to send for you when I knew it was safe."

"Is it not safe?" I ask, wondering what he knows, what he might share, but then feel guilty for even thinking it. I don't want to spy on Aiden.

He hesitates before answering, though, raising my suspicions. "This is a new court, and we are essentially a new country. Things are stabilizing, but there is always risk in something new. But you are safe here. No one will hurt you." I nod my head and let him pull me into a hug, but his words stick in my mind. These are things my group will want to hear. Is that a betrayal of trust, though? "I never want to be parted from you again," he says quietly before kissing me, his lips soft and feeling like home.

"I'm glad you didn't forget me," I whisper against his lips, letting my vulnerability show. He leans back and looks down at me, alarmed.

"Forget you? Never, Aloura. You are mine, and I have never forgotten." He pauses a moment before saying the next part. "I did write a letter. It wasn't right away, but you probably passed it on your journey here. It didn't explain everything, but it did tell you that I was okay and to be ready because I was going to come for you." I kiss him again, delighted that he was planning to send for me, until he finally pulls back and rests his forehead against mine.

"I must go and talk to my brother, but we will see each other tomorrow. Maybe after breakfast we will go into town and we will spend the whole day together. Or have a picnic lunch, just the two of us." He smiles down at me before kissing my forehead and letting me go. "Good night, my love."

I quietly enter my room, not surprised to find Coraline still up and waiting for me. "Well, I take it the reunion went well," she teases, and I give her a shy smile. I'm sure I look thoroughly kissed. "I can see why you were determined to cross the country to find him."

I clear my throat and search my mind for another topic. "He did say that things are not as stable as they look here," I say, before silently cringing. *Maybe not the safest topic*, I think, remembering the prince's request that I spy for him. *It's not like this is secret information, though* I reason, trying not to feel like I've already betrayed Aiden.

"We assumed as much with a new court," she says, easing my guilt a little. "Everyone is trying to find favor with the new king, and I'm sure there are a few unhappy with the choice who thought they should wear the crown even if he is blessed. We will just have to keep our eyes and ears open, like my brother said." She stands up and stretches her arms over her head. "I think tomorrow will give us some excellent opportunities," she continues. "I'm sure there will be activities, and I doubt Aiden will leave your side for long," she teases again as she walks toward her room, but then stops and faces me with a serious look on her face.

"I know we are asking a lot, but please find out where Aiden's loyalties lie. Jude is sure he is up to something. Nothing in his words or actions seemed wrong, but something about him didn't sit right. His actions and words felt practiced, and if the court has taught me anything, it is to spot when people are being insincere. If Aiden knows anything and is willing to share, it will help greatly, but if he is loyal to his brother, we don't want to tip him off to any of our suspicions."

With that, she bids me good night. I sit for a moment before getting up to enter my room and prepare for bed. A maid is waiting to help me out of my dress and into a nightgown. I dismiss her before unpinning my hair and slipping into the softest bed I have ever been in. I settle down into the pillows, but I still can't sleep. My mind replays the events of the day, and my gut twists as I think about what I have to do tomorrow. I love Aiden and will not betray him, but something keeps telling me that his brother is more dangerous than he appears to be.

My mind wanders to my family, and I think of my father. What would he tell me to do? I close my eyes and reach out to The Eternal. "If you're there, and if you're listening, please help me use my gift that you apparently gave me to know what to do. I feel that if there were a time I needed guidance, it would be now." After some tossing and turning, I slip into a dreamless sleep.

Chapter 20

I wake up to a knock on the door. Light already streams through the window. I can't remember the last time I slept so late. A maid walks in carrying a beautiful green gown as lavish as the princess's creations.

"A gift from Prince Aiden," she says as she lays it out. It is the same shade of green as his eyes and matches the rug on the floor of my room. The maid helps me bathe and dress before plaiting my hair into an elaborate style. It feels good to have the dust of the road washed off me, but the clothes feel foreign, leaving me uncomfortable despite the smooth fabric. I wander out of my room to the common area to find that someone has delivered breakfast. I am the last to arrive.

"Aloura!" Gareth says, spotting me. "Did you see him?"

"Yes, it was quite the shock last night, but it turned out well," I say, as I wander over to a side table spread out with food. I take a plate from the end of the table and place a few exotic fruits and pastries on it.

"We sparred this morning. He had a few strong words for me for letting you come, and a few bruises too," he says, rubbing his arm. "But I do think he is glad to have you here. He said that the court is full of power-hungry people who are trying to get as close to the crown as they can. I think he needs some genuine friends." He snags a round orange fruit before wandering over to a chair to peel it.

I nibble on some sweet pink fruit from my plate as I think of his words. I knew I needed to be here, and Gareth's words confirm I made the right choice. Aiden needs us as he adjusts to this crazy new life, and I plan on staying by his side. He can count on me, and I will make sure he knows it.

"An itinerary has arrived for today," Coraline says, patting the seat next to her. "It seems that we are to take a tour of the city." She holds a piece of parchment and looks at it with a frown.

"What's wrong?" the prince says, walking over and taking the paper from her without waiting for a response.

"I was hoping for a meeting with the king today," she says, disappointed. I feel like I'm eavesdropping on a private moment and get up to leave the siblings to talk, but the prince passes the parchment to me. Surprised, I set down my food and take the paper. I glance down at the paper and read. Aiden will be our guide in the city, and in the evening, the king has requested a private dinner with me and his brother. It looks like the welcome feast is postponed until tomorrow. I look up to find both royal siblings looking at me. "Oh dear," I squeak out. I'm not ready for this, but I know I won't have a choice. Not that the siblings would force me to go, but I can't disappoint Aiden.

"You will be fine," Coraline says, sensing my distress. "From what I saw last night, Aiden is head over heels for you. He will make sure you are okay." She takes my hand, pulling me back down onto the couch beside her.

"I know, I just... Aiden thinks so highly of his brother, but he is the king, and he puts you guys on edge, which puts me on edge. This is going to be a mess." I ramble, getting up to walk to a window. The view overlooks a lower garden, and I want to run down and explore, forget my worries, get lost.

"I acknowledge that this puts you in a difficult situation," the prince says, "but I encourage you to think about what service you could do to your country if you decide to take advantage of this situation. Any information you can share would put us in your debt."

His words sound stiff, like he is talking to a stranger, and I frown. I don't want the crown to be in debt to me. I want to say no. This reunion is supposed to be personal, not a reconnaissance mission, but with Coraline looking at me with such sympathy and Rupert and Gareth with understanding, it is hard to deny the request.

"I will think about it," I say before excusing myself. I need a moment to think, but I don't get one as a knock sounds on the door. It opens to admit a smiling Aiden dressed in his new role as a prince.

"Hello, my friends!" he says, walking into the room and straight to my side. "Are you ready to see the capital?" He leads us out of the palace to waiting open-top carriages.

Aiden's commentary is lively as he points to interesting sites. It is clear he knows the city well as he talks about some efforts going on to recover from the war. He almost seems like a new person; the weight that always seemed to sit on his shoulders is gone, and a new light shines in his eyes.

"Over there, we are building a new temple that will be plated in gold," he says as we pass a construction site. "We have been recruiting refugees to help build on the promise of fair pay. We need many people, including artists. They are going to make a statue of my brother and put it out front, also made of gold."

"Out front of the temple?" I ask, surprised. I am sitting next to him, facing backward, with the prince and princess across from us. Gareth and Rupert follow behind in a separate carriage.

"Yes. He says it's too much, the people's trust in him is all he needs, but they like the reminder that he was chosen by The Eternal to fight for them," he says with a shrug. The Aiden I know never put much weight in the teachings of The Eternal, and I wonder if that has changed since we have been apart. I know my faith has.

"Have you become religious in my absence?" I ask, genuinely curious.

"It's a work in progress," he says before he moves on, pointing to the next site. This is a conversation we will have to revisit. The city folk stop and stare as we pass, occasionally waving. A little girl looks up in awe, and I hesitantly wave down at her as we pass. I feel like a princess.

When he isn't pointing out a new site, Aiden has his arm around me or leans in to give me little kisses when the others aren't looking. I want to enjoy it, but every time I make eye contact with the siblings, it's awkward. I've never had a problem with public displays of affection before, but in front of the prince, it feels weird.

"Why don't we stop by the market?" Aiden says, directing our driver to pull over. "Go explore," he encourages the siblings. "We will meet here at the next bells," he says, looking up at a nearby clock tower. "That gives us about an hour, and then we head back to the palace."

Everyone disperses, and he takes my hand, leading me among the stalls. I admire the beautiful craftsmanship of several of the stalls, and Aiden insists on buying me something. "Let me spoil you," he says. He is so eager to shower me with gifts that I can't tell him no. We stop at almost every shop, and pretty soon my arms are full of gifts. I have a wooden flower pin in my hair, a scarf draped over my shoulders, and a new bracelet on my wrist.

"However will I get all this home?" I laugh after he tries to buy me a large vase with pretty white flowers painted on it. Instead of joining me, though, Aiden's face is serious. He pulls me out of the flow of traffic into a quiet side street. All of a sudden, I'm nervous.

"Aloura, I can't leave," he says, looking down at our entwined hands, and I realize this is it—the talk I have been waiting for. "I just found my brother, and it's not like he can leave," he says with a little humorous smirk, but this is not a funny conversation.

He takes a deep breath and continues, "I'm a prince now. I have responsibilities, and until David is married, I'm technically his heir." My mind whirls, processing the information, but he is not done. "We are doing so much good here," he says excitedly, pleading with me to understand. "We are fixing so many problems that the old monarchy had. My people finally have a voice, and I get to be a part of it. So you see, I can't leave."

"But what does that mean for us?" I ask, "Before you left, you asked me to marry you, to plan a wedding for when you returned... But you're not coming back, Aiden, so are we still engaged?" My heart is pounding. Was all of this for nothing?

No, I tell myself. Whatever his next answer is, I need to be here to hear it so I can move forward with my life, whether with Aiden or without him. I fortify myself as I wait for his answer.

"I always planned on returning," he says earnestly, placing a hand on my cheek. I lean into it, relieved at his words. "I would have come back to you. We could have married in Ileria if you wanted, and then I would have brought you here, to Alberon, to be with me. I don't want to be parted from you."

"What?" I ask, surprised, but I should have seen this coming. I've always planned on being by Aiden's side forever. If he couldn't remain in Ileria, I would have chosen to go with him. "But what about my father?" I ask, overwhelmed by the sudden direction my life seems to be heading.

"Well, we will bring him here. He won't have to work again. I will take care of you, both of you." His eyes are wide, pleading with me to say yes, to confirm that this is a great idea, but I can't answer yet. After a moment of silence, he pulls me close. "I know this is a lot. We were just reunited yesterday, but it's always been you, my love. You don't have to make a decision right now, but know that I am going to ask you again, and it would make me very happy if you say yes."

He leans forward and presses a kiss to my stunned lips before leading me back into the square. "Come on," he says, looping his arm around my side and squeezing it, "let's just enjoy the day and the fact that we are together."

"Okay," I respond, but my mind is now in crisis mode. Aiden wants me to stay. He wants to marry me and bring my father here, and we will live in a palace, happily ever after. It's a dream, a fantasy I never thought could come true, but here it is.

The only problem is, something in my gut tells me not to trust his brother. Could I live here if there is something nefarious going on? Could I turn a blind eye if I found out something I shouldn't, if it meant being with Aiden? *We don't even know if there is something to worry about*, I tell myself as we make our way over to a little cafe for a cup of chocolate, but my gut is telling me that all is not right.

Aiden leads me to a table and goes to the counter to fetch our drinks. It's not cold outside, but I'm told that the drink is worth it even if it is warm. My mind circles through my concerns as I stare out at the street, not truly seeing until an odd moment catches my eye. I look closer and realize I'm looking at John. We make eye contact for a moment, and then he is gone.

I stand up abruptly as Aiden comes back with our drinks. "Aloura, what's wrong?" he says, setting down the cups and touching my elbow.

"I thought I saw… I thought I saw John," I say, looking around the market, but he is probably already gone.

"John?" he asks, brow furrowed, "But that's impossible. He is in an Ilerian prison."

He's looking at me concerned, like the heat has gone to my head. I scowl at him before spitting out the next words. "He escaped and has been tracking us. He was involved in the attempted kidnapping."

"That is concerning," he says, but it seems like he is not quite taking this as seriously as I would like him to.

"If you don't believe me, ask Rupert," I say, fed up with this. I want to do something. I feel like a sitting duck. "I'm ready to leave," I turn toward the carriages, not wanting to wait another moment. Aiden follows me, and within a short amount of time, we are back. Rupert is already there with Coraline.

"I'm fine," she says while fanning herself with a new fan. "I just needed some rest."

"What happened?" I ask as we approach a new spike of fear running through me. Did they run into John or any of his accomplices? Was there another attempted kidnapping?

"I think the heat is getting to Coraline. Ilerian fashion is not suited to the heat of this region," Rupert says, looking sternly at the pouting princess. "I am trying to convince her we should head back early." Relieved that is all, I catch his attention to make sure he hears my next words.

"I saw John." Surprise flashes in his eyes before he goes back on the alert.

"Are you sure?" he says, looking around like John might pop out from anywhere. "Why don't you go with Coraline back to the palace? I will find the prince and Gareth, and we will head back as well."

"Come, Aloura," Aiden says, lifting me into the carriage. "When you return, I would like to speak with you," he says to Rupert, who gives a nod before the carriage rolls away.

Aiden leaves us in our rooms when we arrive back at the palace with a promise to come and walk me to dinner with his brother. I am a complete mess as I wait for news from Rupert.

"I'm not crazy. He was there," I say as I pace the room while Coraline drinks tea.

"I believe you," she says for the hundredth time. I am not fit for conversation right now, but I'm grateful for her company. "Why do you think he is following you?" she asks, and I try to repress the shiver that creeps down my spine at those words.

"I don't know," I say, flinging myself down on a couch in an unladylike fashion. "I keep going over it in my mind, but I just don't get why he would be after me."

"Walk me through it. Maybe I can help you," she says, taking a dainty sip of her tea.

"Fine," I say, sitting up. "I keep going back to that first attack. He was drunk, which is why I think it happened. He never liked me, but he was never prone to violence, just mean comments. Aiden never believed me. It's like he never heard them or ignored them." I frown down at my hands. Did he just ignore them? I have to wonder.

"Aiden and John got along?" Coraline prompts, and I nod my head.

"They were both from Alberon and were refugees from the war."

"I didn't know John was from Alberon," Coraline says, her brow furrowed.

"Yes…" I trail off, thinking about the few weeks before Aiden left after we found out about the opening of the border. "He was very supportive of Alberon's king and spoke highly of him. I remember he once said David is a better king than your father."

"Well, it would make sense that he would make his way to Alberon then, wouldn't it?" she says, setting down her cup, her expression troubled. "Tell me more about the actual attack."

"It was dark, and he was drunk, and he grabbed me." I close my eyes, trying to focus on his words and push down the emotions that came with the attack. "He taunted me, telling me Aiden was going to leave me and never come back." I open my eyes and look at Coraline.

"It sounds like he knew something about Aiden," she says, and I have to agree. We sit quietly until Gareth enters to let us know they are back.

"Rupert, Aiden, and your brother are in a meeting with Aiden to fill him in on our journey, especially the kidnapping," he informs us, coming to sit down by me. "I volunteered to come talk to you and keep watch for now." Coraline offers him a cup of tea, but he shakes his head.

"Why were we not included in this meeting?" she asks, taking her own cup back into her hands. "As the ones who have been most directly affected by this person, we should be there." The princess takes a sip of tea, and I realize her manners are a sort of armor for her. She uses them to hide her true feelings.

"I know it's annoying to not be there, but I'm sure your brother will fill you in as soon as he is back," Gareth says, making himself comfortable. "He was upset about John's attack back in Ileria. It was a real betrayal." He glances over at me. "I'm sure Aiden will do everything in his now-considerable power to keep you safe."

An idea sparks, and I'm hesitant to ask, but after Coraline and my conversation, I can't get it out of my head. "Do you think John is working for the king?" I ask her.

"I don't know, but you said he was loyal to him," Coraline says, her brow furrowed in concentration.

"How would he be working for the Alberonian king? He has been training Ileria's guards for years. He started with Machiavelli just before Aiden and I did," Gareth says, looking confused.

"Yes, but do you remember how much he talked about Alberon and how the new king was going to make it a better place? Maybe..." I pause as another idea comes to me. "Maybe David sent John to look for Aiden."

"And then he watched over him until the time was right to bring him back!" Coraline says, following my line of thought. Warmth fills me, and I know we have solved part of the puzzle, but it fizzles as quickly as a bucket of water with my next thought.

"Do you think Aiden knew?" I ask Gareth, who looks troubled.

"I don't know, but they were always close. Aiden enjoyed talking with him about Alberon and the war. If he did know something, he never mentioned it to me." I want to believe the best of Aiden, but I wonder if I truly knew him. How many secrets has he been keeping? Is this why he never talked about the future with me?

"We need to tell my brother," Coraline says. "I'll inform him and Rupert when they get back from their meeting."

"And I'll talk to Aiden," I say. I have to talk to him. I came all this way so we can figure out our future together, and we can't do that with secrets between us.

"Just be careful, Aloura," Gareth says. He looks hesitant to share his next thoughts. "Aiden loves you, but he idolizes his brother. Just be careful how you ask him. We have no proof that his brother is doing anything against us, and he won't take kindly to wild accusations."

"I know that," I say harshly, irritated. He voices my fears that I didn't want to acknowledge, but he doesn't deserve my anger. "I'm sorry," I say, softer this time. "Please trust me to know what I'm doing." I try to sound more confident than I am, but Gareth's pity shows me I'm not.

"Let's get you ready for dinner," Coraline says, drawing my attention. "I have just the perfect dress for you. When Aiden sees you, he won't be able to keep anything from you!" she says with a wink, leading me into her room, but despite her cheery attitude, I can't shake the cloud of dread settling over me. This dinner has become very complicated.

Chapter 21

My slippers hardly make a noise as I walk around the courtyard, waiting for Aiden to come and escort me to dinner. Rupert and the prince have still not returned, and Coraline has retired to her room after helping me dress. She assured me that she would talk with them, but I would have felt better if I could have seen them. A knock sounds on the door before Aiden enters. Taking a deep breath, I approach him.

"You look beautiful," Aiden says with a brilliant smile, taking my hands. I look down at my new gown, a soft pink dinner dress from Coraline. Tomorrow we have an appointment with the seamstress.

"Thank you," I say, keeping my head down. *Why am I so shy?* I wonder. I glance up at him. He looks different in his princely attire rather than guard leathers. "You look very dashing yourself." He lets go of one of my hands, lifting my chin so I have to meet his eye.

"Thank you," he says, leaning down to give me a soft kiss before tucking my hand into the curve of his elbow. "Shall we go to dinner? David is eager to get to know you." With my nod, he leads me out of our guest wing. We walk in silence the whole way, and it feels strange. With these clothes and this setting, I don't feel like my usual self, and he feels like a stranger. We enter a set of doors with guards on the side who bow their heads as we pass. We walk through a large hallway that branches off in several sections and take one on the right.

We enter through a door into a private dining room. The space is small, with a low table and pillows on the floor. Aiden leads me over to one of them before helping me sit. The room is open on one side, showing a view of the lake, and a moment of homesickness sweeps over me.

"Are you okay?" Aiden asks, sitting next to me, but before I can respond, the king sweeps into the room.

"Make sure we are not disturbed," he says to a servant before walking to the table, plopping down on a pillow, and removing his crown. I have to work to keep my mouth from dropping open at the lack of propriety from this intimidating man. Instead, for the first time, I feel like I'm truly seeing Aiden's brother.

"I hope you don't mind, but tonight is going to be informal," he says, giving me a tired smile before closing his eyes like he could fall asleep at the table. I can see the weight of the kingdom sitting on his shoulders, and a feeling of sympathy moves through me.

"That bad?" Aiden teases, reaching towards the meal placed on the table. "Who knew being king could be so rough?"

The corner of David's mouth lifts in an amused smile before replying with his eyes still closed. "I think that's why I got the job. All the other old guys realized they didn't want to be the ones to do it."

"I thought it was because you were divinely called," I say before biting my lip and waiting for his reaction. I watch as the king slowly opens his eyes, looking at me with amusement.

"Well, that is the true reason, but the other is probably why it was uncontested." He reaches for the food as well now, but I can't eat. My curiosity is piqued.

"You were uncontested?" I ask in complete surprise.

"You haven't told her the story?" the king says, looking surprised at his brother.

"I didn't even know the story until a little while ago," he grumbles a little, and I would laugh if I weren't so intrigued. "Plus, we were only reunited yesterday. We've been a little otherwise occupied." He sends me a wink, and my cheeks flush as the king gives me a knowing look.

"I guess it's up to me then," he says kindly, moving on from his brother's comments and gesturing for me to eat. The meal is full of exotic foods, such as a pink fruit that has an interesting smell and a type of flatbread that I watch as they fill rice and beans into before eating. I hesitantly take a bite as the king starts talking. "Has Aiden told you about our father?" he asks before taking a bite of steaming food.

"Just that he was a rebel leader and... not very nice," I add, the last bit of an afterthought, but that's all I know about him. Aiden always changed the conversation whenever he came up. I glance at him now, but he is eating and staring out the window. I wish I could read his emotions.

"Ha!" the king barks, startling me. "He was a brute, but he had a strong conviction in the cause. In a failing resistance, that was valued." He pauses to take another bite of food before continuing, "The only thing of value he had were family records going back generations. They showed that he came from royalty, a disowned princess, a few generations ago. The rebellion latched onto it because it gave their rebellion validity. Here was someone who could claim to rule."

"Was it true, though?" I ask before finally taking a bite of food. The spicy flavor explodes in my mouth, distracting me from his answer. I take another bite and enjoy the blend of beans with the spiced rice. The bread helps keep the spice from being overwhelming. I look up to find both men staring at me, smiling.

"I knew you would like it," Aiden says, taking another bite of his own food.

Embarrassed, I take a bite of the fruit, recognizing it from breakfast, before repeating my question. "Are you descendants of royalty?"

"The records are in the library. After the takeover, we checked them for validity, and yes, his claim was true, but at that point, it didn't really matter," David says, looking at me as I take another bite. "He was a hothead, but he had a claim to the throne. They gave him responsibility, but he never had any ideas. He was a weak puppet for weak leaders," he says with a sneer on his face.

"What happened?" I ask, leaning forward, enraptured in the story, drawing a smile from the king.

"I think the weight of his incompetence caught up with him. After Mira and Aiden disappeared, he drank heavily. That made him reckless and sloppy. He died during a raid." I look back and forth between the men, but neither one of them shows much emotion from the passing of their father.

"And then you took over." It's a statement.

"Yes. I was old enough and had the same claim to the throne as my father," he says, trailing off, lost in thought for a moment.

"And how did you realize you had The Eternal's blessing to rule?" I ask carefully. I feel nervous for some reason, like the wrong question could set him off.

"Are you religious?" he asks me instead of answering right away.

"Yes?" I say, and he raises an eyebrow. "It's... a developing thing."

"Hmm," he says with a smile before sitting up and leaning closer to me like he is about to share a secret. Nerves flutter in my stomach, but I stay still. "I was not religious at all, but something happened. My first raid after my father had passed away, I was angry. I fought hard, but when anger clouds your judgment, mistakes are inevitable. I made a fatal one. As I lay there bleeding out, I pleaded with The Eternal to see my brother one more time, and if I could, I would follow His direction. My men found me, I survived, and I have sought The Eternal's wisdom ever since. He helped me clear my mind and make plans that succeeded. Soon we were winning."

We eat in silence for a moment. Each of us lost in thought. I don't ask about his battle or how he won, and he doesn't elaborate. His reputation, though, sits in my mind, stories we heard back in Ileria about how brutal and bloody the battles were for the nobility. His goodness and mercy toward the citizens, who were more than happy to support him. The rebellion grew swiftly, and then it was over.

"Now that I am king, I want to continue following The Eternal's will. I want to create a better country that takes care of its people. I think The Eternal helped put me in the best position to do so." He makes it sound so simple, but there has already been so much bloodshed. I watch the king as we finish our meal. My gut tells me there is much more to him than meets the eye.

"You saw some of the amazing things we are doing," Aiden says excitedly as he helps himself to dessert, some sort of moist cake that smells of fruit. His ease makes me want to relax as well, but my mind cannot stop wondering about David's story. Would The Eternal bless his actions even if they required so much sacrifice of life? "With trade up again, the economy is really coming around, and David is working on a way to keep taxes low and a budget on a more efficient way to use that, so it goes directly back to the people," he says. His brother's good work clearly captivates him, but I remain unconvinced.

"Aiden has been invaluable as well with his insights on how to help the homeless population," David says with sadness and pride as he looks at his brother. It's a look that tells me Aiden has shared his hardships with his brother and that he truly does care about Aiden. It's a look that suggests his feelings are similar to mine about Aiden, particularly his strength and resilience. "I have been going on about myself for too long, though," the king says, turning to me. "Tell me about yourself. I want to get to know the woman my brother has been talking nonstop about."

I smile softly at Aiden, who leans over to kiss me. My heart is full to know that he was talking about me. That I was on his mind and not shameful to him because of my inferior status.

"I'm nothing special," I start, not sure what to say. "I grew up in a little town near the capital until my mother died. Then, we moved to the capital to be closer to family and to reduce travel for my father. He owns a carpentry shop, and his work is highly regarded in many wealthy circles. It wasn't long after we moved there that Aiden found me. I was lost, and Aiden helped me find my way home. After that, we adopted him into the family. I know my father loves him like a son."

Aiden's eyes find mine, and he scoots closer, pulling me into his arms. "And I love you both. You were my family when I had none." I can't help but tilt my head to kiss him. He beams down at me after we part. His joy is infectious, and I smile back. "Now we are living a life we couldn't have even imagined. We will marry and live here. I can't wait to bring your father over as well. I want David to meet him," he says, turning to his brother, who gives him an indulgent smile. I also smile, but his words still don't sit right with me. I have yet to agree to his proposal, but he talks as if it is going to happen. I can't bring myself to correct him.

"I think now would be an appropriate time for your gift," David says, giving Aiden a look.

"Of course," Aiden says, kissing me on the cheek before standing. "I'll be right back," he smiles and hurries off, leaving me alone with his brother. I watch him leave as my nerves come back in full force. I avoid looking at David, but he has no such reservations. He reaches out and takes my hand.

"You lied," he says, and my eyes snap to his face in a panic. I meet his face and see the teasing smile on it, but unease sits in my belly as I look at him. "You said you were not special, but it is not just any girl who could catch Aiden's attention. Goodness knows the court girls have been trying, but you captured his heart long ago."

I should smile at his words, but they sting instead. They remind me of how much our situation has changed. We are not simply Aiden and Aloura, but a prince and a nobody.

"I want my brother to be happy, and you make him happy. My marriage will have to be a political one, a fact that I have accepted. But there has never been anyone who has tempted me away from my duty." He is patting my hand now, and I want to pull mine away, but I don't know how to do so without being rude.

"I want you to know that you will be provided for here. You will want for nothing. We will bring your father here, and we will live as a genuine family." I want to believe him, but my instincts are screaming at me that something is not right.

"I haven't said yes yet." It comes out in a whisper, but he hears it anyway, his face losing its smile. His hand squeezes mine, and I wince.

"You will," he says, and it sounds like a threat. "I need Aiden, and Aiden wants you. If you love him, then you will stay here with him. You can help with our work. The Eternal is not done with us yet, and I plan on moving forward to fulfill His vision." His intense look softens, and he loosens his grip again, stroking my hand with his thumb before he lets go.

"You have a soft heart, Aloura. I can tell. You will make a great princess. Trust me; you will find great fulfillment serving The Eternal and his children alongside your prince," he says, standing, and I quickly follow, not liking the feeling of him towering over me.

"If you don't believe me, ask The Eternal. I'm sure He will tell you I'm right. Follow your heart, Aloura," he says before leaving.

I plop back down on the pillows, shaken. *What was that?* I wonder as I look out the window. Another wave of homesickness hits me. I want to go home to my father and to the familiar everyday problems that I am used to. I am not meant to play games with kings and princes.

I suck in a breath and close my eyes, trying to control my emotions. *Please help me*, I plead to The Eternal, but my emotions are still turbulent when Aiden walks back in.

"Aloura! I have…" he says, but trails off when he sees me. "You are not well." He kneels beside me, taking my face in his hands.

"I am tired, is all," I say, trying to bring a smile to my face, but weariness consumes me, and I let it drop.

"I have a present for you," Aiden says, looking down at a little box in his hand, looking torn for a moment before looking back at me. "I think it would be best, though, to let you rest. I will find you tomorrow and give it to you then."

He stands before pulling me to my feet and leading me back to my room. We are quiet as we walk back. He is disappointed, but I can't muster the energy to apologize. With a quick kiss good night, he leaves me alone. I open the door, expecting to see people still up, but it is quiet. I call a maid to help me with my dress before I climb into bed. Despite my troubled heart, the excitement of the day has exhausted me, and I fall asleep quickly.

I wake with one thought—I need to find a quiet place to pray. I rise and dress in one of my new gowns we got in town. Its design is simple and Alberonian, with ties in the front so I can dress myself. The fabric is flowing and soft, perfect for a morning stroll in the hot climate. After combing my hair, I wander out of my room.

I must have slept late because Coraline's room is empty. A note sits next to the breakfast spread, explaining that Coraline has been called away for meetings but promising to find me later. I grab a pastry and debate my options. I don't have any responsibilities now while Coraline is in meetings and Aiden is busy being a prince. *What is my purpose now?* I wonder, brushing off the crumbs that stick to my hands. With nothing else to do, I slip out the door to explore. I don't make it far before Gareth finds me.

"Aloura," he says, matching his stride to mine as we make our way out of the guest wings. "I am to be your guard today while you are out of your rooms," he informs me with a smile.

"I didn't realize I needed a guard in the palace," I say, taking a set of stairs down, looking for the gardens. Outside is calling me.

"We decided it would be best until we can confirm your safety. We have sent scouts to look for John in the city, and Aiden has agreed to send some of his guards as well to look since they know the city better than we do."

I frown at the reminder. After the dinner with the king last night, I had forgotten that I had seen a glimpse of John yesterday. A shiver travels down my spine as I slip out of a wide archway into a courtyard with a fountain and lovely plants, but it is not what I'm looking for.

"We will keep you safe," Gareth assures me, taking my silence as fear.

"I do not doubt that I am well looked after," I say, sparing him a smile before continuing on my search.

"What are you looking for?" he asks, finally catching on to my search.

"The gardens," I say with a frown as we enter another courtyard with fountains and plants, but not a veritable garden.

"This palace is a maze," Gareth says with a laugh before flagging down a servant and asking for directions.

Finally, we arrive at the formal gardens, and I am not disappointed. The air smells like dirt and sunshine, with a smattering of fragrant flowers. The paths are almost overgrown with big green leaves stretched out over them, and brightly colored flowers to give it variety. They are not neatly organized and groomed like in Ileria. These gardens feel wild, like the jungle outside the city walls.

We start wandering down the paths until I hear the trickle of water. I am drawn to the sound as we pass small groups enjoying the gardens. They all give me curious looks, but I don't stop to engage with them. I take a smaller path that looks less used and find myself in a secluded oasis next to the palace wall. A bench sits by a quiet pond fed by a stream that leads farther into the property. A wall of wild bushes surrounds the area, giving it shade and privacy.

"Would you mind giving me a moment alone?" I ask Gareth, who agrees to wait just out of sight at the entrance of the little area. I wander over and sit on the bench, closing my eyes. The birds chirp, and the stream trickles nearby. I breathe deeply, and peace fills my soul. *This is what being in harmony with The Eternal feels like*, I realize. This is not how I felt last night with David.

I am pondering this when Aiden finds me. "I see you found the hidden pond," he says, surprising me with his presence.

"It's enchanting," I say, looking toward the entrance, but there is no sign of Gareth. We are alone.

"It is," he says. I glance over as he walks towards me. His eyes are on me, not the garden, and it sends a thrill down my spine. He sits next to me, drawing me into his arms. "But my favorite thing about it is it's private, which is perfect for my plans," he says, leaning down to kiss me. All thoughts vanish into the background as his mouth dominates mine, taking my breath and making me weak. "Aloura," Aiden says, pulling back and looking into my eyes, "you have been my best friend, companion, and family when I've had none for years now. I never thought I had much to offer you, a broken man with a tangled past and nothing to his name, and you loved me anyway."

Aiden stands, stepping back before kneeling and taking my hand. "But now I can give you the life you deserve. Please make my life complete by agreeing to marry me here in Alberon. Become my princess and rule by my side."

Feelings overwhelm me. This is what I have wanted for years. It is the reason I am here, to see what type of future Aiden wanted with me, but this was not the life I had always imagined. I've never wanted a palace and riches; I've only ever wanted this man.

"I don't know how to be a princess," I say, trying to stall as I sort out my feelings.

"I've never been a prince before, but I'm figuring it out. We can figure it out together," he says, looking into my eyes. "Say yes, Aloura."

"Yes," I whisper, my desire for a life with him finally winning out over my reservations. "You never needed a palace to be enough for me. I just want you."

Aiden stands and sweeps me into his arms, spinning me around and bringing a smile to my lips. He sets me down and kisses me softly. "You have made me the happiest man," he says reverently before reaching for my hand and placing a beautiful emerald ring on my finger.

"David took me to the treasury soon after you arrived and offered me my choice of rings. If you don't like it, we can pick a different one, but I thought you would like the green," he says, peering into my face to see my reaction.

I stare down at the obnoxious-sized jewel without words. It is more than my mind can comprehend. I've never owned anything so expensive. "I love it because you chose it for me," I tell him, because this is the life I have to get used to if I want to keep him. He is no longer just my Aiden. He is a prince, but I would rather take him as a prince than lose him forever. I kiss him again, and we spend the rest of the afternoon lost in each other's embrace. But I can't help the little voice in my head that tells me all is not as it seems.

Chapter 22

"Since everyone is here, let's begin our meeting before we have to get ready for the banquet," the prince says, glancing around the room. This is the first time we've all been together in two days, and we have much to discuss. Gareth has joined us and sits next to me on a couch with Coraline on the other side of me. Rupert stands near the entrance to the courtyard, and the prince stands at attention, facing us.

He looks tired, and I realize we haven't had a conversation since we have gotten here, my time being taken up by Aiden. I don't know when it happened, but at some point, Prince Jude became a friend, and I miss him.

"I talked to some of our scouts today," Rupert begins his report. He has been attending meetings as an advisor to Coraline, but as someone without a title, he has a little more freedom in his free time and has taken control of our security here.

"They have confirmed sightings of John in town. He is keeping a low profile, but they have been able to locate him a few times, coming and going from meetings. If either of you ladies want to leave the palace, please make sure you have some of our men with you," he says, looking at me especially. I nod my consent, but I can't hide my grimace. Once again, John has stolen my sense of safety.

"I think we can safely say he is an errand boy for somebody," Rupert continues, obviously not happy that John has been running about. "We just need to know who and why," he says, and the prince thanks him for his report. Coraline takes my hand, and I smile at her, grateful to have her with me.

"Aloura," the prince says, drawing my attention. "You had dinner with the king and Prince Aiden last night. Is there anything we need to know?" he asks, looking at me and then glancing down at my hand. I've been fiddling with the ring, its weight still foreign to my finger.

"Well, you already knew Aiden and I were engaged," I start, but I can feel the heat rising to my cheeks as everyone's attention is drawn to the ring that I quickly cover with my other hand in my lap. "This afternoon, he asked me again as a prince of Alberon, and I said yes."

The news is met with congratulations from everyone. Coraline gives me a hug, and Rupert and Gareth smile, but I can't keep my eyes from darting to the prince and noticing the troubled look on his face. It passes quickly, smoothing out back into his mask of indifference, but I know it was there.

"Tell us about the dinner," he requests when everyone quiets down.

"It was very informal. We ate in the style of the lower classes, on pillows with a low table. King David told me a little about how he became king. Did you know they have a claim to the royal line?" I ask, not sure what they already know.

"Yes, the king has the records in the library behind a glass case for anyone to see. He took us there on a tour as a break from one of the meetings," Coraline says.

"It's very strategic of him to help keep any doubt of his legitimacy at bay," the prince remarks. The thought had never even occurred to me, and it hits me how far out of my depth I am when it comes to political maneuvering.

"Besides that, nothing significant happened," I say, but that statement doesn't sit right. Nothing truly happened, but when I was left alone with David, something just felt off. I'm not sure how to explain it.

"Are you sure?" the prince asks, and I look up. Our eyes meet, and I know he can see my unease.

"It's just a feeling," I say, not wanting to say anything wrong. "After dinner, I was left alone with the king. He..." I fade off, thinking again about our interaction. "He told me that he wants his brother to be happy and that I make his brother happy. He never said anything threatening, but I felt uneasy. Like if I didn't accept his proposal, the king would have made me."

The room is quiet as I look up from fidgeting with my ring again, each of them with a concerned face.

"I'm sure it was nothing, but it just felt weird. He said that The Eternal still has work for him to do. He wants me to be a part of it, but I don't know. It didn't feel like The Eternal was there with us," I say, looking at my companions again. Rupert and the prince share a look while Coraline grabs my hand.

"We trust your feelings," Coraline says, and a wave of relief hits me. I didn't realize how nervous I was that they would think I was silly. "I have also felt like things are not all what they seem, but there has been no evidence of anything nefarious," she says, looking up at her brother.

"The people all seem happy, but everyone here in the palace has gained power because of him. His court is all new, merchants and the like, who have been rewarded for their efforts in the rebellion. No one will speak out against him."

"Not to mention the people think he is a saint. They are building statues and altars to worship him," Rupert adds. "But he is a man. He doesn't dispute their claims, though, and that worries me. I don't trust him one bit."

"You said he claimed that The Eternal still has work for him?" the prince asks thoughtfully. I give my confirmation as he starts to pace. "He could mean bettering his kingdom, but I feel like it is more than that. We must be diligent and careful as we try to figure this out," he says, looking at each of us.

"Rupert, keep tabs on John. I have a feeling he is more involved in this than we know. Gareth, talk to the soldiers in the morning during sparring. They might let slip some things. Aloura, if you hear anything that could help us, please share. Coraline and I will keep our ears open during treaty and peace meetings to see if we can ascertain any of his plans that might affect us," he says, dismissing us to finish getting ready for dinner.

Everyone splits up, but before the prince can leave, I catch his attention. "I'm not a spy," I say as soon as we step to the side. "I've already told you I won't spy on my fiancé." He gives me an exasperated look.

"I'm not asking you to, but honestly, Aloura, if you heard that Alberon was planning on invading Ileria, would you keep that from us?" he asks, his eyes piercing me.

"No," I say. He is right. I don't want my friends in danger.

"You don't need to spill all his secrets, but if your feelings are telling you that what you learn is wrong and will hurt someone, I trust you will tell us." It's like he can read my soul. His harsh look softens for a moment before he turns to go, leaving me feeling bare.

"Come on, we must get you ready," Coraline calls from the hallway to our rooms. I follow her to her room, where a maid has already laid out some dresses for us to wear. She must have been waiting outside the door. In quick order, I find myself in a borrowed dress. The seamstress had been waiting for me when I came back from the gardens to take my measurements, but new dresses won't be available tonight.

I pick the green one, thinking of Aiden. He always liked me in green. He says it turns my gray eyes green to match his. This one is a lovely sage color with minimal ornamentation, but it has a sheer cape that falls from my shoulders and attaches with a loop to my fingers, making it spread out like wings.

The maid styles my hair in a large braid down my back with some small white flowers scattered throughout it. I look at myself and smile. I feel like a princess. The thought sobers me as I realize I will be a princess. I look down at the emerald on my finger. It's all surreal.

A note arrives from Aiden to meet him down at the banquet, so I walk down with Rupert.

"I'm happy for ya, lass, truly," he says before leaning close and dropping his voice, "But don't forget we are in a foreign place. I know it is Aiden, but I don't trust his brother. Be careful."

I give him a small smile, knowing his words to be wise, but they still make me want to pout. My heart wants to soar with the fairy tale I'm living, and I don't want anyone to bring it down. I am about to get my happily ever after. Still, my head shouts caution, and I know I should listen.

Aiden meets us at the door. "You look incredible," he says, kissing me lightly before looping my arm through his. Rupert slips away into the hall, leaving us alone. "We will wait for my brother and enter just before him," Aiden tells me, pressing another kiss to my head. The door opens again, and I hear the sound from inside. It sounds like a crowd, and nerves flood my belly.

I don't know if I can do this and am ready to beg Aiden to let me slip in ahead of him, but before I can, David walks up with Coraline on his arm, Jude following behind.

"I'm glad we are all here," the king says, smiling when he spots the ring on my finger. "Let us enter."

Aiden and I enter first, followed by Jude and then the king and Coraline. Aiden leads me to the head table, leading us to the right side of the king. Jude and Coraline will sit on his left.

"We are pleased to have Prince Judian and Princess Coraline of Ileria here as our guests. We look forward to creating a stronger bond between our two countries," David says after he takes his place in front of his throne. The prince and Coraline dip their heads in acknowledgment as the crowd cheers.

"We have another guest as well, one that brings me much joy," he says, turning to look at me. My cheeks turn red as all eyes in the hall turn to look at me. Aiden places his hand around my waist to support me, but it just makes it worse as whispers break out. I swear I can feel the glare of the young women in the room.

"As many of you know, my brother, Prince Aiden, lived in Ileria for many years before we finally reunited. When the Ilerian delegation came, they brought a special guest, a woman who is not only friends with the princess but holds my brother's heart." Aiden smiles down at me for a moment before looking back out at the crowd, enjoying their stunned expressions, but I feel faint.

"I am pleased to announce the engagement of Prince Aiden and Aloura of Ileria. Please raise a glass as we wish them happiness as we prepare for the wedding, which will take place in two weeks. The Eternal, as always, desires our happiness, and I know this match will bring great prosperity to the kingdom."

My jaw drops as the crowd roars in approval, drinking to us. I look up at Aiden, who is smiling pleasantly at the crowd, seeming unfazed. He squeezes my side, leaning down to whisper in my ear. "Smile for the people, darling. We will talk about this later." I try to smile, but I know it's strained.

"Did you know that was going to happen?" I inquire of Aiden as we take our seats. The attention has turned to the food for a moment, but I know eyes keep sneaking glances at us.

"No," he says, but he doesn't seem concerned. I don't have a chance to talk to him privately for the rest of the banquet, between congratulations and entertainment. It isn't until he is walking me back to my room that we finally get a real chance to converse.

"I just said yes today," I say as we approach my room, grateful there is no one else in the hallway. "Isn't it too soon?"

"Why? Have we not waited long enough?" he asks me. "Wasn't it you who was pushing to get married just a few months ago?" He smiles down at me as he cages me in against the wall.

"Yes, but everything was so simple then." I look up at him, begging him to understand, but he leans down and kisses my neck instead.

"It's still simple now." His words are a whisper against my skin, eliciting shivers. "I love you," he says between kisses as he makes his way up to my jaw. "And you love me." He pulls back to look into my eyes, and I am mesmerized. "Then why should we wait to get married?" His eyes darken before he takes my lips. I let them distract me from my worries, but they come back too soon, and I break the kiss. If only it were so simple, but we are not nobodies anymore, or at least he isn't. I look up at him and the simple circlet in his barely tamed curls.

"He said The Eternal told him our marriage was good for the king-dom. Do you believe that?" I ask him as he pulls back. His arms drop, and he steps back.

"Does it matter? We want to marry either way. It's late. You should go to bed, and we will talk more tomorrow."

"Okay," I say, needing time to think away from his distractions. I enter my room with a promise to see him tomorrow, my mind spinning with all that has happened. Apparently, I now have a wedding to plan, and I only have two weeks to do it.

Chapter 23

I have concluded that I am not a fan of dress fittings. The seamstress has me up on a chair in a new gown fit for a princess. The dresses are amazing, a variety of rich colors and fabrics, but I would rather be out in the garden or anywhere else.

"Hold still, my lady," she says for the millionth time as I try not to fidget.

She is pinning the hem of my ball gown, the one I will wear for a ball to celebrate Aiden and me. The dark-green bodice fits snug around my curves and then flows out at my hips into a full skirt. The sleeves are little ribbons that fall just off my shoulders. I smooth my hands down the sides as I look at it. The color is an exact match of the royal green of Alberon. The color makes me feel claimed. I am Ilerian, but Alberon is claiming me as one of their own by dressing me in their colors. I wonder if that is why Aiden loves the color so much—because it belongs to his home country.

Coraline and Jude are with David and Aiden, discussing the new terms of a peace treaty between the two countries. I would much rather be in the meeting than here trying on dresses, but this is my current duty: to prepare for my wedding.

"You may step down," the seamstress says, and one of her assistants helps me down and out of the dress and into another new dress that has already been adjusted. "I will be back next week to start fittings for your wedding dress. Any requests before we start to put it together?"

"No," I say, "these gowns are lovely. I trust your judgment." She quickly packs up and leaves, but I can feel her pleasure from my compliment. I wander to the window, sitting on the little cushioned ledge, and look at the dresses a maid is carrying to my room. They truly are lovely. Lana would die of envy to see them. When it comes to my wedding gown, I had always thought I would wear a fixed-up dress of my mother's, but they are all in a chest in Ileria with my father.

I decide to walk around our little courtyard, the movement helping me think. We met as a group this morning before the royal siblings had to leave for meetings to discuss last night. All expressed shock and concern for me. Jude offered to speak to the king today to ask him to postpone the wedding until my father can be fetched, but I don't know if he will change his mind.

It's not that I don't want to marry Aiden. As he said last night, I love him, so why should we wait to get married? But as I thought about it more, it's not that simple. Our marriage is not just between us anymore. It has political ramifications that I don't even understand yet.

And then there is the fact that I miss my father and even Lana and her family. I want them here to witness my wedding, but if it takes place in two weeks, they will miss it. It took us a few weeks to travel here by carriage one way, and I know it's only slightly quicker by boat. There is no way for them to be here with such a short timeline.

I am restless and leave the room to wander the gardens, an Ilerian guard trailing behind me. David offered to have his guards watch us, but we all feel better keeping our men close. I take a new path in the gardens, but my mind is not on the flora and fauna that I pass.

No, my mind is now drawn to the king. The mouthpiece of The Eternal here in Alberon. Something about that just doesn't sit right with me. The peace that I should be feeling about following His will is absent, even though David claims that this is the way.

Frustrated, I turn around to find the hidden oasis I enjoyed yesterday, but I am lost in the vast gardens and have no idea where to find it. I have to wonder why I care. I'm not responsible for either country. I could let myself fall into the bliss of this princess treatment and finally plan my wedding to my love, but nothing feels right.

Determined to figure it out, I head back inside. I need to talk to Coraline or someone who can understand my fears. I ask for directions to the council rooms and find them just before lunch. I hope they will take a break for lunch, and I can catch someone to hear what news they have.

The chamber doors open, and my heart speeds up as Coraline and Jude walk out. Coraline sees me first and smiles, walking over. Jude nods in acknowledgment before moving on without stopping to talk. I frown after him but shake it off when Coraline reaches me. "I didn't expect to see you here," she says, taking my arm as we walk toward the dining hall for lunch.

"I was anxious to hear how the meeting is going, and I finished my fittings for my ball gown. They are starting on my wedding dress next."

She widens her eyes and leans in, talking quietly, "The king insists that the wedding is nonnegotiable. He says The Eternal has plans, and your marriage must go forward. His councillors fully support him, and your prince, Aiden, would marry you today if it were possible," she says, and I blush. Pleasure and a touch of embarrassment flood me with how eager Aiden is to marry me, and I think again of his words and kisses last night. "Plus, how can we argue against The Eternal? We were not given authority over Alberon, so we have no say in how the king wants to run his country." I can tell she is frustrated with whatever was discussed in the meeting. Whatever it is, she shakes it off to give me a sympathetic smile.

"Of course. If The Eternal wills it," I say, thinking of The Eternal. *Is this your will?* I ask him for the hundredth time, but no warmth comes.

"The king wants to give you a tutor so you can start learning more things about Alberon," Coraline says, interrupting my prayer. "He insists you will need to be prepared to serve them as their princess. He has also assigned one of his courtiers to help you plan the wedding." I can't hide my grimace, and Coraline laughs. "You don't want to plan your wedding?" Her head tilts as she smiles at me, and I can feel her genuine curiosity under her amusement.

"If it were a normal wedding, sure," I say with a shrug. "But this wedding is… big and important. It doesn't feel like it is really mine. To be honest, I feel a little overwhelmed when I think of all the responsibilities I will have. How has my life come to this?" I say with a groan, earning a pat on the arm from Coraline.

"Being a princess isn't all that bad, and you will get to know the court. They will soon feel like yours." I know she is trying to help, but it is not working. We walk in silence for a moment, but I can tell something is weighing on her.

"What else is on your mind?" I inquire, hoping she will share with me.

"There is something else," she says hesitantly. "Aiden insists that your quarters be moved to the royal wing."

I stop and stare at her, surprised. "But we aren't married yet," I say, but after a moment, the shock wears off. I should have expected it. It doesn't surprise me that Aiden wants me close, but what does is the alarm at the separation from my friends. I'm not ready for that change yet.

"I tried to hold him off until after the delegation left, but as his betrothed, he wants you close by. I don't like you being separated from us. Not yet," Coraline says, and I have to agree. As much as I love Aiden, having my quarters close to the king and far away from the support of my friends makes me nervous. It makes it official.

"What was the verdict?" I ask, not sure what I want it to be.

"It was decided that the choice should be up to you. They will have a suite prepared for you to move into as soon as you wish." I am grateful for the consideration, but I'm almost disappointed the decision wasn't made for me.

"I'll think about it," I respond, not ready to make a decision yet. Joy, sorrow, love, and nerves all battled through my body, making the whole situation a confusing mess. I give Coraline's arm a grateful squeeze before leaving to go walk through the gardens again. I have a lot to think about.

"Why won't you move in yet?" Aiden asks me the next day as he shows me my room in the royal wing. He has been giving me a tour, showing me all the nooks and hideaways he uses when he needs a break from being the prince. He hides it well, but I am glad not to be the only one overwhelmed.

"I will be moving in here soon enough." I smile shyly up at him as he pulls me close to him. "I'm not sure you would be able to resist the situation of my sleeping in the next room," I say after looking to make sure we are alone. Servants roam around everywhere, and it is hard to find a moment when one of them isn't wandering nearby.

He gives me a flirtatious look before pressing a kiss to my lips. "You may be right. Well, it just gives me time to have it decorated to perfection for you." The room is large with several doors that split off into a dressing room, a bathing chamber, and a connecting door to his. There is a shared sitting room for entertaining as well.

"These rooms are amazing as is," I tell him, stepping away to look in the bathroom again. He keeps hold of my hand, though not letting me get away.

"Yes, but I'm sure you would like some reminders from Ileria. Just tell me what you want, and I will have my men pick them up when they go to collect your father," he says. He is all smiles, but I feel guilty about the idea of upending my father without warning. I need to send him a letter, but everything has happened so fast, I don't even know how to start one.

"Have them bring me something to remind me of the ocean," I say, avoiding mentioning my father. I'm not ready to talk about him yet.

"As my lady commands," he says with a deep bow, but he glances up with a smile, and I roll my eyes. "Now, let's go find some of the secret passages. There is one in the library." He tugs on my hand to whisk me away to the next adventure before he is called away to more meetings.

He leaves me in the guest wing after exploring, and I am delighted to see Coraline seated on one of the couches. We have both been busy.

"Hello!" she says as I come to sit down by her, accepting the cup of tea she offers. "Has Lady Clara let you have a break?" Lady Clara, the wife of one of King David's chief advisors, is in charge of my schedule. She makes sure I attend my tutoring sessions, meet with merchants, and find appropriate ladies-in-waiting.

"I was actually with Aiden, but I do have interviews for ladies-in-waiting later this evening," I say, taking a sip of the tea. I scrunch up my nose at the spicy aftertaste. Putting it down, I turn to Coraline. "Why don't you have ladies-in-waiting?"

"I do, but they stayed behind for this trip. We weren't sure who we could trust and decided the easiest way to travel would be to not bring them. Instead, I got you, and I am so glad."

"Are things really that bad back in Ileria?" I ask quietly. We are alone in the room, but after Aiden showed me some of the servants' corridors, I realize they could be hiding anywhere, just out of view.

"We are lucky Jude has no ambitions for the throne, but that is why peace with Alberon is so important. We can't have them invade while we are fighting among ourselves." Coraline's words trouble me. I feel foolish trying on dresses and picking out linens while my friends have such heavy burdens.

"Maybe I should sit in on some of the meetings."

"Maybe..." Coraline says, evasive, and I frown. "You have a lot on your plate right now, preparing for your wedding and your future. There will be time for that later. Enjoy this." She stands and smiles at me before walking away, leaving me alone. I know what I'm doing is important, but it feels silly and useless compared to the work Coraline is doing. If I am truly going to become a princess, I thought that training would be much more important than what color of forks are to be used at the wedding.

The thought stays with me all through my interviews and into the next day. "I just don't understand," I complain to Gareth while we are out shopping with Lady Clara for more of who knows what. She has graciously allowed us to take a break while she checks in on something. We are in a little coffee shop, taking a break and enjoying a delicious cup of chocolate. "I feel as if they are purposely trying to keep me in the dark. How can I be helpful if they don't let me?" I ask, exasperated.

"Well, maybe they just don't want to overwhelm you," he says kindly, but I can hear the pity in his voice and scowl. He smiles and sits forward, elbow on the table, and his full attention on me. "What do you think you could do?"

"I don't know, but something," I say, sitting back and folding my arms.

"You have no political training, and when you are a princess, your duties will be here in Alberon. Probably helping the king with his programs to rid the country of the poor," he says, his arm sweeping out to gesture to the surrounding population. My eyes sweep the wealthy shopping district we are in and return to Gareth. "Well, not here, but you know what I mean." He sits back in his chair, extending his long legs in front of him.

"Those are important, but I am Ilerian. Shouldn't I have more say in foreign policy dealing with my country? Maybe I could help with my knowledge of customs or something." I haven't admitted it to anyone yet, but all my lessons make me feel like I'm giving up my country, a part of my identity, and I want to hold on to that.

"Maybe mention it to Jude or, you know, your fiancé," he says, raising an eyebrow, but his gaze softens at my slight frown. "I know this has been a big change for you, but you chose this."

"I know, which is why I want to be more involved."

"But on which side?"

"What do you mean?" I ask, sitting up straight. It's a weird question. What does he mean *which side*? A guilty look flashes across his face.

"Gareth," I practically growl his name when he doesn't respond right away.

"Well, you are marrying Aiden. Who is the prince of Alberon? That is where your allegiance will have to lie," he says slowly.

"That doesn't mean I have to renounce my Ilerian heritage," I protest.

"No, but... listen," he says, running a hand through his hair and sitting forward. "It's not so simple anymore. If you want to embrace your new life, you have to be dedicated to Alberon. Jude and Coraline know it, but they have been giving you space to make the transition. They don't want to put you in a difficult situation," he says, taking my hand. I let him, but I can't keep the hurt look off my face.

"But that's not fair. I'm their friend. Wouldn't fostering friendship between the kingdoms just benefit us all?" I say, trying to understand.

"Yes," he says slowly, "eventually, But right now, they are trying to decide if David is a threat to them or not, and you are about to become his family. It's not that they don't trust you, but it's a delicate situation."

"So, marrying Aiden has put me on the opposing side?" I pull my hand away from his and rub the sides of my head. I am not cut out for the game of politics.

"No, but it is complicated. They don't want to force you to choose," he says, but it becomes clear that they think I already have. By accepting Aiden's proposal, I have lost them as close friends.

"Aiden isn't a bad guy," I state, trying to defend him. I want to say the same about David, but something holds me back. There is no evidence, but my instincts are still telling me that he is hiding things.

"No, he's not. He's been my best friend for years. He is my family as much as yours," Gareth says, looking me in the eye. "That's why I know he is loyal to those he loves, and he loves his brother very much."

"And I love Aiden."

"If David made a move that endangered Ileria, Aiden would probably support him, and then what would you do?" I look away, not sure how to answer that question. My heart wants to tell me that Aiden would not support anything that would hurt my country, but I know it is a wish, not reality.

"We have no evidence that David has any designs on Ileria. The whole reason we are here is to redo the peace treaty."

"We don't know what he is up to, but we know he is up to something," he says. It's only because I'm looking closely that I see the brief look of panic that flashes across his face before he sits back and folds his arms. He knows something that he isn't saying. "Are you done? We should probably head back to the palace." He starts to stand up, but I'm not ready to let this go.

"Tell me," I demand.

"I can't," he says, his eyes darting around. There is no one to rescue him. I don't want to be in the dark anymore. "You're a little too close to the situation," he says, sitting back down and leaning toward me. He opens his mouth a few times like he is going to say more but closes it again. He pushes his lips together, his brows furrowed as we look at each other.

"Tell me," I ask again, quietly. His shoulders sag, and he looks away.

"Fine," he says, and I smile in triumph before schooling my expression. I don't want to rub it in his face that he lost. "Our scouts have been following John, and there was a meeting the other day. One that clearly showed us he is working for the king." My muscles clench at the mention of John. I glance around for a moment, like he might pop out of nowhere and attack me.

"How do you know?" I prompt him, my need to understand making me impatient.

"He was talking to someone undeniably close to the king," he says next, still cryptic like he wants me to give up before he tells me too much.

"Who?" I ask, but he just shakes his head.

"Just trust me on this one," he says, but I can't let it go. The king has so many loyal supporters, whether because he gave them status or because they believe in his sainthood, but no one stands out in my mind.

"Who?" I ask again. He doesn't respond, refusing to look me in the eye. Suddenly, an idea pops into my head. I sit back and shake my head. I want to dismiss it. It can't be, but the more I think about it, the more it makes sense. He has a history with John, and who would be more loyal to the king than his brother? Dread pools in my stomach.

"No," I deny, but his face tells me it's true. "Why would Aiden meet with John, especially after what he did to me?"

"We think he was getting information for his brother, information the king didn't trust with anyone else."

"Maybe our scout was mistaken," I say, not wanting to believe it.

"Trust me. The scout trailing him was good."

"How do you know?" I ask, wanting there to have been a mistake.

"Because the scout was me."

"No," I whisper again, shaking my head. It can't be. I don't want to believe it, but Gareth would not lie about this. I have to know what happened. I lean forward, grabbing his hands. "What happened? Did you hear what they said?" I am desperate for information. There has to be a mistake.

"I don't know what they said, but Aiden looked angry when he left. It's clear he isn't fond of John right now."

Good, I think. Maybe he was telling him to leave and never come back, but my instinct tells me he was there for his brother. A bitter feeling surfaces at the thought. I suspect that if he had to choose between me and his brother, he would choose his brother.

"I need to leave," I say, standing suddenly, needing to get away. Without waiting for Gareth, I stand and start walking down the street. I don't know where I am going, but I need to be alone.

I walk through the city instead of waiting for the carriage. The palace is easy to see, and we are in a relatively safe area of the city. I can't get lost, and so far, no one knows who I am yet unless they are from the palace. My troubled thoughts follow me, running around my head in a never-ending loop. Aiden loves me, but he loves his brother more. I love Aiden, but can I love him even if he is choosing things that go against my friends, my home?

My brain hurts, and I stop, feeling lightheaded as I realize my breathing is coming in panicked gasps. A man yells at me as he drives his cart around where I have stopped in the middle of the road, jarring me enough to notice my surroundings. To my right is a large temple, and I turn to enter.

The temple has a few petitioners inside, but all is quiet. The bustle of the city outside is muted and fades away as I walk deeper inside. I wander toward the few benches at the back of the temple. Sitting down, I take in the tall arched ceilings and stained glass windows letting in colors that shine on the walls from the fading afternoon light.

Not wanting to be disturbed, I close my eyes and find myself praying. It's not an eloquent prayer or one even with words. It's more of a wish sent to the heavens that all will be well. That Aiden will be good and choose me. That David won't be evil, so he doesn't have to choose, and I don't have to choose between him and my friends.

I have a special gift for you.

The words come to mind as I close my eyes. They make me think of Mama. *How did she do it?* I wonder. At the end of her life, she was still so sure that everything would be okay. That The Eternal had a plan for her still.

"Is this truly your plan for me?" I ask quietly, not expecting a reply. Just the act of thinking of Mama helps calm me, and I find peace even if I still do not have answers.

I keep my eyes closed, basking in the quiet until I sense a presence sitting beside me. For a moment I wonder if it's my mother but quickly dismiss the notion. It is probably just a priest. I crack open my eyes to find Rupert, arms crossed and legs extended in front of him.

"What are you doing here?" I ask, surprised, just barely remembering to keep my voice down.

"I was coming to fetch you in the market when you took off. Gareth is outside. He told me, you know, and I thought you could use a friend."

"Thank you," I say quietly, appreciating his familiar presence. We sit in companionable silence for a moment before I recall an interesting fact about Rupert. "You were in the king's guard," I say to him, drawing his attention.

"That's right," he says, looking over at me, brow furrowed. I can tell I've confused him.

"They can't be married, but you're married." The statement doesn't clear anything up. Luckily, Rupert is a good sport and goes along with this line of questioning.

"That's true," he says. "They have to dedicate their lives to the crown, and a spouse and children would be a conflict of interest."

"So, how did you choose?" I ask. His brow smooths out, and a small smile tells me he's made the connection. "How did you decide between love and serving the king?"

"Ah, well, that was not an easy decision," he says, looking at me. "I was loyal to the king. I had made an oath to serve him, and I planned on sticking with it. Even when I met Ruth and I knew a pretty kitchen girl had stolen my heart, I couldn't turn my back on him."

"So, what happened?" I ask, intrigued. I had met his wife before and knew they were deeply in love.

"The king was my friend. When the twins were born, His Majesty turned to me and told me that there was no greater feeling in the world than holding his precious babies, and he hoped I had the same experience. I was confused, and he laughed at my bewildered expression before he gave me his blessing and told me if I don't seek out my love, I am a fool." He smiles, lost in the memory. My eyebrows are lost in my hairline, though, at the thought of the Ilerian king being a romantic. Rupert's expression becomes sadder, though, and I know he is thinking about his wife and their struggle for children. The boys in the guard are the closest they have.

"Do you regret it?" I ask quietly.

"No," he replies without hesitation, looking back down at me. "Even though we haven't been able to have children, I still would choose her again. I'm glad the king still thinks to call on me when he needs aid, but I am grateful I have a companion in this life that brings me joy."

"So even though you had to change your whole life for her, it was worth it?"

"It was worth it for *me*," he says. We are silent a moment longer as I contemplate his words before Rupert speaks again. "I know you're struggling, Aloura. I love Aiden, too, but this is bigger than going from one guard post to another. Choosing him means choosing a whole new life, one that is controlled by David. He will be your king, and you will have to answer to him, unless Aiden decides to renounce his right to the throne and live a simple life with you."

"I don't know if that will happen. He loves being a prince," I say quietly, looking ahead.

"Then you have to decide if Aiden's love is worth your new life," he says. A tear falls from my eye, and I wipe it away.

"Thank you," I say quietly. He's given me a lot to think about. I thought our love was strong enough to cross countries, but is it strong enough to compromise my identity? Am I willing to change and become a new person for him?

We sit in the chapel a little longer until the light fades, signaling it is time to get back before dinner. I walk quietly, lost in my thoughts. I have a fiancé to interrogate. I'm tired of not knowing what is going on and who to trust. I'm going to find out the truth no matter what.

Chapter 24

The next few days pass in a blur of wedding preparations. My mind is a mess as I try to figure out what the king is up to, what Aiden is involved in, and what I'm going to do about it. All the preparations have kept us apart when all I want is a moment to talk to him and have an honest conversation, to reassure myself that I'm making the right choice.

I have taken to spending most of my time in the gardens or the library when I'm able to escape for a moment. The incessant questions of Lady Clara and an etiquette tutor who is trying his best to cram dance lessons into a short time are all overwhelming and happening so fast that I just need to breathe. I have taken to hiding from it all as much as possible.

Today, I slipped out while Lady Clara talked about place settings for the banquet after the wedding with several of the court's new noble ladies. They were distracted enough that they didn't even notice when I slipped out the terrace door and into the garden to explore a new path. This one led to a lookout over the sparkling lake.

I have to admit that I enjoy the gardens here in Alberon. They are different from our green grass and simple flowers. These are filled with big leafy plants and trees, streams, and ponds. Rocks create designs off the paths, and large, brightly colored flowers leave heavy perfumes in the air.

I stop and take in the view of the lake from a balcony. It's peaceful out here, and I swear that when I close my eyes and listen, I can almost grasp what path The Eternal wants me to take. If I were truly given the gift of guidance, then I need it now.

"There is my beautiful bride," Aiden says, surprising me as he sweeps me into his arms, spinning around and startling a laugh from me. When he sets me down, he gives me a long kiss. I press into him, loving the feeling of his soft lips on mine and his warm hands at my waist. I rest my hands against his chest, fighting the urge to grab fistfuls of his shirt and pull him closer. His kisses make me forget my troubles and remind me that this is the core of what I want and why I am here.

Aiden pulls back with a sigh but keeps me in his arms, resting his forehead against mine. "Can you believe it?" he whispers. "After all these years, we are finally getting married." I can hear the joy in his voice, causing a smile to come to my lips.

"I am glad it is finally happening, although I wish that it didn't have to be such a production." I try to keep the annoyance out of my voice, but I know I failed.

"Oh, come now," he gently reprimands, pulling back to look at my face. "It's not that bad."

"It's just all too much. The ball, the wedding, the feast—all of it. I just wanted something simple at a temple with my father. I miss him."

"I know, but isn't the most important thing that you will finally become mine?" he asks, trying to soothe me. It doesn't work. "It doesn't matter really who is there or how it is done; in the end, it is just you and me and the rest of our lives together."

"Yes," I say hesitantly, pulling out of his arms and leaning back against the balcony again. "I guess it would be easier to bear, though, if I understood the reason why it has to happen so quickly. Why can't we wait a month or two until my father can be brought here?" Aiden comes towards me, pulling me close once again, cupping my head against his chest as more tears spring to my eyes.

"I know, my love. This is hard for me too." He soothes me, his fingers combing through my loose hair, his other hand holding tight at my waist. "I don't quite understand it either. My brother insists that this is the will of The Eternal. I... I am working on understanding because he believes it, and I don't believe he would lie to me," he says, and I take hope from the conflict in his voice. I hate that he is also struggling, but I hope it means he is willing to listen to me.

"Let me distract you for a while," he says in my ear, his breath giving me goosebumps. He starts to kiss me behind my ear, then down my neck, and to my exposed shoulder. I turn and meet his eyes, and the desire in them leaves me breathless, but as much as I want to let him take my cares away, we need to talk before the wedding, and I realize this may be our only chance.

"Aiden." His name leaves my lips like a breath, and he takes that as an invitation to continue our kisses, but at the last second, I turn my head, giving him my cheek. "Aiden," I repeat, my voice firmer as my resolve strengthens. "We need to talk."

He sighs against my cheek, resting against me for a moment before finally pulling back and letting me go again. "I hate those words, but I have to admit you are right. What is on your mind, my love?"

"I've heard something concerning," I say carefully. "I've heard that it has been confirmed that John is still here in the city." I watch him carefully for his reaction.

"I've heard," he says, frowning before looking at me with sympathy. "Don't worry. You are safe here," he says. "It would make me feel better, though, to have you under my protection. I would like to have an Alberonian guard follow you and maybe move you into your room in the royal wing."

"But I already have a guard," I say, gesturing to the Ilerian soldier who stands far enough away to give us privacy.

"Yes, but you have already been kidnapped on their watch." His annoyance with Ileria is clear, and I pull out of his grasp.

"It's not their fault," I say, defending my countrymen, but that was the wrong thing to say, and it sets Aiden off.

"You were attacked in Ileria. He escaped from their jail, and you were attacked on the way here. Obviously, you need more protection, and they are not able to offer it." The intensity of his emotions startle me. He turns toward the lake, running a hand through his hair before gathering himself once again. "You are precious to me. Let me protect you, be my queen."

I step back, his uncharacteristic outburst making me wary. He matches my step, though, placing his hands on my upper arms as he looks into my eyes. "Listen, I don't know about this whole religious stuff, but David has no heir, and he is not planning on it anytime soon even though his councillors keep pushing their daughters at him." He rolls his eyes, smiling at me like I am supposed to find this a joke, but I don't. "At the ball, I will officially be announced as the Crown Prince and will take the oaths during our wedding. I'm sure that is why he wants us married, so there is security of the royal line," he says triumphantly.

I know I am supposed to congratulate him and be happy about this, but I am stunned. This changes things. Aiden is fully committed to Alberon, and if I marry him, I will need to be as well.

"I see," I say, trying to be cheerful, but Aiden knows me well.

"Aloura, this is a good thing," he says. He is sure of himself and his position. He wants this.

"What if I don't want to be a queen?" I ask quietly.

"This is who I am now. I cannot turn away from it," he says, and I know he is telling me I have to choose. If I want him, this will be my life, and if I can't handle it, then I am saying he is not worth it. Our love is not worth it.

Even still, I can't help but ask, "Cannot or will not?" The question hangs between us for a moment. His expression is hard, and I worry I have pushed him too far. I want to take it all back to apologize, but I have to know: is he choosing this, or is it because his brother has asked it of him? His expression softens, and he rubs his hands up and down my arms, the tense moment breaking.

"Aloura, I have been looking for my brother for such a long time. He is the only family that I have left. I will not turn my back on him."

"I am your family," I say. "And Papa, Rupert, Gareth..." We have been there when his brother was not.

"Of course you are," he says gently, "but why can't we be a family here? All of us together. We can make a new home here. David is sending for your father, and even though he won't be here for the wedding, he will be here soon," he says, trying to make me feel better, but I keep fishing for any sort of loyalty to his old life.

"I know, but I miss home. Don't you miss home, too?" I ask, and he lets out a big sigh. "Aloura, that wasn't home for me. My mother took me away from my home, and while you and your father welcomed me in and helped me make the best out of a bad situation, this is my home now, in Alberon with my brother and now you."

"Oh," I respond dumbly, not sure what to say. I so wanted to believe that he harbored good feelings about our life before. "It is all I've ever known," I say, thinking about my feelings for my country and my home. "All my father has known. Our family and traditions come from there. It's... it's hard to think about leaving."

"Why are you so loyal to that country?" Aiden says, pulling away, his expression turning hard again. "Why do you have to be loyal to a country? It is just land; it is just a language, but I am here. Why can't you just be loyal to me?" His words are like a slap in the face.

"I am loyal to you! Why do you think I am here? I have crossed a continent to be with you, and that is why we are having this conversation," I say, upset that he would question my love.

"Aloura," he says, his hard tone gone in the face of my anger. "Listen, I understand this has been a lot. A lot of changes and stress. Why don't we take a breather for a moment? Cool our tempers and return to this discussion later. I will see you for dinner," he says, kissing my forehead and walking away. I just watch him, feeling betrayed as I question if this is the life I truly want.

The ball is upon us before I have a chance to truly talk to Aiden again. I almost dread attending. My emotions are still mixed up from our fight, and we are supposed to marry tomorrow, but I can't help but hope the magic of the night might lend us healing.

"That man is insufferable," Coraline says, sweeping into our common room with the men behind her. The meeting must have ended early today to prepare for the ball.

"What has happened?" I am ready to be distracted from my troubled thoughts.

"King David has made a request of you for a wedding present. He says that The Eternal needs you and Aiden to take a wedding tour of Coati. It so happens that those are the lands he has been asking to gain access to," she says, plopping down onto a sofa. I stare at her for a moment. It's a strange request. Coati is a jungle where the only thing of interest is the ruins of the old castle. It's a destination of interest for pilgrims seeking to grow closer to The Eternal and those seeking warmer temperatures during the cold season in Ileria, which is still a long way off.

"Why would he want us to go tour the cursed ruins?" I ask. There has to be a reason behind his request, especially since he says The Eternal desires it.

"They are not cursed," she says, picking at the tea tray that was brought in earlier. They have done a great job of keeping us fed. I guess she would know, though. They have probably been there plenty of times. "They are just sacred."

"This is a major clue as to what David could be planning. After meeting the man, I know he is not satisfied with ruling Alberon. He has bigger plans. I just don't know exactly what," the prince says, drawing my attention to him.

"And you want me to figure out why while I'm there?" I ask listlessly. I don't have the energy to worry about espionage when I am worried about the war in my heart. At this point, I am not sure there will even be a wedding trip.

Almost as if sensing my mood, the prince moves closer and gently responds, "No, we won't ask any more of you."

"But…" I respond, surprised. I know that this could be important information, and I will be in a position to get it. Why are they not asking me?

"We won't ask you to spy on your husband," Coraline says gently. I still hesitate, though, and realize that I am considering doing it anyway. I'm not ready to turn my back on Aiden yet, and that is why I can't tell them yes. I understand their decision, but it still hurts to be pushed out.

"We are going to see if Gareth might accompany you. Once you marry, you will officially be under Alberonian rule and protection, but Gareth is a friend to both of you, and it would not seem strange."

"And you would be willing to spy on your friend?" I ask, turning to Gareth.

"If it protects my country, then yes," he says, determination in his gaze. I wish I were as sure of my loyalty as he is.

"I understand," I say, standing to go get ready for the ball, but then I stop. There is a piece of information I can share since it will be made public tonight. "Just so you know," I say, facing the royal siblings, "Aiden will be announced as Crown Prince tonight, and the oaths will be taken tomorrow during the ceremony."

They look at each other for a moment, a silent communion before turning to me. "Thank you," Coraline says. "That is good to know."

I turn to leave again, but a thought enters my mind. A memory from the tavern in Ileria. It's a long shot, but maybe it has value in this situation. "You should ask Rupert about Coati. He told us a story about it right before all this happened. Maybe he will have some insights into why David wants us there."

Chapter 25

The maid tugs at my hair, pulling it back into elaborate braids and twists, leaving just enough hanging down to soften the look. The dress that was delivered earlier is a beautiful, flowy piece in emerald green, the color of Alberon royalty.

"You look gorgeous," Coraline says, stepping into the room. I step back to take in the full look as I stand in front of the full-length mirror. "Aiden will not be able to keep his hands off you." She gives me a wink as we meet eyes in the mirror. I try to smile back, but I can't help but ask myself if I even want that anymore.

I gulp in a breath as panic sets in. I am to marry Aiden tomorrow, but I'm still wondering if I should. *What am I going to do?* I ask myself. Needing to move, I walk quickly over to the vanity, picking up the necklace that goes with the dress.

"Do you need help with that?" I am startled by the deep voice that is obviously not Coraline's. I turn around to see Aiden standing in the doorway, dressed to match my gown in a dark-green doublet, blank pants, and boots. His curls are combed back, but a few are already trying to escape and curl on his forehead. His green eyes sparkle as they take me in, and I blush as much from the guilt of thinking about calling off the wedding as from the delight in Aiden's eyes as he comes and takes me in his arms. Coraline slips out of the room with the maid, giving us a moment of privacy.

I look up at him, and he gives me a soft kiss, making all other thoughts leave my mind. "Let me help you finish getting ready," he says against my mouth before turning me and trailing his mouth down my neck, kissing my bare shoulder and eliciting a shiver from me. I know we still need to talk about our fight, but we still have most of the night to do that, so for now, I ignore it.

This is right, I tell myself as he takes the necklace from my hands and brings it around my neck, giving me another kiss where he rests the clasp. *Are you sure?* another voice whispers as I step away and turn around, setting the jewel above the slight show of cleavage. Aiden's eyes follow my hands, looking hungry before he sighs and holds out his arm, giving me a charming smile. "Come, my lady, it would not do for us to be late to our ball."

We are announced at the top of the stairs, and before we descend, I take in the magnificence of the room. Gold and white decorate the room in ribbons and tablecloths. Banners of the Alberonian green cover the walls. Large chandeliers hang from the ceiling, lighting the room, the candles creating rainbows as they reflect crystals hanging near them. The many doors leading to the gardens are open, letting in the warm desert air.

The room is already full of people dressed in their finery, who swarm to us as we descend, begging introductions and giving congratulations. When we have a moment, Aiden points out an older lady who could be mistaken for a bird with all her feathers in her hair and dress. We both smother a laugh, and my heart leaps with joy. This is what my heart has been missing.

I reach my hand up to touch Aiden's cheek, sad that my silky black gloves create a barrier between our skin, and look into his eyes, trying to convey how much I have missed him. Keeping his eyes locked on mine, he turns his head slightly, kissing my palm. I feel the heat of it even through my glove, making me shiver. He smirks before leading me over to the dais, where King David waits for us. It is time.

"My people," David calls, and the crowd falls silent. He lets the silence sit for a moment as he looks around, taking in his people. "I am so pleased that you are here with me tonight on this joyous occasion." He smiles at them, and I know why his people love him. He is one of them; he is the poor boy, the military leader, the charming noble, and he knows how to play to his audience. It is mesmerizing to see him gather in the crowd, making it feel like you are having a conversation with a close friend instead of one of the hundreds.

"Of course, we are glad that our friends from Ileria can join us, but they have brought an even greater gift than they ever realized. As many of you know, my brother, Prince Aiden..." The title startled me, and once again, I am reminded that Aiden is no longer the same Aiden that I had loved a few months ago—close but not the same.

The king continues sharing how we were reunited, but my mind has wandered, only to be brought back when Aiden brings me forward to the king's side. I smile at the crowd and then duck my head a little in embarrassment at all the eyes on me.

"As many of you have realized in my short reign so far, I care greatly about all of my people and want your happiness, and I especially want all the happiness in the world for my beloved brother who never gave up looking for me." The tenderness in David's eyes as he looks at Aiden cannot be mistaken, but it does diminish the calculation in them. "Therefore, I am pleased beyond measure to congratulate him on his wedding to the newly appointed Ilerian ambassador, Lady Aloura." Everyone cheers as Aiden pulls me close and kisses the side of my head, eliciting a few more cheers from everyone. David smiles at us before bringing up his hands to call attention back to him.

"That is not all. A kingdom without an heir is weak, and I am not in a position yet to give you one," he says with a little self-deprecating smile. The crowd gives a good-natured laugh while several young ladies flutter their eyelashes up at him. "Therefore, it is important that we have a clear line of succession. The Eternal has encouraged me to name Aiden my heir and any of his offspring until the time I can have my own." The crowd cheers once again, and my cheeks flush at the attention and implication of that statement.

"Let the dancing begin!" David calls as Aiden takes my hand and leads me to the dance floor to begin the first dance. We had been practicing for the past few days. My nerves flutter like butterflies in my stomach as Aiden places one hand at my waist and lifts the other over his head, palm out, meeting mine as I hold out my dress in one hand and lift my other to press against his. We will be the only ones on the dance floor for the first few measures before other couples join us.

The music starts, and the dance begins. Our arms swoop, we spin, and I look up into Aiden's eyes. The joy in them is contagious, and I find myself lost in the moment with him and the music, trusting him to keep me from making a misstep. I am so caught up in the moment that I don't even notice when more couples join us on the dance floor. The song ends, but Aiden sweeps me up into the next dance as well. I lose track of time in his arms. It's like a fairy tale, a dream come true. For this moment, I forget what is to come, the heavy mantle that is now placed on our shoulders, and I enjoy the fact that we are here now together.

After our third dance, I need a break. Aiden escorts me to the refreshment table, where eager nobles fight for our attention, flattering and congratulating us once more.

I smile politely as another person starts in, but I can't respond, leaving it to Aiden. It is hot in the ballroom and even as I sip my lemonade, it feels suffocating. The dancing was magic, but reality is back, and I feel like I'm going to scream.

"I need a moment," I gasp to Aiden before stepping away and out the open doors to the gardens. My feet carry me past one or two couples through the public gardens. I'm sure I am lost, but the path begins to look familiar, and I find myself in the hidden garden. I collapse on the bench beside the pond, burying my head in my hands. I am overwhelmed with everything.

Can I truly be queen of a country that's not mine? Can I support Aiden as a wife if he is involved in things I don't agree with? I think of his work he is doing for the homeless population and all David is doing to rebuild his country. They are doing good things, but does that make up for any bad?

I've given you a special gift. You know what you need to do.

The voice is familiar, one I have been hearing more often of late. The Eternal is speaking to me. "I don't," I whisper out loud, but we both know that is not true. The reason I am having trouble is that what I want is contrary to what I need to do.

You know what you need to do

The words repeat themselves in my mind, and I let the tears come. I grieve for my broken heart. I grieve for the life that is lost to me. I cry for what feels like hours, but it can only be minutes, pouring my heart out silently and begging for some hope that something can change. I am about to give up before I realize I am not alone.

The hair on the back of my neck prickles with awareness. My eyes search the darkness, and I call out, "Hello? Who is there?" There is only one exit to this garden, and I can't remember if a guard followed me out here. Slowly, a dark figure pulls itself away from the shadows at the entrance into the pale light of the moon. I stand helplessly as the figure approaches. It's a man, tall and thin, and my pulse rises.

"You just don't know when to give up." My blood chills when I hear his voice, and then the moon lights his face. John stalks towards me, a cruel smirk on his lips. I step back, but there is nowhere to go. I try to recall my self-defense lessons, but my mind is panicking. All I can do is repeatedly think, *Not again*. I am a little mouse frozen in fear as the cat stalks me. "I warned you back in Ileria that you are not good enough for him, and yet here you are. Aiden is a prince. You are just a little nobody."

A whimper escapes my lips, and he laughs, coming even closer as I back up, almost stepping into the pond. He has me trapped. Desperately, I try to reason with him. "You can't hurt me now. I'm engaged to Aiden. He will be looking for me."

"Ha, like the king would let his precious brother marry you." His demeanor changes. He is no longer teasing. He is angry now. "You are just a distraction, a thing to be discarded when a better prize comes along."

"You're wrong. Aiden loves me, and even his brother says it's the will of The Eternal," I say, although I no longer believe it.

"Yeah right, like The Eternal cares about you." His words ignite something within me. *It's a lie*, the voice tells me, but I don't need its confirmation. I already know that I'm precious to Him.

"The Eternal is aware of all His creations. I am not a nobody to Him. He was aware of me before I was even born."

"You are a fool," he spits out, seething with anger. I can see he has lost reason, but I can't hold back the tide of words coming out of my mouth.

"No, it is you who are the fool. You have been given so many opportunities by The Eternal to live a happy life, and still you reach for things that are not given to you." The words fill me as the warmth of The Eternal fills my veins. He is guiding my words. "Just because those in power here in this world make you feel like nothing doesn't mean The Eternal does. Walk away, John. There is still time to choose a different path, but if you attack me now, you will be severely punished." The fire in my soul gives me confidence, and I lift my chin and move to walk past him. I hope my bravado will put him off, but I misjudge his sense of preservation, and he grabs my arm in a bruising grip.

"It's only a matter of time until I will be proven right. Things are in motion, and you can't stop them," he sneers, his rancid breath making me gag.

"Aloura," says a familiar voice, and I pull my arm away as he lets go, causing me to fall.

"This isn't over," he hisses as Prince Jude walks into the garden, pausing to take in the scene. I stand and rush to him as a dagger is produced from somewhere on his person. His free arm encircles my waist as I bury my face in his chest, grateful for the familiar presence.

"You are under arrest," the prince says, gently pushing me behind him and placing himself between John and me.

"You have no authority here." John pulls himself up, puffing out his chest, thinking he won. The prince's hand pushes me back again. He wants me to go. I turned to leave, only to run into Aiden, who looks from the prince with his dagger and John with no weapon in his hand.

"What is going on here?" he commands in a voice I have never heard before. He sounds like a prince, sure that he will be obeyed. John quickly bows and, on his knees, starts talking.

"I saw the girl run through the garden and wanted to check on her."

"Lies," I cry, turning to Aiden before remembering that he supposedly had met with John here in Alberon. I look at him, desperate for a sign that he has not betrayed me. "You know he attacked me in Ileria, and he came here to taunt me and threaten me." I try to meet his eyes, but he doesn't take them off of John. Prince Jude looks between Aiden and John before looking at me.

"This man escaped an Ileria prison for crimes committed there, and now he is threatening your betrothed. I demand his arrest," he says, breaking the stare-off. I don't know whether to be grateful or upset that he intervened.

His demand is clear: John is brought into custody, or we will have an international incident. Aiden looks from Jude to me to John, his shoulders tense and his eyes calculating before he relaxes. "Of course, you are right, Prince Judian. This man has caused grievous offense between our countries and against me by harming my beloved. Guards!" he calls, bringing a few men running, "Arrest this man!"

John tries to protest, but it is of no use. He glares as he is walked out of the garden, but he can't help but give a few parting words: "You know who you are and what you deserve," he says to Aiden. "You can't outrun your destiny."

We watch in silence as he is escorted out. Aiden's arms come around me, and I let him support my weight, exhausted from the evening. John's last words leave a lot of questions to be answered.

"I would like a meeting with you and your brother," Jude declares before I can ask my questions. "There is obviously more going on here, and I am worried about the safety of our people. We will leave if we are in danger."

"Of course," Aiden says, his arm prompting me to begin moving. "Let me escort Aloura to her room, and I will send a message to my brother to meet in his study."

"Wait!" I halt, although Aiden continues to try to corral me towards the palace. "I deserve to be at the meeting."

"Aloura," Aiden says, but I am tired of being pushed around.

"No, I am part of this, and I will not be pushed off to the side and made to wait for others to make decisions for me. I will be at the meeting."

I can see he wants to fight it. It would be easy to claim that I'm exhausted from my ordeal, and he wouldn't be wrong, but I hold his gaze. By the slight drop in his shoulders, I know he gives in. I glance over at Jude, and I swear I can see pride in his eyes as he nods his head.

"Fine. I will send for my brother, and we will meet in his study," Aiden says, retaking my arm. It's time for some answers.

Chapter 26

The king's office is full. Prince Jude left Aiden and me to gather Rupert and Coraline. Aiden escorted me straight to his brother's office, sending for him and a pot of tea. When Aiden's brother arrives, they step to the side for a private conversation.

"Are you okay?" Coraline asks, coming to sit by my side as soon as she is in the room.

"I will be," I say, pouring her a cup of tea while everyone finds a spot.

"Is this everyone?" King David asks, taking a seat behind his desk. Aiden follows and stands behind his chair on his right. "Prince Judian, will you please tell me why I was pulled away from my ball?"

"There was a man who escaped Ilerian custody and has followed us here, who has attacked Aloura twice now. We also believe he was involved in the attempted kidnapping of my sister." I glance around the room, and Rupert meets my eye, silently asking if I'm okay. I give him a small smile. Surprisingly, I am.

"So now we are dealing with Ilerian incompetence," the king says. No one makes a sound, but all the men are standing, their shoulders tense.

Coraline frowns at the king but also keeps her peace, glancing at her brother.

"Pardon me, Your Majesty, but I think it is Alberonian incompetence we are talking about. How did he get onto the palace grounds?" Jude asks, not giving in to whatever game David is playing. Aiden bristles at the disrespect, but David's hand stays any words he might have offered.

"My apologies. I am irritated to be missing the party, but that does not call for rudeness. You are right. There must have been a failure in our defenses. He most likely slipped in with a group of servants or vendors for the party." It makes sense, but my feelings tell me that he knows more than he is willing to share.

"Now I have a question. Who is this man, and why is he after my brother's bride?" the king asks, looking from the prince to me.

"I think that might be a better question for your brother. There is a history there," Jude says, and all eyes turn to Aiden. A brief look of contempt for the other prince passes on his face for a moment before he smooths it out, turning to his brother.

"John was an instructor for Machiavelli's guards. He was also a refugee from Alberon. I'm sure after he escaped, he decided to come here, to his home. As for his actions, I do not know why he has chosen to act as he has. We were not that close." Aiden says, crossing his arms.

I'm not sure what to believe. I glance at Gareth, but he looks away, a frown on his face. Sure, we knew Aiden had talked to John, but we still have no idea what the conversation was about. There is no proof to call his lie. And it is a lie. Anyone who knows Aiden and John knows they were closer than he is admitting. The king looks at me next, and I realize he wants an explanation from me.

"I don't know why John doesn't like me. I think all along he knew that Aiden was going to be a prince. He thinks I'm unworthy of him," I say, keeping my eyes on the king. I don't want to show weakness anymore.

David's face turns thoughtful at my words, and a little smile tugs at the corner of his mouth. I don't trust it. "Ah, a religious zealot, probably. While I do think that The Eternal has been guiding me to take care of His creations here in Alberon, some of my followers have been swept up in the idea that I am a saint. I try to help them understand that I am just a man, but I can't control their belief," he says, sitting back and folding his hands. "I'm sure when he found out Aiden was my brother and decided he was also gifted from the divine that he took it upon himself to separate him from what he deemed a weakness." The king turns his sympathetic eyes to me. "I am sorry that you have suffered from my failings. I'll be sure tomorrow to let the people know that The Eternal has blessed your union." He is lying. This man is no more influenced by The Eternal than John, but how to prove it? "I promise that we will address that concern in the future. We will interrogate him sometime after the wedding."

"I would like to be there for the interrogation," Jude says. The king looks like he is considering the suggestion, but Aiden is the one who responds.

"He is now in our custody. You can wash your hands of this." I am surprised by his words. It was a reasonable request, and now I can't help but think he is trying to hide something.

"He has endangered my citizens, and I would like to know why," Jude continues, as calm as ever. In the face of that calm, I can see Aiden's frustration building. He glares at Jude.

"This is about me and my fiancée. I can guarantee you that she will be taken care of. You do not need to worry," he responds. All of a sudden,

I worry about Aiden and what he will do to John. He is not normally prone to violence, I thought, but the look in his eyes feels wild.

"She is still a citizen of Ileria, and there is the matter of his being involved in kidnapping my sister," Jude responds, but he has lost his relaxed posture. He stands up straight, shoulders back and squared, looking like the military leader he is.

"She will be a citizen of Alberon tomorrow, and you don't have proof of his involvement." Aiden has stepped forward, and if there weren't a desk between him and Jude, I'm sure they would be toe-to-toe.

"That's what I'm trying to get." Jude's tone is as frustrated as I've ever heard him. His mask is still there, but it is cracking. I can see the tightness of his jaw, and his fist is clenched at his side. This is so unlike both of them. I'm about to intervene when another delicate throat clears. Both princes look at Coraline, who sits tall, hands clasped delicately in her lap next to me.

"Your Majesty," she says, focusing on the king. "I would like to humbly request that Prince Jude be allowed to interrogate the prisoner for any crime committed on Ilerian soil. My attempted kidnapping happened just before we crossed the border, and it's in our treaty that we have a right to be present. I'm sure I can find the section if you need me to."

"No need for that," the king responds. He does not seem at all bothered by Coraline's bringing up the treaty. He seems amused, but Aiden folds his arms and looks away. I know him well enough to know he is bothered that he got so riled up. "We will hold the interrogation the day after tomorrow. I would hate to ruin a beautiful wedding with unpleasant business."

Jude hesitates for a moment before he nods, and we all file out of the room. Coraline has her arm looped through mine, and we turn to head back to our suite, but a hand on my elbow stops me.

"Aloura, may I have a moment?" Aiden looks at me imploringly, and I nod, letting go of Coraline before taking Aiden's arm. I'm tired, but we need to talk before tomorrow.

"I'm sorry that I failed you," he says after we are alone. His tone surprises me, and I look up into the anguish on his face. "It took me too long to realize you slipped away, and I didn't have a guard assigned specifically to you tonight, figuring you would be with me the whole time. Why did you leave?" he asks, and I immediately feel guilty.

"I was overwhelmed," I admit. "I needed some air."

"I would have gone with you if you would have told me."

"I know." We are quiet for a moment, and I decide I need to be brave if I am to get any answers. "What did John mean when he said, 'You know who you are and your destiny?' He said something similar the first time he attacked me."

Aiden stares down at me silently for a moment, and I worry he won't answer me. In the garden, I knew that I couldn't marry him if he held on to his secrets. If he can't share with me freely now, I will have to call off the wedding. I can see the debate in his eyes before he glances around and quickly maneuvers us into a quiet sitting room. He's going to tell me, and my stomach swoops in anticipation as my heart rejoices.

"This isn't common knowledge," he says, taking my hands and looking into my eyes. "David is not ready for it to get out, so I'm telling you this in confidence, okay?"

I nod, trying not to look too excited as he leads me over to a couch where we sit facing each other, knees touching. "David mentioned that we are descendants of the Alberonian royalty, right?" he says, leaning towards me.

"Yes, I remember." I lean forward too. If I lean forward just a little more, I could kiss him, but I keep my lips to myself so I can hear the information.

"Do you also remember the story Rupert told about the shipwrecked prince?"

"The one from Coati?" I ask, clarifying. I knew that was important, and I hope Jude and Coraline talked to Rupert about it. The puzzle pieces start to click in my mind as Aiden continues.

"One of the rumors was that he survived and married an Alberonian woman, the disowned princess. He never revealed himself to be a prince, and so when she decided to marry, they disowned her. Their family and their children grew up as commoners," Aiden confirms.

"What does this have to do with Coati?" I ask, but I think I know.

"We are not just descendants of the Alberonian family but descendants of The First Family," he says. I am struck mute for a moment, but Aiden continues excitedly. "My brother wants to find the Inheritance Stone that proves he has divine rule not just of Alberon but over all Lumina. We are doing so many good things here, and he wants to bring them to the whole continent," Aiden says, and the joy on his face is nothing compared to the shock on mine.

"He wants to rule all of Lumina?" I ask in a horrified whisper. This was David's plan all along: to find the stone, to give him a foothold, to form an empire.

"Not exactly. He doesn't want a hostile takeover. He has had too much bloodshed over corrupt governments." Aiden says, brushing off the fact that his brother wants to take over everything. "That's why he wants the stone to help him. When people see it glow, they will have to give him a chance to show them the amazing system we are establishing here. As they start working, we are going to see the elimination of poverty and government abuse." He truly believes this. I watch as he explains excitedly, and my heart breaks just a little as I see the naive little boy who worships his older brother.

"I honestly don't know what to say," I express when he waits for my response. I need to get to my room to share what I know with the delegation.

"It will be great. You shall see. Tomorrow we marry, and then you shall join us in our mission to exterminate the bad and make the world a fairer place."

"I'm tired," I say, looking for an excuse to leave. I need to talk to Jude.

"Of course," Aiden says. "You have been through quite a day, and tomorrow shall be another big one—the day we finally become one." He gently takes my face in his hands and kisses me, but I don't respond. I should tell him the wedding is off, but my mind is preoccupied with thinking of how to tell my friends. We will need to leave tonight. Aiden pulls away before helping me stand and escorting me from the room. I'm so caught up in my thoughts that I don't realize we aren't in the right hallway until it is too late.

"This isn't the way to my room," I say, trying to turn around, but Aiden just pats my hand.

"This is your room. You will get better rest here tonight, and it would make me feel better to have you close," he says, leading me into my suite in the royal wing. My wedding dress is already hanging in the wardrobe. I want to cry. This is all too much to take in. "I figured you can rest here tonight since you will be getting ready in here tomorrow anyway." I open my mouth to protest, but he cuts me off with a soft kiss. He points to a set of doors off to the other side of the room. "I'm just through there if you need me," he says before leaving me alone.

I wait a moment before walking to the door and poking my head out. Guards are standing at the end of the hallway, and I suddenly feel trapped. I walk back inside and look around, spying my dress, a beautiful sage green and silver creation with a slim skirt into a train and delicate embroidery across the square neckline and down the long sleeves that come to a point at my fingers. It makes me feel willowy, which is a feat for my short and moderately curvy stature, but I can hardly think about wearing it tomorrow.

I make my way over to the window and take a seat on the bench underneath, opening the window to glance at the night sky. The air outside is hot and humid, but there is a slight breeze that cools my face.

I stare up at the stars, my brow wrinkling as I think. I have important information to share, and no idea about how to get it to my friends. I could take the servants' passageways, but the entrance to that is in the hallway. I have no doubt that my actions are being watched. I could send a note, but that could be read or intercepted at any point.

Help me, I plead to The Eternal. Whether He has guided David or not in his conquest, I don't think he has gone the way The Eternal has wanted him to. I don't know how long I've been asking before I hear a single word.

Wait.

Frustrated, I open my eyes and gaze back at the stars. *Wait for what?* I ask, but I only receive the same answer.

Wait.

Chapter 27

My eyes flutter open, and it takes me a moment to remember where I am. The quiet sound of voices alerts me to the fact that I am not alone. I sit up and stretch, my body stiff from sleeping on the window bench. I look around and am relieved to see Coraline admiring my wedding dress that hangs on the wardrobe.

"Oh, thank goodness you're here." I stand and rush over, grasping Coraline's hands. "I have so much to tell you."

She pulls me into a tight hug. "We were so worried when you didn't show up at your room last night. Jude wanted to go find you, but Rupert stopped him," she says, stepping back but not releasing my hands. I am grateful for the connection.

"I'm fine, but Aiden told me the plan. David wants to find the Inheritance Stone," I say quickly. I don't know how much time we will have alone.

"What are you talking about?" Coraline responds, and I want to groan in frustration.

"The stone that glows for The First Family. Rupert told us a story about it. I think I mentioned it a few nights ago," I can see the light ignite in Coraline's eyes. She knows what I'm talking about, but then her eyes narrow.

"That's just a fable. The Coati line died out before being absorbed into Ileria. Plus, the stone was said to be lost for generations before that," she says, but if Aiden is right, he and David are descendants of that line.

"He claims to have proof that he is a descendant of the last prince of Coati. That he survived the shipwreck and married the princess here." I remember the records in the library, and I would bet that David has proof somewhere that also confirms him as a descendant of the last ruling family of Coati.

"If that's true and if the stone is real, how would he even know how to find it?" she asks skeptically.

"I don't know," I say in frustration. "But that's not what's important right now. We need to leave right away. He wants the stone because it would give him the right to—" Maids burst in at that moment with hot bath water.

"It's time to start your preparations," one of them says in a no-nonsense tone. As they push me into the bathing room, I know my chance for privacy has been lost. I want to tell them to stop the preparations, that the wedding is off, but each time I open my mouth, that voice comes into my head.

Wait.

Some time during the preparations, Coraline slips out only to return in her gown. She meets my eyes, steady and deliberate, and I know she has shared what she could with whomever she could. I hope that the men are prepared for a quick getaway because I have a feeling that things are going to be changing quickly.

I stand and look at myself in the full-length mirror. I am breathless for a moment at the sight. My hair is pulled back at the nape of my neck in an elegant updo, and a crown of white flowers sits on my head. I look like a princess.

If I were truly getting married today, I would look perfect, but instead, I want to cry. This had always been my goal for years, but now that dream is dead.

Maybe I can convince him to come with me, I think in a desperate grasp to preserve our love. *Maybe that is why I am being told to wait.*

Even after the information he revealed last night, I don't think he is a bad man. He is confused, wrapped up in the vision of his hero brother. Maybe I can help him see the truth, and then we can still have our happily ever after. The one I've always dreamed of.

There is a knock at the door, and I know that it is time. I send up another little prayer to The Eternal, asking for comfort and guidance to get through this. Coraline opens the door and steps aside for Rupert to enter. As our gazes meet in the mirror, I almost burst into tears.

"My, I wasn't sure I would see the day ya were to marry our Aiden," he says, coming in while the room empties. "I figured I would come walk ya down the aisle since yer father's not here." I want to fling myself into his arms, but I hold it together.

"I am so glad to see you," I say, walking over to him to take his arm. Rupert looks me over, and I can see the tears forming in his eyes.

"You are a vision, lass," he says, and I break, turning to fling my arms around him. I know Rupert has seen Aiden as a son for many years, and he has always felt like a beloved uncle.

"He is still in there, lass," he says, returning my hug. "I see it every time he looks at you. I know the road ahead will be hard, but I think you two will be able to weather it, and if you can, then you can weather anything. You are young, but your heart is in the right place, and I know it will work out. Don't lose hope." His words settle in my soul. I take a deep breath and as I let it out, I stand tall, confident. I take his arm and walk out of the suite.

The walk down to the throne room seems short, and we arrive at the doors sooner than I expect. "Be ready for anything," I whisper to Rupert before inclining my head toward the guards standing at the doors. I am ready. The guards reach for the doors.

"Wait!" I turn to find Prince Jude striding towards us.

"I just need to talk to you for a moment, privately." Rupert looks at me, and I give my consent before he steps away to give us some privacy. "Listen, I know this is probably not my place, but I needed to make sure you know you don't have to do this. You have other options."

I'm surprised, and it takes me a moment to find my voice. I had started to think of him as a friend, and now I know he cares about me too.

"Thank you," I say with a smile, reaching out and placing a hand on his arm. "I need to talk to you," I say quietly, aware of the guards close by. "I need you to be ready to help me. I don't know what is going to happen when I get in there, but... I can't support David. He says this union is blessed by The Eternal. I know it's not, though. He has blessed me, and this is not His will. Not like this."

He looks at me, his eyes searching my face before finally, he places his hand over mine, still on his arm, and gives it a gentle squeeze. "I trust you. Whatever you need."

"We need to be ready to leave at a moment's notice," I say, glancing once more at the guards. They are watching us openly. I let go of Jude and take a step back, beckoning for Rupert.

"We will be ready," Jude says as Rupert comes to my side once again. We turn as Jude leaves, and I tell myself that he will see to it that we are ready. I just need to give him enough time.

The doors open, and I am stunned by the beauty of the room as we start down the long aisle. Afternoon light shining through the throne room windows bathes the room in a glow. The aisle is lined with green fabric, and someone has gathered white flowers everywhere. I glance around at the large crowd gathering, but all I see are strangers before I turn my eyes forward.

The walk is long. A string quartet plays as we walk slowly. My train drags after me, and I have to remind myself to breathe. I squeeze Rupert's arm and am grateful not to have to do this alone. As we get closer to the throne, I see Aiden. He is handsome in a black tunic and pants with silver trim and embroidery. A green sash crosses his chest, and a silver coronet sits in his hair, making him look like the prince he now is.

His eyes are on me, his face radiating pride and joy as he takes me in. I smile at him, but I worry it doesn't reach my eyes. *Maybe whatever is supposed to happen will happen after we are married*, I try to tell myself, but my gut tells me it won't. As soon as I get to the front, something is going to happen.

We arrive at the stairs leading to the dais, where Aiden and his brother wait for us. I kiss Rupert's cheek before taking Aiden's hand.

"Thank you for being here for me," I whisper to Rupert before I grasp Aiden's hand. Together we walk up the stairs to the dais.

We stand in front of his brother, who waits to perform the wedding. I meet his eyes as we walk up, and I can't read the emotion in them. He glances at Aiden, and his gaze softens, which makes me feel worse. No matter what he is up to, I know he cares for his brother.

David looks at each one of us before addressing the crowd. "We are gathered here today before the eyes of The Eternal to join these two souls together. This is an extra special occasion because of how long they have waited to become one." I glance around the room, waiting for something to happen, but there is nothing.

I look at Aiden across from me as his brother continues talking about the blessings of our union, but I am having a hard time paying attention. This all feels like it is moving too fast, and all I have for direction is to wait. *Wait for what?* I want to shout, but I already know what my answer would be.

"The Eternal has spoken to me," David says, catching my attention again, "and he has a great work for us to do. To protect our country and our sacred family line, I officially name Aiden as my heir. Please kneel," he says, and Aiden kneels next to me. I look down sharply at Aiden. I thought this took place after the marriage, but he doesn't look surprised.

Aiden starts repeating his vow to watch over and protect the realm. *Wait.* The voice comes again, and I let out a breath. The Eternal is still with me. David places a crown on Aiden's head, and he stands once again next to me. "And now for the marriage. May they help secure our line for the next generation," David says.

It's time.

"Do you, Aiden, take Aloura..." David starts to say, but I can't let him continue.

"Wait!" I say, stalling the ceremony.

"What is it?" Aiden asks, his eyes full of concern. Tears come to my eyes as I look at him.

"I'm sorry," I whisper before raising my voice for all to hear. "I can't go through with this wedding." Hurt and confusion flash across Aiden's face, but it is David that I am truly watching. His eyes meet mine, and they are harsh with disapproval.

"What is the matter?" he asks. "You don't want to marry my brother?" His voice is loud as well, projecting to the entire audience.

"I do," I say, "But not like this." I glance at Aiden, begging him to understand before I turn back to his brother. This is between me and him.

"You spurn the will of The Eternal?"

"No," I say, the words coming to my mind a moment before I speak them. "You do." A gasp runs through the crowd at my words.

"You don't know what you are talking about," he says, glaring at me like I am a stupid child. "I have communed with The Eternal. He has granted me this kingdom to rule over in His stead, and soon He will grant me the world," he says. His voice is still projecting, and the audience hears him and his declaration. They break out into murmurs, and I can see the moment he realizes his mistake.

"The Eternal is displeased with your ambitions," I say. Warmth fills my heart and then my whole body as I repeat the words in my mind. "He has blessed you with a kingdom, and yet you reach for more. I am here to warn you before it is too late."

Out of the corner of my eye, I can see the Ilerian delegation standing at the bottom of the stairs, but I can't focus on them as words flood out of me. I couldn't hold them back if I tried. "I give you this warning through my servant: If you continue down this path, it will only lead to death and war. The people that you are trying to protect will suffer, and My vengeance shall be turned upon your head."

David is red with fury, and Aiden just stares at me in shock. "Enough!" David roars. "You know not what you are talking about. I had hoped that you would be a boon to my brother, a blessing at his side, but I see now you have been deceived. The Eternal has blessed me, and I will have proof of it, just you see," he says.

"You are the one who seeks to deceive." My voice isn't the only one I hear. A second quiet voice has joined it, speaking in time with mine.

"You have been warned, David. You have fallen out of favor with The Eternal. Be happy with your lot or be destroyed." With that, the warmth leaves me, taking my energy with it. I fall to my knees, unable to hold my weight any longer.

"You lying witch," David says, pulling a ceremonial dagger from his belt. "I can't let you continue to spew lies!" he says, raising the dagger. I look up into his eyes and see the rage and fear in them. He steps toward me, but before he can plunge the dagger into my heart, Aiden steps in front of him.

"I can't let you do that," he says, and my heart leaps. "Let me take her away from here," he says quietly, leaning toward his brother so the audience can't hear their words. "Don't kill her in front of everyone."

"You just want to protect her, but I won't let her poison your mind anymore." I glance up at his back, wanting to see his face, but he keeps me behind him as he looks at his brother. I try to stand, but my legs are still shaky. A hand grips my elbow, and I look to see Jude at my side. Coraline, Rupert, and Gareth are down below.

"Come," Jude says, silently backing down the stairs. I lift my dress and follow after him, but we don't get far before David spies us.

"Guards, arrest them!" he yells, pushing Aiden to the side. "Keep the prince and princess alive; kill the rest."

"No!" Aiden shouts as the room erupts into chaos and the guards leap into action. They ignore the Alberonian court and head toward us. The rest of our group circle up quickly with swords out, the ladies in the middle. We will be overwhelmed in minutes.

"Quickly," Aiden calls out, "this way." I see the hesitation as the prince looks between Aiden and the approaching guards, but Rupert is quick to act and starts pushing me and the princess towards Aiden. "Follow me," Aiden instructs, taking my hand and rushing out a side door. I look back and see the rest of the group following, Jude bringing up the rear, and he swings his sword at a guard.

"I have a place where you can escape," Aiden says, pulling me along. "It's an tunnel in case of emergencies. I found it when I first got here. I don't know if David knows about it yet, but it's not guarded. I didn't explore the whole thing. I don't know the state it is in or where it comes out, but it may be your only chance."

By this point, Jude has caught up, and Rupert with him. Gareth makes up the rear guard. "We need to gather the rest of our party," Rupert says, thinking of the guards.

"I've already contacted them. We have a rendezvous outside the city," Jude says, turning to Aiden. "Where do we go?"

"Head to the library," Aiden instructs as he checks around a corner, leading us away from the throne room. Someone must have barricaded a door because they aren't right behind us. "The back left corner has a little alcove with a tapestry with a lion on it. There is a door behind it. It looks like it doesn't have a handle, but pull the torch next to it. It should trigger the latch. Make your way to the tunnel as quickly as possible," Aiden says, pushing me in front of him. "I will create a distraction."

"No," I say, reaching back for his hand, but Rupert holds me back.

"How do I know we can trust you?" Jude asks. It's a valid question, but I know in my heart that Aiden is good. That's why he is helping us get away. I can only hope that he will come with us.

Aiden looks at me before meeting the prince's eyes.

"Trust that I want to save her," he says. The moment is tense, but then Jude nods, and our party splits. As Rupert herds me away, I pray that we will see each other again. Despite everything, I can't deny I still love him.

Chapter 28

he way to the library is teeming with guards looking for us. "How are we going to make it to the library?" Coraline whispers as we hide in an alcove.

"Come this way," I say, realizing that because I haven't been in the meetings, I've had more of a chance to explore. "We will take the servants' halls. I've seen several entrances as I've been exploring, and I'm sure I can find the right ones." I look around before leading them over to an unadorned door that marks the servants' passageway.

The hallway is empty. Most of the servants are still down in the kitchen preparing for what was to be the wedding feast or off celebrating until they were called on to serve. As we approach the royal quarters, I realize we will have to leave the servants' halls.

"I'll lead," Jude says, sliding past everyone to the front of the group. "You follow behind to direct me."

"This dress is not the most practical for running away," I say as I hold the train close. It still restricts my movements, but at least no one will step on it. Jude looks down at me in the tight quarters before he nods, making a decision.

"You're right. We need to get you a change of clothing. Where is the best place to go?"

"All of my things are in the royal wing, and I don't know where any extra clothing might be stored. I know how to get to the library from there," I say, biting my lip. We are wasting time.

"Then to your rooms it is," he says, taking off in the direction of the royal wing.

"But what if they think I have come up to my room?" I ask, following behind him.

That's a risk we are going to have to take. Our guards should have had bags ready with some provisions they could grab at a moment's notice, but we should get you ladies changed if possible."

We poke our heads out into the main hallway. I smile in triumph when I realize we made it to the opening right across from my room. "It's all clear," Jude calls, beckoning us out and across the hall, where we quickly close the door. I run to the wardrobe and quickly try to find the plainest dresses.

"This would be so much easier if I still had my serving dresses," I grumble as I pull out a few morning dresses that only have simple embroidery, even if they are still made out of expensive fabric. I shove a garment into Coraline's hands before selecting one for myself. I am grateful to find the men facing the door talking quietly as Coraline helps me undo the buttons down my dress. "Quickly," I whisper, feeling the urgency to get going, but this is not a dress to be removed quickly. I blush a little at the thought that it was meant to be Aiden undoing them after our wedding.

I'm both sad and relieved that the wedding was interrupted, but I don't have time to dwell on these feelings as the dress becomes loose enough to slide over my hips. I quickly help Coraline with her dress while the men quietly discuss options.

"The library is here in the east wing. It should be simple to get there from here," Rupert says while Gareth stands by the door listening.

"Do you think there will be guards patrolling over there still?" Jude asks, walking over to peek out a window, but it only leads to a private garden, the wall too high to see over.

"There will probably be some, but hopefully most will be outside hoping to catch us in the gardens or something," Rupert says, folding his arms with a frown. "That's probably where our men will try to escape, so they will help with creating a distraction for us to take the tunnel."

"I wish they were with us," Coraline says softly by my side. Silently, I agree with her.

"I think I hear movement," Gareth says by the door. It's time to go.

"Come, we will leave through Aiden's rooms," I say quietly. It will be unexpected, and the hallway entrance to his rooms is around the corner, closer to the library.

"Wait," Jude says, touching my shoulder. "The flowers in your hair," he says, reaching up and plucking them out. "They will fall out and leave a trail if we aren't careful." His hands are quick to remove them, and I quickly step away, opening the connecting door to Aiden's room.

I try not to let myself get distracted as I walk through, but I can't help but look for touches of my Aiden. His room is as opulent as one would expect for a prince. I can't see many personal touches. *Maybe he never truly settled here*, I think, for a moment before shaking my head. We don't have time for that, and I thrust it out of my head to think about later.

"If we go to the right and past David's door, we can head down the back passageway into the east wing. The library will not be far from there," I say. A servant had shown me there the first time when I had had a restless night and needed a book, but I've been back a few times. This is a little different angle than the guest wing, but I am sure we are headed in the right direction. We walk quickly, the carpeted hallway masking the sound of the men's boots.

We are lucky to hardly encounter anyone, only having to wait around a few corners for a servant or a set of guards to pass. As we approach the main hallways once again, we slow. Our luck is about to run out.

I can hear the guards searching as we come down a little hallway connecting to the main hall, where the library can be found. We pause, crouched under windows behind some potted plants. Voices are coming closer, and I hold my breath and send a silent prayer that we will not be discovered when we are so close. I think of Aiden and how this would be a good time for that distraction he was trying to create, and I pray for his safety as well. He never promised he would find us again.

"We will come down this way. You do a sweep of the library," one of the voices says as they come closer. Guards, for sure.

"Why would they be there?"

"I don't know, but do you want to be the one to tell the king that we didn't search every corner of this palace?"

"So I will sweep the library and meet you out in the garden?" There is a murmur of agreement, and then only one pair of steps walks closer to our hideout. I cross my fingers that he will walk past our hallway, but no such luck.

The guard walks around the corner, but Jude is ready. As soon as the guard passes the first plant, Jude steps out and hits him over the head with the hilt of a dagger, rendering him unconscious before he even has a chance to register our presence. Gareth quickly grabs him under the arms and drags him behind the plants to where he hopefully won't be seen.

Faint shouts go up outside, and I worry that they have seen us from the windows, but a glance outside shows in the fading light of the evening sun that this is the distraction Aiden promised. I knew that was Aiden buying us time.

"The guards are running toward the front of the palace," I say, watching as a squadron runs past down below.

"Whatever Aiden did seems to have worked," Coraline says, peeking over my shoulder.

"Let's go," Jude commands, leading us into the main hallway.

"What about the guard who was supposed to check the library?" I ask as we hurry across the hall and down a few doors, sticking close to the sides where we can quickly duck behind a pillar or plant.

"We will just have to dispatch him like we did his friend," Jude says, not even looking at me as he continuously scans our surroundings. Preparing myself, I slide into the library. It is quiet. Everyone must still be in the throne room at the wedding. I hope that even the librarians were given the day off. We can't afford for anyone to spot us as we sneak out of the castle.

"Where did Aiden say the entrance was again?" Coraline asks, but my attention is taken up by the display in front of us. A large podium stands in a beam of orange sunlight with a book and a scroll on it. I wander closer, drawn to it despite the time constraint. My eyes trace the royal record first, tracing the lines back until I spot the disinherited princess. Esmeralda was her name. On the scroll, her name is written at the top next to the name Fredrick, the last prince of Coati, and follows the line down. There is a smudge on David and Aiden's father's name, probably from dirty fingerprints, and it has had to be rewritten for legibility, but it is there with David and Aiden written underneath.

"Quick, we don't have time for this," Jude says, making his way to the hidden door Aiden told us about.

"Do you think these records are true?" I ask Coraline as she comes to my side.

"The royal archive records are true, but I do wonder about that scroll. Do you see the smudge and how the name has been rewritten?" she asks, pointing it out.

"Yes, do you think their father falsified his name there?" I ask. If that is true, then they have no claim to the throne except from the people who gave it to them.

"I don't know, but it does make his claim questionable," she says.

"Come on," Gareth calls to us from a far wall. "We found the entrance."

Aiden did a good job of describing the secret door to us. It blends into the surrounding wall, but with a hidden latch, it opens into a tunnel. It is dark and damp.

"We will need some light," Jude says, and Rupert leaves to find a torch. Jude stares into the dark, a grim expression on his face.

"Are you okay?" I ask, coming up to his side.

"If we can get out of here safely, I will be," he says before turning to look at me. "I hope my men make it out okay. Do you think Aiden can be trusted?" He searches my face, looking for the answer.

"He stopped his brother from killing me and created a distraction. I think we can trust that this tunnel will get us out."

"I sure hope so."

We enter the tunnel single file, with Jude in the lead. I'm glad we can see where we are going, as the tunnels are not as straightforward as Aiden led us to believe. Other tunnels branch out along the sides, but we keep straight, trusting his directions. As a bug crawls across the moss-covered stone wall, I almost wish I didn't know what was in front of us. A faint glow tells us we are nearing another light source, but a shout slows us down.

"I'll go scout ahead," Gareth says, creeping forward. I don't know what he hopes to see in the dark, but I'm grateful to him anyway. It feels like a long time until he makes his way back, but it is probably only minutes. "There is an exit this way. Quickly. I think Alberon's guards have entered another tunnel," he says, ushering us forward toward the faint light.

The tunnel ends in a trapdoor in the ceiling, faint light creeping through the gaps in the wood. Jude starts the climb, handing the torch to Rupert, who will wait at the bottom and climb up last. The door opens up into a warehouse. It is packed full of boxes, probably merchandise ready to be shipped to who knows where.

"We are still in the city, at the northern edge," Jude says, giving us the information on the situation. "Across the way is a little gate that leads out, but it has a pair of guards standing there guarding the door."

"How many?" Rupert asks as he climbs and joins the rest of our party, closing the door behind him. Gareth pushes a box on top. We have three fighters with us, although they might be able to count Coraline and me if we can find a weapon.

"Only two," Jude says, and a glance out the little window in the door confirms it. "Let's go before word of our escape reaches them and reinforcements arrive," Jude says, leading the group to gather up. With only a signal, Jude and Gareth break from the group, moving in to take out the guards quickly before they can raise an alarm. Unfortunately, right as they approach the guards, another squadron of five rounds the corner of the building.

Chaos breaks out as our group engages them. Swords are clashing, and we need to finish this quickly before more guards are called by the noise. I am unarmed and try to stay out of the way, but as I back up toward the building, a man comes up and grabs me. "Hello, deary." I look up into the face of a guard. "I won't harm a lady, but you are coming with me back to the palace," he says, pulling me in the direction of the palace.

"Unhand me," I demand as I struggle and tug away, but his hold is firm. I can't believe this is happening again. I am tired of being the damsel in distress, and instead of my normal panic, I get angry. I recall my training. I've been doing the exercises that I have been taught, and it's time to put that training into motion. I go limp and drop to the ground, waiting for the right time to strike.

"Fine, be difficult," the guard says, dropping my arm. "We will do this the hard way." He reaches down to pick me up, but he's too late. I am already up and ready to flee. I turn, but he is quicker than I anticipated and wraps both arms around me. *I've trained for this*, I remind myself before I lose my bravado, and stomp down on his foot as hard as I can. He howls in pain but doesn't let go, so I do the next thing I can think of. I fling my head back into his face, hearing a satisfying crunch before his arms loosen around me.

I break free and turn, ready to continue trying to defend myself, but I find it unnecessary as Aiden hits him over the head, effectively knocking him unconscious. I'm stunned, and he smirks at my confused face.

"I was just coming to save you, but you hardly needed me," he says, coming towards me and giving me a quick kiss.

"I've been practicing," I say, stunned and relieved to see him here. A shout goes to us, and we turn to see that the gate has been opened.

"I can tell," he says, pushing me towards the gate. We take off at a run to join the group. We are the last ones out, but Aiden turns back and pulls at the heavy wooden doors. "Quick, help me close it," he commands, and several of the men help, grunting at the effort. He grabs a sword and wedges it across the handles. "It won't hold them for long, but hopefully, between the fire in the stable and that, they won't be coming after us anytime soon," he says, coming to join us as we hurry to the edge of the jungle on this side of the city.

"The fire in the stables?" I ask as he comes up and takes my hand, pulling me further into the shadows where we cannot be easily seen from the walls.

"I'll tell you about it later," he says. We will have a lot to talk about later, but for now, I see that most of us have gathered.

Jude, Rupert, and Gareth are arguing when we show up about where we are to travel. "We can't take the main roads. They will be looking for us," Jude says.

"We could always take a ship. Otherwise, we have to go around the whole lake. On a ship, we can sail through the lake down the River Sal and out to the ocean. From there, we can either sail straight to our capital or disembark in Coati and travel from there," Rupert says, nodding toward the lake.

"We will want to travel on foot first to another little village before we find a boat. We can't find one here at the Capitol," Aiden says, stepping right into the conversation.

"And why should we trust you?" Jude says, his voice calm, but in the faint light of the moon, it is easy to see the lines of tension in his body.

"Listen, I have been searching for my brother for a long time, but he is not who I thought he was. He is not who I remember," he says, and my heart aches for him. "As much as I loved him and still want to love him, I can't stay with him. I care too much about Aloura to stick around. I know she is safer with you, and by her side is where I belong." I melt into him as he grabs my waist and pulls me close.

"I trust him," I say, although I know in this case that may not hold a lot of clout as I am firmly pressed into Aiden's side.

"He has a fair point about the ports," Rupert says, his eyes jumping between Jude and Aiden. I can tell he sees trouble brewing, but I hope they can put it off long enough to get us to a safe place.

A shout from the city tells us we are out of time. "Fine," Jude says, leading us deeper into the jungle. "We will follow your lead to the next town and then reevaluate from there."

"I also have something else that may be of value," he says as we start walking.

"And what is that?" Jude asks, walking behind us.

"My brother's information about the Inheritance Stone. I think I can find it."

Epilogue

AIDEN

Aloura sits cuddled up at my side, falling asleep. I don't know how she manages to sit so close to the fire on the hard ground in this heat. I won't lie; it feels good to have her back in my arms. If we were alone, I would pull her close and kiss her until we both forgot everything that had happened today.

It would be foolish to say I wasn't disappointed that the wedding was never completed. If everything hadn't fallen apart, we would be on our way to Coati in comfort with servants and all the luxuries that I can give her, but nothing went to plan today.

Luckily, all is not lost. I am still on my way to Coati, but instead of traveling in comfort with a beautiful wife at my side, I am traveling with no provisions and a group of people who hardly trust me. If it weren't for Aloura, I would be gone, making the journey on my own.

Aloura snuggles closer, and I pull her onto my lap, giving her a light kiss. Her eyes flutter open, and she gives me the look that makes me feel ten feet tall. The Ilerian princess calls her, and she gives me another light kiss before going to her.

Tomorrow, we will enter the little fishing village on the far side of Lago de Sal. There, we can make it quickly back to Locura, where the rest of the guards will meet us, and we can make a plan.

I can feel the journal pressed against my chest, tucked safely inside my tunic. I won't trust anyone else with it until I have more time to study it. I catch the eye of the Ilerian prince, his eyes dark as they watch me across the fire. He doesn't trust me, and with good reason.

I've seen the way he watches Aloura, and when I was talking David down from his panic, he was the first to reach her. He has been her protector, but it is time for him to step aside and give her to me. She has always been mine anyway.

I listen to the jungle, hearing the sounds of the wildlife. We are close enough to a town that we won't have to worry about the animals coming too close, but that's not what I am waiting for.

A soft birdcall comes from the darkness, and I know my brother's scout is out there ready with my instructions. I'll have to wait until my turn for guard duty and hope that the prince isn't the one to stay up with me. Maybe I'll ask for Gareth. He trusts me enough that a moment or two of being out of sight won't set off his radar.

I stare into the fire and think of my last conversation with my brother before we escaped.

I reenter the throne room, trying to think of a distraction, but am distracted myself by David sitting on his throne in the now empty room.

"I wasn't sure you would come back," he says, and immediately guilt hits. I'm not sure what I am going to do either, but I can let him kill her.

"Why did you do it?" I ask, confused as to why he let his anger take control. It reminds me of our father. "You still could have saved the situation, but now you have played your hand." I'm frustrated. He had a plan, a good plan to do good things, but now he has ruined them by being rash, just like our father.

"I'm sorry," he says, looking weary. "Her prophecy shook me." He's not the only one. I have never been a devoted person, but I have always believed in my brother's vision of a better world. I've even been able to see the evidence of it working here in Alberon, but Aloura's prophecy was something else. I don't understand it.

"Aiden," David says, standing up and coming closer. "I know my actions seemed rash, but you don't understand yet. I have handed you an opportunity." He places a hand on my shoulder.

"What opportunity?" I ask, aware that time is not on my side right now if I want Aloura and her friends to get out. "We are going to let the Ilerian delegation try to escape," he says, surprising me. "And you are going to go with them."

He reaches into his doublet and pulls out an old leather journal. I know what it is right away. "I have been sending scouts for years now to try to find this stone, but I think it has to be you. A descendant of the bloodline. Go with them and have them help you find it. Win over your girl, bring her back, and then we will show everyone that we are the rightful rulers of the nation. We will fix this world like we have been called to do, and you and Aloura will help me rule over it all." The idea sounds appealing, but I still have doubts.

"The prince doesn't trust me," I say, even though I know I'm going to go anyway.

"No, but Aloura does, and he trusts her. So does Rupert. You are charming; you can win the others over."

"Okay," I respond, taking the journal and tucking it into my shirt. I turn to leave, but he calls after me.

"I'll be keeping an eye on you," he says. "I won't lose you again."

I almost feel bad for having set the stables on fire but it felt nice to destroy something of his when my emotions had still been so close to the surface. I glance up at the moon and notice it's almost time for my shift. Aloura comes, pulling me out of my musings, and kisses me good night before going to her bedroll by the princess. I rise to stand at my position for my watch. I can't help but let my thoughts wonder if, at the end of this all, she will still love me and if we will finally find our happily ever after as rulers over all.

Acknowledgements

This work has been a long road as I have learned the ropes of writing a novel. Thank you to my husband for his patience and support as I have pursued this dream of writing and publishing a book.

A big thank you to my parents, who have also played an important part in making this come together, from listening to my progress and offering a little financial support to more.

Thank you to my editor, Jacob. This was his first novel, too, and we have learned so much from each other. Thanks for taking a chance on me. And thank you to my proofreader, Alicia, who polished up the grammar and made this book pretty. Thank you to my beta readers. The version I sent you was rough, but without your feedback, it wouldn't be where it is today. You helped me find the true story with your comments, and hopefully it's turned out much better for it.

Thank you as well for all my friends who listened to me in the early stages as I started this book. You helped me keep up my motivation when it felt hard. I couldn't have done it without you!!!

About the author

KD Call lives in Arizona with her husband and three children. A lifelong lover of stories, her passion for fantasy began as a child when her father read The Chronicles of Narnia and Harry Potter aloud to her. With a vivid imagination and a head full of worlds waiting to be explored, she finally decided it was time to put them to paper. Love and Loyalty is her debut novel—just the beginning of many adventures to come.

www.ingramcontent.com/pod-product-compliance
Lightning Source LLC
Chambersburg PA
CBHW060848250626
47159CB00013B/2808